Jake's Return

by

Liana Laverentz

Jake's Return

Contact Information: info@thewildrosepress.com

Cover Art by *Kim Mendoza*

The Wild Rose Press
PO Box 708
Adams Basin, NY 14410-0706
Visit us at www.thewildrosepress.com

Publishing History
First Champagne Rose Edition, 2007
Print ISBN 1-60154-124-4

Published in the United States of America

Jake stood at the front desk, his left profile turned toward Rebecca and the rest of the main reading room. He looked tall, dark and rangy in faded denims and a black T-shirt that matched his windswept hair. The clerk behind the desk finished checking out a patron with two small children. A short, stout, no-nonsense woman who had never married, Eunice Lee Larmer had been with the library for as long as most of the town could remember. She looked up at Jake and froze, her eyes rounding with recognition. Her face two shades paler, she stepped back carefully.

The sight of Eunice's fear sparked a surge of protective anger in Rebecca, taking her by surprise. Damn. She'd thought she was prepared for this.

Obviously not. Telling herself she was rescuing the situation—not Jake—Rebecca started forward just as Jake turned her way. His expression stopped Rebecca in her tracks. He looked completely out of place. Completely unapproachable. A lone wolf barely tolerating the trappings of civilization.

An eternity passed as she bore the weight of his sharp scrutiny from across the now suffocatingly silent room. Rebecca would have sworn she actually felt his cold, dark gaze move from the top of her French twist to the tips of her navy pumps.

She shivered.

Sounding as if it were right next door instead of three blocks away, the daily noon wail of the firehouse siren pierced the unnatural silence. The familiar sound seemed to nudge everyone back to life. Rebecca swallowed hard and braced herself to meet Jake again, to speak with him for the first time in eight years.

The first time since the night he'd given her Katie.

Amid a rising tide of rustles and scandalized whispers, Jake seemed to recall why he'd come to the library. As he slowly wended his way across the crowded reading room to where Rebecca stood, neither of them smiling, a paralyzing thought struck her.

What if he still doesn't want anything to do with us?

Dedication

To Louis
Thank you for being my best friend.

Chapter One

Rebecca Reed would never forget the sound of Jacob Donovan walking back into her life. The sharp hiss of startled gasps that suddenly swept across the town library's main reading room was enough to grab anyone's attention. She frowned and straightened from where she was shelving books in the children's section, looked to see what had happened, and felt her heart stop.

Omigod, she thought. He's here. He's really here. In Warner.

Her heart jerked to a start again, and she was sure every soul in the building could hear its wild, erratic beat in the shocked silence that had settled over the room.

Jake stood at the front desk, his left profile turned toward her and the rest of the main reading room. He looked tall, dark and rangy in faded denims and a black T-shirt that matched his windswept hair. The clerk behind the desk finished checking out a patron with two small children. A short, stout, no-nonsense woman who had never married, Eunice Lee Larmer had been with the library for as long as most of the town could remember. She looked up at Jake and froze, her eyes rounding with recognition. Her face two shades paler, she stepped back carefully.

The sight of Eunice's fear sparked a surge of protective anger in Rebecca, taking her by surprise. Damn. She'd thought she was prepared for this.

Obviously not. Telling herself she was rescuing the situation—not Jake—Rebecca started forward just as Jake turned her way. His expression stopped Rebecca in her tracks. He looked completely out of place. Completely unapproachable. A lone wolf barely tolerating the trappings of civilization.

An eternity passed as she bore the weight of his sharp scrutiny from across the now suffocatingly silent room. Rebecca would have sworn she actually felt his cold, dark gaze move from the top of her French twist to the tips of her navy pumps.

She shivered.

Sounding as if it were right next door instead of three blocks away, the daily noon wail of the firehouse siren pierced the unnatural silence. The familiar sound seemed to nudge everyone back to life. Rebecca swallowed hard and braced herself to meet Jake again, to speak with him for the first time in eight years.

The first time since the night he'd given her Katie.

Amid a rising tide of rustles and scandalized whispers, Jake seemed to recall why he'd come to the library. As he slowly wended his way across the crowded reading room to where Rebecca stood, neither of them smiling, a paralyzing thought struck her.

What if he still doesn't want anything to do with us?

She beat back her own wave of fear, and focused on Jake. He was leaner now, harder and tougher-looking than she remembered. True, he'd always looked tough, but his toughness as a teenager had been a façade. One she'd seen through from the start. But this was different. This was no small town bad boy trying to make the best of his messed-up life alone. This was a grown man who'd spend most of his adult life in hell.

With a sinking sense of dread Rebecca realized she'd made a mistake. She was staring into the face of a stranger.

"Hello, Rebecca."

His voice was rougher, deeper than she remembered. Deep enough to send a shot of awareness down her spine. "Jake."

"Been a long time."

Rebecca knew exactly how long it had been. Counting Jake's four-year stint in the army, with the exception of those few unforgettable hours they'd shared in Pittsburgh eight years ago, they'd been apart for almost twelve years.

Before that, they'd been the town outcasts together.

"You're looking good," he said quietly.

"Thank you. You look...fit."

He arched a dark brow. "Considering I spent the last eight years locked up, you mean?"

Rebecca flushed. A nearby cough reminded her everyone within earshot would shamelessly repeat anything she or Jake said, first chance they got. A town like Warner had precious few secrets, and Jake obviously didn't intend to play down his recent parole from prison.

She squared her shoulders and offered Jake her most professional smile. "Would you like a cup of coffee? My office is right behind the desk."

"Your office?" He looked blank, then over his shoulder at the checkout desk, the open door that led to the tiny office behind it. The eavesdroppers' expressions ranged from indignant to shocked.

Frowning, Jake turned back to Rebecca. "You're head librarian?"

She understood his confusion. She wasn't even supposed to be in Warner, much less working at the library. The last time he'd seen her, she'd had much bigger plans. "For three years now."

Jake stared at her a moment longer, then ran a slow, speculative gaze over her short-skirted navy summer suit and heels. Just as slowly, he smiled. "Well, I'll be damned."

Rebecca's knees nearly buckled. His smile was vintage Jake. Reckless, unrepentant, and sexier than black satin sheets. Her heartbeat soared, her palms broke into a sweat. With what she considered an amazing amount of grace, given the state of her nerves, she managed to smile back neutrally and avoid tripping over anything as she led Jake past their astonished audience, and into her office.

Once inside, she made a beeline for the coffee pot, then forced herself to take a deep breath before she handed Jake a steaming mug of coffee. "Black still okay?" Her hand only trembled a little.

His slow half-smile hovered between some private amusement and pleasant surprise. "You remembered."

Rebecca looked into his gunmetal gray eyes and wondered how he thought she could forget. Then wondered if she was losing her mind. Jacob Donovan was no longer part of her life. By choice. His choice, and hers. She had to remember that.

"I was...floored to find out you were back in town," Jake said, his voice surprisingly deep and uneven. "Things, ah, seemed to be going pretty well for you in Pittsburgh."

Rebecca blinked at his oblique reference to the engagement that had never happened, the life she'd walked away from— because of him. She ignored the questions in his eyes and retrieved her own cup of coffee, now cold, from her desk. "I came back a few years after I graduated from Pitt. There was an opening at the library, and before I knew it." She waved a hand in the direction of the big, airy room that lay beyond her open office door, to indicate the rest was history. Rebecca didn't care to discuss the reasons she'd returned to Warner. Not yet. First, she needed to take this new Jake's measure. She eyed him as she took a sip of coffee.

"I want to thank you for everything you did at the house," he said.

"It was nothing."

"Rebecca, the place never looked half that clean, even when my mother was alive. You must have spent weeks on it."

She shrugged, uncomfortable with his gratitude. Her motives hadn't been entirely altruistic. "I thought you might be tired when you got home."

"How did you know I was coming?"

"I ran into your parole officer." Jake stared. Rebecca couldn't tell if he was more shocked or angry. "I was...checking on the house when he stopped by about a month ago. He said you were being paroled and had listed the house as your home address. Apparently, he was just checking things out."

Jake swore softly, running a hand through his hair. He looked up at Rebecca. "I'm sorry you had to have anything to do with him."

"He didn't seem so bad." Rebecca was more worried about what information the man might have relayed to Jake. Information Rebecca wasn't ready to share. But Katie had run back to their apartment on the other side of the hedge that separated her back yard from Jake's to get something for Rebecca just before the parole officer had stopped by—and stunned Rebecca with his news. Rebecca had pretended to ignore the pink and white bicycle her seven-year-old daughter had left lying in Jake's front yard, and the parole officer had politely followed her lead. "Pretty decent, actually."

Jake's eyes hardened to flint. "Yeah, well, that's because he doesn't have the power to snatch your butt off the street and bury you so deep you won't know if it's day or night." Abruptly he looked away, and in the small confines of her office looked...trapped. "Listen, I've got to go."

Rebecca wasn't surprised by Jake's sudden need to escape. He'd never been one for revealing much of himself. She was surprised he'd let her see as much as he had.

"Sure," she said, and suddenly recalled the last time she'd seen him. He'd just gotten out of the army, had bought himself a Harley and was filled with dreams of enjoying his newly acquired freedom. Freedom from the military, freedom from responsibility, and—simply by association—freedom from her. "I'm sure you have some settling in to do," she said, ignoring the familiar stab of pain at the knowledge that he didn't love her, and never had.

"Not really, since I don't plan to stick around any longer than I have to."

An unexpected wave of bitterness welled in her, startling her with its intensity. Damn it. She thought she'd dealt with all of that. Determinedly, she squashed it. "I see," she said impassively, while her mind grappled with the reality of what he'd just said. Jake intended to leave Warner again, as soon as he could.

But as a parent, she couldn't in good conscience tell him he was a father until she had some kind of idea as to how he'd take the news. If she sensed his reaction would in any way be harmful to Katie...

"Well, thank you for stopping by," she offered politely, slipping back into her professional mode. "It was good seeing you again. Take care," she added, nearly choking on the words. "In case I don't see you before you leave."

There. That sounded reasonable enough. Logical enough. And truly idiotic, to be honest about it. She hadn't taken all that time and effort to clean the man's house just so he could say thank you and be on his merry way.

But what could she do? Confront him here and now? Walk off the job and follow him out the door? Demand to know why he'd left her without a word eight years ago in the street if she had to? The town would really enjoy that.

She forced herself to turn away, reach for her reading glasses and slip them on. The rough draft of the budget proposal she'd been working on for the past two weeks was waiting.

"Ah...Rebecca?"

She looked back to find Jake watching her closely. The distancing feel of her glasses helped her maintain her professional smile. "Yes? Was there something else you wanted?"

His eyes darkened for a moment in what Rebecca would have sworn was masculine frustration before he shook his head. "No. Not really. I was just wondering how you got to be so...so..."

She lifted her chin, positive she knew what was coming. Cold. Bitchy. "Got to be so what?"

"Beautiful." Jake shook his head. "Never mind. Listen, Becca, would you like to have dinner tonight?"

She stared at him in stunned surprise. Jake was calling her beautiful and inviting her to...

"Dinner?"

He swore at her disbelieving response. "Forget I asked. Bad idea. I just wanted to thank you for cleaning the place up and having the power turned on. Last thing I expected when I got here was a light on in the window. Kinda spooked me, if you want to know the truth."

"Oh." She'd wondered if leaving the living room light on for him was over the top, but in the end had done it anyway.

"Thanks for leaving the casserole and pie, and…all that other stuff, too. I really appreciate it."

By "all that other stuff" he probably meant the linens and soap she'd left in the bathroom, the staples in the kitchen, the note that had told him the casserole and pie were in the freezer. Had she really done all of that? It seemed unreal, now that he was actually standing here, thanking her for it. "Oh."

"Like I said, bad idea."

"No! I mean, no…not at all. Dinner would be great," she added more sedately, her mind finally moving past "Oh" and racing to catch up. There wasn't a place in town they could go that wouldn't cause a stir, but she didn't have time to worry about that. Jake wasn't staying in Warner. This might be her only chance to get the answers from him she and Katie deserved.

She met his eyes, pure determination straightening her spine. "Just name the time and place."

Jake actually blinked in surprise. "Okay…" he said slowly, almost warily. Like he knew something was up, but not quite what. "How about my house, six o'clock? Bacon cheeseburgers on the grill sound like a plan?"

He sounded the tiniest bit uncertain, like he wasn't quite sure how to handle her any more. Good. The thought pleased her. Maybe it was time Jacob Donovan learned to expect more from her than blind adoration.

She smiled, and apparently jolted him all over again. "Perfect."

6

Chapter Two

Rebecca arrived just as Jake was carrying the burgers out to the small hibachi grill he'd dug out of the basement and set up at the end of the driveway closest to the back of the house. Suddenly appearing at the right side of the now six-foot tall hedge that bordered his back yard, she took him by surprise—in more ways than one.

"Hi," he said, unable to take his eyes off of her. She looked drop-dead gorgeous in a swingy yellow sundress that showed off her tan. Her red-gold hair was still tucked up in the sophisticated twist she'd worn at the library. Just looking at her made Jake wish for a thousand things that could never be, starting with a whole different life. "Where'd you come from?"

She smiled. "The apartment."

"Oh." So she was living in her great-aunt Martha's garage apartment again. Practically in his back yard.

Doesn't matter, Donovan. You're not gonna see her again after tonight.

"Thanks." Jake reached for the bowl of salad greens Rebecca carried. "I forgot about the salad." He nodded toward the ancient pair of vinyl lounge chairs he'd found in the basement and scrubbed clean, along with the grill. "Thought we'd eat out here, if it's all right with you."

Jake knew the instant she made the connection between prison and needing all the fresh air he could get. All the freedom. The gentle understanding in her eyes made him want to strangle something. Pity was the last thing he wanted, from anyone.

"Sure," she said. "What can I do to help?"

Several ideas surged into his mind, most of them involving getting naked, and half of them illegal in several states. "Nothing. Just make yourself at home. I'll bring the rest of the stuff out once the burgers are cooking." He refused to invite her into the house with him. Having her that close and looking that good and not being able to touch her would be sheer torture.

He offered lemonade, she accepted. Their fingers brushed when he handed hers over, and Jake felt a damning jolt of sexual heat. He looked up and caught a faint flush in Rebecca's cheeks. Their eyes locked. Apparently she'd felt something, too.

Great, Jake thought. Just great. If he thought for one second she'd go for some hot, no-strings-attached sex, they'd be halfway upstairs already.

But that wasn't Rebecca, and never had been. Rebecca came with all kinds of strings.

"The yard looks nice," she said.

"Thanks." He'd spent most of the afternoon working on it. "It'd look better with some grass instead of these ratty clumps of weeds, though. I'll have to look into seeding it."

"I thought you were leaving right away."

"Can't hurt to fix the place up a bit before I unload it."

Strong emotion flashed in Rebecca's eyes, startling him. The unexpected flare-up passed too quickly for him to be sure, but Jake would have put his money on anger—or maybe bitterness.

Bitterness? Over his selling the house?

Maybe she expects you to stay.

She couldn't. If she knew him at all, she couldn't.

"You weren't by any chance around when Mickey died, were you?" he asked, changing the subject.

"I was with him."

"You? With him? When he died?" Jake didn't know what to say. "Why?"

"He didn't have anyone else, Jake. He collapsed in Tim's Tavern. He was in the hospital nearly six weeks before he died. I couldn't let him die there alone."

Jake stared, rocked to the core. Rebecca had liked his dad, sure. Pretty much everyone had like Mickey Donovan—when he was drunk and feeling fine. Which had been most of the time, even before his former socialite wife had taken a fist full of sleeping pills.

But after Eileen's funeral, after Mickey's showdown with old man Dillenger himself right there in the living room of the house where she'd killed herself, the secret showdown nobody but Jake knew about, Mickey had changed.

Still, Jake was pretty sure *he* was the only one who'd spent any time up close and personal with the dark side of his dad. The side that had kept Jake's inheritance from his mother—and God only knew what else—from Jake for over twenty years. "Then I owe you a lot more than a simple thank you," he said quietly. I'm sorry. I'd have come back if I could've."

"Would you?"

He caught the edge in her question, but couldn't have taken offense if he'd wanted to. He hadn't been there. Rebecca had.

Forty-five minutes later Jake polished off the last of his second bacon cheeseburger with a satisfied grunt. "So how's Aunt Martha doing?"

In the lawn chair beside him Rebecca started. Apparently he'd caught her woolgathering. "Oh, she's still as active as ever. She and Ka—she and a—a friend are spending the week visiting friends in Erie."

"A friend?" Jake frowned, watching Rebecca's color rise. "As in male friend?" She turned even redder. Jake couldn't help but grin. "Rebecca," he teased. "Do you have a problem with your, what is she now? Seventy-five year old aunt having a boyfriend?"

"Of course not! And she's seventy-eight."

"Then what's the problem? Then again, this is Warner. Land of the perpetually closed minds." He switched to a more appealing subject. "Aunt Martha still make the best berry pies in three counties?"

The smile that flooded Rebecca's face was a reward in itself, even if it did hold more than a hint of relief. "Matter of fact. Taught me everything she knows, too. So if you're looking to snag yourself one, you'd be wise to be nice to me."

Jake couldn't help but grin back at her. "I'll consider myself warned. You know, I stopped by her house today, to ask after you. Never occurred to me you'd be living in the old place." He paused, half waiting for her to jump in with an explanation. No such luck. "Anyway, I'm standing on the doorstep and this little old lady next door comes out to get her mail, squints over the rhododendrons at me and asks, "Can I help you, sonny?" Jake rolled his eyes. "Made me feel like I was in second grade, selling candy bars all over again."

Rebecca hooted. "You? Selling candy bars?"

"Yeah, well, that was before your time." Before he'd learned that no matter what he did, it wouldn't be good enough.

Rebecca's laughter faded, but a breathtaking smile remained in her eyes. Jake could have stared into them all night long without any problem at all.

But he didn't have that right. Not after what he'd done.

"So you met Mrs. Schneider and she pointed you to the library," Rebecca was saying. "I wondered who had. I guess she assumed you already knew where I lived."

Jake pulled his thoughts away from his regrets and chuckled dryly. "Truth is, after seeing you today, all decked out in your power suit, I expected you to be living in one of those places up on The Bluff, overlooking the bay."

The smile in Rebecca's eyes vanished. "Your mistake."

Ouch. "Jeez, Becca, last I heard that's what you wanted out of life. How many nights did we spend down at Dillenger's Marina, me skinny-dipping while you sat on one of the loading piers, dangling your feet in the bay and spinning your dreams?" He recalled how across the bay they could see the condos on The Bluff, their floor-to-ceiling windows glittering like big diamonds. How further down the shoreline were the secluded mansions of Glenhill, where his grandparents lived in a house just like the one Rebecca had always dreamed of owning. Big, expensive, and probably filled to the gills with antiques.

Jake wouldn't know. He'd never been inside.

"What happened, Rebecca?" Jake asked softly, unable to hold his curiosity any longer. "Why did you come back to Warner?" Had that rich Pittsburgh dude she'd been planning to marry dumped her? Decided she wasn't good enough for him and his family full of lawyers after all? Just the idea of it made Jake's blood boil. "You had such big plans."

Her expression never wavered. "Plans change."

"Oh?" If she was hinting he was responsible for any of the changes in her life, she couldn't be more wrong. He'd done what he'd done to spare her a wasted life, not push her into one. "Care to explain that?"

Rebecca continued to stare at him for what felt like an hour, then closed her eyes. She leaned her head against the back of the lounge chair and blew out a heavy sigh. "No. I wouldn't."

"Suit yourself." Jake looked up at the stars and regrouped. After a few minutes of silence, he stole a glance at Rebecca's profile. Moonlight had always done great things for her skin, but tonight she looked awesome.

And totally torn up about something. *Probably being with you, Donovan. Wondering if you're going to pull another hit and run on her.*

"I don't suppose old man Feeney's still got his Gulf station out on the triangle," Jake wondered aloud. The triangle, a prominently located patch of land at the east entrance to town, split the road in two, one branch heading downtown, the other around Dillenger's Bay and into Glenhill. Jake had always thought the triangle was the perfect location for a service station. The first one you hit coming into town, the last before you left. Feeney's had been the busiest place in Warner when Jake had been a teenager. A regular gold mine.

"Are you thinking of going back to work there?"

Hell, no, but no point in beating the subject of his leaving to death. Jake's lips tightened at the memory of Sheriff Sutter's visit that afternoon. Warning him he was being watched.

That's all right, Sheriff. I'm used to being watched.

God, how he hated it. Feeling like he was living in some damn fishbowl. "You know anyone else in town who'd consider hiring me?" he tossed out more roughly than he intended.

Rebecca's hesitation didn't surprise him. But her answer did. "I know you didn't kill that woman, Jake."

He straightened, stunned by the conviction in her voice, in her eyes. For the first time in eight years, Jake felt the weight of another's trust, of another's belief in him. That it was Rebecca believing in him humbled him beyond words.

It also made him feel good inside. So good he felt ashamed of himself. He didn't deserve Rebecca's trust.

"Yeah, well you're wrong on that one, babe."

Rebecca went white as a sheet, then shot to her feet, empty plate in hand. "This is ridiculous. I have work to do."

Nice move, Donovan, now you've scared the shit out of her. Rising to his feet, Jake kept his plate and took hers. "How about I walk you home?"

She gave him a startled look. "It's just on the other side of the hedge, Jake."

He offered up his most non-threatening smile. "Not if we take the long way." He figured he could stretch it to a twenty-minute walk or more if he handled it right. Suddenly it was important to him to make every minute count. To part on good terms. "You can fill me in on the local gossip."

Rebecca just stared at him, not seeming to know what to say.

"Never mind," he muttered, turning toward the house in self-disgust. What was he *thinking*?

"Jake, wait."

He looked down at Rebecca's hand resting on his forearm, and flashed back to their night together in Pittsburgh. Heat pooled in his groin as he remembered the feel of those fingers in his hair, on his skin as he poured himself into her.

"What?" he growled, feeling confused and not liking it.

11

"I'm not afraid to be seen with you."

Gripping their dirty plates tighter, he met her cornflower blue eyes.

"We have a history, Jake," she said quietly.

"As kids, Rebecca. Kids." He refused to bring up their night in Pittsburgh. It shouldn't have happened, and he'd roast in hell before he'd let it happen again. Rebecca deserved better. So much better. "We're adults now. Adults on the opposite ends of the social spectrum—and not just in Warner. You're a pillar of the community and I'm a convict on parole. You think mamas are going to let their little darlings anywhere near your library if they think there's even the slightest chance they might run into me?"

Her fingers tightened on his arm, the pressure almost painful. "Then why did you come back, Jake? Why did you invite me to dinner?"

"Temporary insanity. I thought…" The heat from her hand spiked the heat in his groin. The look in her eyes demanded answers. He swore and pulled away, ignoring her hurt expression. "The truth is I wasn't thinking at all. If I had been, I never would have done it."

"Come home or invited me to dinner?"

"I didn't even know you were in town until I got here," he shot back defensively.

"So if you'd known, you wouldn't have come back to Warner, is that it?"

Jake took a moment to corral his emotions. He turned away briefly and set their dirty plates on the cold grill in the darkness at the end of the driveway. "Listen, Becca, I don't know what gave you that idea, but..."

"You've been avoiding me for eight years, Jake. I think it's a reasonable assumption."

"Avoiding you? I've been in prison. For *murder*."

She flinched, but didn't back down. "They don't allow convicted murderers pens or paper in jail? Stamps or envelopes?"

He looked away, ashamed of his attempt to intimidate her, ashamed he'd stopped writing to her after all the letters they'd sent back and forth while he was in the army. "I thought it would be best if I stayed out of your life," he said quietly.

"You thought wrong. We're family, Jake."

"Family? Is that what your cozy little homecoming set-up was all about? Because if it was, you're way off base, Becca. Way off. There's no way in hell we can go back to being buddies. Not after that night in Pittsburgh."

Rebecca flushed violently. Jake swore in bitter frustration. Now he'd done it. Why couldn't he have just kept his mouth shut and let her go?

"Was it that bad, Jake?"

The pain in her eyes, in her voice, stabbed into his heart. "Bad? Of course not. It was the most." Terrifying experience of his life until that point, including his time in the army. And he'd been some scary places in the army. Four years apart, and within hours of seeing her again, Rebecca had turned him inside out. In one short night she'd made a complete sham of everything he'd convinced himself of concerning their buddy-buddy relationship, made his soul ache for everything he was never going to have. Her. A big house on the water she could fill with antiques to her heart's content. Kids. The whole shebang. He shook his head. The less said, the better. "No. It wasn't bad. Believe me."

"Then why did you leave without saying goodbye? Why did you run straight to another woman's bed?"

He stared, knowing he hadn't. Not by a long shot. It had taken him a solid week of hard riding—riding like the hounds of hell were snapping at his heels—to reach that dive in Wyoming. A vision of Christine, the long-legged, red-haired, blue-eyed rodeo widow who'd come on to him that night flashed across his mind. She'd said she was lonely—he'd been game. Several beers and a handful of slow dances later had them walking to her trailer in the court behind the bar, then kissing like there was no tomorrow on the kitchen table.

Until he'd realized what he was trying to do.

Until he'd realized Christine wasn't the red-haired, blue-eyed woman he wanted.

"It wasn't like that, Rebecca," he said wearily.

"Then tell me how it was."

"No. It's over. The woman is dead. I've paid for it with eight years of my life. I don't want to re-hash the reason why. I had acres of time to cover that ground in prison."

Just then a car eased into the driveway, its headlights off. Suddenly a girl's voice screamed, "Oh, God, it's *him*!"

Jake swore as two more screams split the evening air and the driver hit the gas. He grabbed Rebecca and pushed her against the side of the house, putting himself between her and the car. The dark sedan lurched forward, hit the hibachi grill and knocked it over before screeching into reverse. Gravel sprayed the back of his jeans as the car peeled backwards out of the driveway. Tires squealed as the vehicle roared down the quiet residential street.

Neither Jake nor Rebecca moved for a good ten seconds. His arms were around her to protect her back, her hands gripped fistfuls of his shirt. Both of them were breathing hard.

Slowly Rebecca relaxed her hands and Jake stepped back, still holding her elbows. "Are you all right?"

"What was that all about?"

Jake willed himself to keep moving backward, away from the tempting warmth of her body, the sweet strawberry smell of her hair and skin. The urge to pull her close again and lose himself inside her unbelievable softness was just shy of painful. "Teenagers. Looking for a cheap thrill, I guess." His fingers tightened on her elbows. "You sure you're okay?"

"I'm fine. Just spooked." But she was still breathing hard.

Simmering with residual anger and fresh regret, he forced himself to let her go. "I'm sorry, Rebecca. I never should've invited you over. I forgot how fast news travels in Warner. And how little there is for kids to do on a Friday night."

"It doesn't matter, Jake. And it was just kids." She started brushing off her dress. Jake caught a flash of cleavage in the moonlight as she bent forward. He damn near cracked his molars gritting his teeth against the surge of need that boiled up inside him.

"It should matter," he snapped. "Cell phones were probably burning up minutes all over town after my visit to the library this afternoon."

She stopped brushing and looked up at him. "So?"

He raked his gaze over her, making sure she couldn't mistake his meaning. "We both know I wasn't there to check out books, Rebecca."

She straightened slowly. "The town doesn't run my life, Jake. I do."

She looked so beautiful standing there. Tall and proud and completely sure of herself. Time had given her a confidence and maturity that looked good on her. Damned good.

"Give it a few days," he growled, then looked away, disgusted with himself and the whole sorry situation. He never should have come back to Warner. Never should have stayed once he'd realized Rebecca was here. "Then tell me again."

"All right. I will."

Jake looked back at her in surprise.

"I have to work tomorrow, but I'll be over on Sunday around eleven to help you seed the yard," she said, with what Jake would have sworn was blue fire in her eyes. "And as long as you're planning to fix up the place, the house needs to be painted. I'd suggest white. There's a sale on at Hull's Hardware. They open at ten tomorrow morning."

With that, she left. Jake watched her sail across his barren back yard, her sunny yellow skirt swinging sharply against her spectacular calves, and felt blindsided on too many levels to count. Apparently the quiet little bookworm he'd taken under his wing eighteen years ago had turned into a woman who didn't take anyone's crap.

Especially not his.

Chapter Three

Jake thought he was ready for Rebecca the next time she rounded the hedge that separated their yards. He was wrong. He watched her stride over to where he stood on the back porch, enjoying the warm Sunday morning breeze and considering his options on how to get rid of her when she showed up—and knew he didn't stand a chance.

"Hi," she said, planting her hands on her hips and looking up at him with what had to be her best head librarian look. "Where do you want to start?"

He hadn't seen her since Friday night, guessed it was because the library was open on Saturdays until three, and she went to church on Sunday mornings. Apparently she knew as well as he did that getting together again on Saturday evening would have been a big mistake.

And so would today, especially with her looking as good as she did in shorts.

Mentally, he sighed. She wasn't going to like this at all. "Listen, Becca, I want to thank you again for all your help, but I'm a big boy now. I can handle things on my own from here on out."

Her pretty pink nails flashed up at him as her fingers drummed against her nicely flared hips. "I'm sure you can, big boy. But look at it this way. The sooner you get your house fixed up, the sooner you can ride off into the sunset."

He'd have to be blind, deaf and stupid to miss her cool sarcasm. But he had to admit she had a point. The sooner he was done, the sooner he could book. He studied her again, her red-gold hair a thoroughly tempting mass of soft-looking curls pulled up and back with one of those monster hair clips, and dressed for dirty work in a baggy Tim McGraw T-shirt and faded thigh-high denim shorts that showcased her mile-long legs.

More than enough woman to drive a man who'd spent the last eight years in the company of men insane.

"Did you get the grass seed?" she asked.

Apparently she hadn't noticed the supplies propped against the back porch wall at her feet. Jake nodded in their direction and said dryly, "And the lime, fertilizer and straw. Hull's delivered it yesterday afternoon." On credit, which had amazed him. Turned out he'd made a few trips to Holton Hill with the woman behind the counter way back when. He didn't remember them, or her name, but he'd gratefully accepted the credit she offered.

"Great. Aunt Martha has a spreader we can use."

"I'm surprised you didn't show up with it."

Her delighted laughter reminded him painfully of simpler, happier days. "Feeling a little cornered, Jake? You never did care for the idea of being pushed into anything until you were darned good and ready."

When he didn't respond, her eyes and voice softened enough to make him hard. "I'm sorry. I only meant to help."

How was he supposed to keep his mind on his work and his hands to himself when she looked at him like that?

"Then let's get to it," he practically snarled. He wanted this *over*.

They spent the next seven hours busting butt in the smothering heat. Rebecca's aunt not only had a spreader, but a couple of rakes and an ancient rototiller. The thing was cranky from dampness and disuse, but Jake, who'd been tearing machines apart and putting them back together since before he could read, soon had it oiled and running.

Feeling as if he were jackhammering concrete, he plowed up his hard-packed yard so the grass seed would have a fighting chance. Behind him, Rebecca raked smooth the clumps of dirt he'd left in his wake. Now and then she slipped into the house to get them something cool to drink. Once, she went over to her place and came back with a snack tray of fruit, cheese and crackers. Together they spread straw over the grass seed and fertilizer as the sky darkened and the wind picked up. The first rumble of thunder echoed in the distance as they returned the gardening equipment to her aunt's garage.

"Hungry?" Rebecca asked, after he'd pushed the rototiller back into its cobwebbed corner.

"As a bear, but I don't—"

"Good. I found some canned stew and enough flour and yeast to make baking powder biscuits in the house. The dough's already risen so it won't take but a few minutes to roll out a batch."

She turned and left the garage. Feeling annoyed, Jake followed her back to his house. Enough was enough. He wasn't frigging helpless. He entered the kitchen, planning to tell her he could make his own damn supper. "Rebecca. Hold up a minute."

She opened the refrigerator, and released a blissfully cool burst of air into the room. As she looked at him over the door she smiled, and the warmth in her eyes turned his brain to mush. "What's up?"

Jake lost his breath. The dirt smudges on her left cheek and chin and stray bits of straw in her hair practically begged for his attention. He shoved his hands into his pockets and looked around the room, desperate to focus on anything but her. "Nothing."

"Would you rather skip the biscuits, have an omelet instead? It is kinda hot and sticky to be turning on an oven. You could save the biscuits for morning."

So much for declaring your independence, eh, Donovan?

He forced himself to meet the genuine warmth in her eyes. Warmth born of a friendship forged during many home improvement projects they'd cobbled together as kids, trying to hold their homes together while their parents could care less. Rebecca wasn't acting any differently now than she had back then. He couldn't count how many meals they'd shared while fending for themselves. Saltines and ketchup being one of the more common choices, by default. Until he'd started working at Feeney's, there hadn't been much else they could afford to eat between the times her Great-Aunt Martha invited them in for a treat.

"Stew and biscuits sound good. The storm'll probably cool the air down." He knew better than to hope the same for himself. Especially when all he could think about was how much he wanted her, about what he wouldn't give to drag her upstairs for a long, cool, shower, then get hot and sweaty with her all over again. Some kind of friend *he* was. "Uh, thanks for stocking the fridge, by the way."

She'd left eggs, bacon, bread, butter and coffee—a big can of coffee—in addition to that awesome peach pie and chicken casserole in the freezer. He'd practically gorged himself on both his first night home.

"You're welcome. I know how it feels to come home to an empty refrigerator."

That she did. Jake winced with fresh guilt as she turned away to knead the dough she'd made earlier. Rebecca had never known her father, and her mother had taken off when Rebecca was sixteen, shortly after he himself had been 'strongly encouraged' by the local law to join the army. He hadn't wanted to go, to leave her to fend for herself, but…

Next thing he knew, he was in boot camp, feeling lonely as all get out, writing his first letter to her out of sheer desperation for someone to connect with he could trust. She'd written back immediately to tell him she'd come home from school one day to find her mother had cleaned out her closets and left.

Somehow Rebecca had pulled herself together and gotten on with her life, earned herself scholarships to both the local two-year college and the University of Pittsburgh…where Jake had tracked her down for a few unforgettable hours, then, as abruptly as her mother, pulled his own disappearing act on her. As he watched Rebecca cut the rolled dough into biscuits with a jelly jar, Jake wondered if he'd fallen into the Twilight Zone. By rights, the woman should hate him for what he'd done. Instead here she was, acting like none of it had ever happened.

Why was she being so nice to him?

"I got the paint," he said, unwilling to ask the question that was really on his mind.

"You did?" Rebecca looked over her shoulder. She seemed genuinely surprised. Jake ached, as he had for most of the day, to release her monster hair clip and see if her hair still fell to her hips.

"You said it was on sale."

"I know, but…I didn't really expect you to do it."

"You didn't?"

She turned back to her biscuits. "Of course not," she said breezily. "Since when have you ever listened to me?"

Jake stared at her slender shoulders and back, stumped. Obviously the woman had no idea of the impact she'd had on his life, of the decisions he'd made, by and large, because of her.

Then again, you've never told her.

If you have any sense left, you never will.

As they sat down to dinner, Jake squelched a grimace of pain. The souvenir gunshot wound he'd brought home from a not-so-quiet trip to a military hot spot not on the general public's radar was letting him know he was pushing his physical limits. He looked up at Rebecca, buttering a biscuit across the table from him. A lone tendril of red-gold hair slipped free of her hair clip and she swept it back, curling it behind her ear. Even under the harsh glare of the fluorescent light they'd turned on as the sky darkened, her hair shone like burnished gold shot through with fire. Jake recalled how he'd wrapped her silky curls around his wrists in the moonlight and lost himself in her big blue eyes as he buried himself inside her so deeply he…

Hell. Jake shifted in his seat, then burned his tongue on his stew. Half an hour later, Rebecca put away the last of the dishes, cheap iridescent gold glassware Jake recognized in mild amazement as the stuff he'd brought home from Feeney's fifteen years ago. The station had given them away free with fill-ups.

"I'd better get going," Rebecca said as Jake finished wiping the kitchen table. "That storm's about to break loose and my windows are open."

As if on cue, a low rumble of thunder rolled across the sky. Jake glanced out the window and tossed the dishrag into the sink. "I'll walk you."

They paused on the back porch. The air crackled with electricity as another wave of thunder rolled over them. Jake studied the charcoal sky. Considering the sweltering heat, Jake was sure he smelled like a bull, but he'd swear he could still smell strawberries on Rebecca.

The same scent that somehow graced his sheets.

"The furniture upstairs," he said abruptly. "The stuff in the old man's—my room. Whose is it?"

Rebecca didn't answer right away. When she did, it was with a quiet, "Mine."

"Yours? What's it doing over here?"

His sharp surprise had her looking mildly nervous, like she'd been caught with her hand in the cookie jar. "There's no room for it in the apartment. I picked it up at an estate sale six months ago. I needed a place to store it for a while."

And in exchange, she'd cleaned his house. Things were beginning to make sense. "It looks great, Becca."

Her all-out smile did dangerous things to his libido. "Doesn't it? Rosewood. Every last piece of it. Hand-carved."

"Antique?"

"Of course. Can you believe how good a shape that wood is in? It's over three hundred years old. Came all the way from France."

Excitement glowed in her eyes. Unrestrained joy for her lifelong passion of finding treasures other people considered junk. What Jake wouldn't give to be able to put that smile in her eyes, to make her half as happy as her beloved antiques. "I didn't know they made beds that big back then. I mean, weren't people a lot smaller then?"

"This one was custom built. It's somewhere between a queen

and a king size. Impossible to find a mattress for. I think that's why I got such a good deal on it. I had to have a new mattress custom-made and sew the sheets myself."

Jake shifted, suddenly aware that they were discussing a bed. His bed. Rebecca's bed. "What about the quilt?"

Rebecca's smile turned rueful. "A little project I finished up in a hurry a week before you came back."

"You made that quilt for *me*?" The bold red-and-white star pattern flashed across his mind. It must have taken months.

Rebecca frowned at him as if he wasn't quite all there. "No," she said slowly, "I made it for the bed. I started it last winter. I just hurried to finish it when I heard you were coming back. I didn't think you'd be bringing your own bedding." She looked away, out over the yard. "I can have everything moved into storage if you'd rather get your own stuff."

"No. No. It's fine, really. I won't need anything of my own, and you're more than welcome to keep your...things here as long as the place is mine." So the extra set of white sheets with the red satin trim and matching bath towels were hers, too. "I just wondered where it all came from."

Rebecca continued to watch the coming storm. When she finally spoke, Jake had to lean close to hear her above the rising wind. "Most of Mickey's furniture was falling apart, and covered with so many stains, burns, holes and scars it wasn't worth saving. I hope you don't mind that I got rid of it."

Jake didn't hesitate. "Are you kidding? It's a relief not to have to deal with." *Those memories.* "With that stuff."

"I thought as much," she said quietly.

Jake studied her profile, and knew he was in trouble. Even after all these years apart, Rebecca knew him too well. He'd have to be crazy to see her again. To let the feelings he'd locked deep inside himself have any hope of escape.

"Thanks for lighting a fire under me," he said, and slid his hands into his back pockets to keep from touching her. "If you hadn't pushed me into getting started right away, I probably would've slept for a week. Living in prison is like living in a beehive. Between the noise and the total lack of privacy—well, anyway, thanks for the push. And the bed. I've never slept in such a nice one."

Rebecca's grateful smile sent a powerful rush of desire shooting though him. "You're welcome on both accounts," she said, still smiling. "The push...and the bed. I'm glad you like it."

The first fat drops of rain pelted the ground. Jake looked into the cornflower blue eyes that had haunted him nightly for the past eight years and swallowed, hard. "It's great. Really. I wish it were mine."

It could be, if you stayed in Warner.

The thought hit him like a sledgehammer. Jake wasn't sure where the idea came from, but was damned sure it wasn't his. He searched Rebecca's eyes, but found only his own memories of a shared bed in Pittsburgh, and the stirrings of a passion he'd never thought to feel again.

Without thinking, as if it were the most natural thing in the world to do, he stepped toward her and slipped a hand behind her neck. Her eyes widened and her lips parted on a soft gasp, but other than that she just stood there and stared at him like a doe frozen by headlights. Jake smiled and lowered his head, then braced himself for his first taste of ambrosia in eight long years.

Rebecca blinked and placed a searing palm on his chest. "Ah, Jake, I don't think this is a good idea."

His heart felt like it would explode beneath her hand. Their eyes locked, their mouths just inches apart, and Jake heard himself say in a voice so low and gravelly he barely recognized it, "You got a better one?"

She hesitated. "Sure."

"I'm all ears." He waited, caressing her nape with his fingers, and reveled in the silky feel of her skin, the soft strawberry scent of her hair. For a gratifying instant, she seemed to melt into his touch, seemed to sway a little closer. Jake closed his eyes and savored the moment, savored the knowledge she was his, and felt himself rise to the occasion in anticipation of the pure pleasure to come.

"Uh, Jake?"

"Hmmm?"

"Race you to the garage?"

His eyes popped open as she ducked out from under his hand and took off down the steps. He swore at his own stupidity and swung over the porch railing after her. He landed on his bad leg and nearly fell face first into his freshly seeded yard, which was quickly turning into mud. Cursing fluently, he scrambled from his knees to his feet. The rain erupted full force as he reached the six-foot hedge that separated their yards. As he skirted the small, rectangular swimming pool in her aunt's back yard, the gunshot wound in his hip burned with an unholy vengeance. Ignoring the pain, he pitched himself against the side of the garage palms first a split second before Rebecca did the same. "Gotcha."

Half-panting, Rebecca pushed off the garage wall and turned her face to the storm. She'd lost her monster hair clip somewhere around the pool. She reached up with both hands and slicked her soaked mass of curls back, then pressed her palms against the side of the garage and looked up at him, all traces of uncertainty gone from her eyes.

Rebecca the head librarian was back in control.

"You made good time, Donovan."

"Considering you cheated, yeah."

She looked at the sky. "I think we'd better get inside."

Just then the wind and rain surged, creating an incredible racket as it pounded on the corrugated plastic roof that covered the steps leading to her apartment. Jake ignored the shooting pain in his hip and sprinted after Rebecca along the side of the garage. A blinding shaft of lightning cracked close enough for him to smell the ozone as he propelled her up the steps ahead of him. An ear-splitting boom rent the air before the sky unleashed another fiery bolt, practically on the heels of the first. Swearing, Jake kicked the door open and shoved Rebecca inside. She stumbled and let out a surprised shriek as he dived in after her, knocking her to the floor.

They landed in a wet, muddy tangle of arms and legs. For several stunned seconds, neither of them moved while the air rumbled around them. Breathing hard, Jake mentally took stock of whose limbs were whose—and where. He figured Rebecca was probably doing the same. He got himself oriented and backed away first, bracing his arms on either side of her as he tried to push himself up. A searing pain shot through his hip when he put pressure on his right leg and he swore sharply.

"Jake? Are you all right?"

"I'm fine. Just give me a minute to regroup."

"You're clenching your jaw."

"I'm in pain, here, Rebecca. Unless you plan to do something about it, I suggest we drop the subject."

A long moment passed before they awkwardly pulled apart.

Rebecca stood first, then swept her tangled hair back and over one shoulder. Turning away, she snagged two bath towels from a pile of folded laundry on the couch and handed him one. She began to towel the rainwater from her hair with the other. Her hair didn't reach her hips any more, but was still long enough to wrap around his wrists. Mid-back was Jake's guess.

More than long enough.

Rebecca noticed him staring and stopped drying. Jake forcibly directed his thoughts elsewhere. "Sorry about your door," he muttered. "And the mud." Thanks to him, it was all over the floor. All over Rebecca.

She looked down at the mud that smeared her chest and legs. Her wet T-shirt clung to her like a second skin. She swallowed, and he saw her cheeks flush bright red. No wonder. He was staring at her like a sugar addict in front of the cotton candy booth at the county fair. The combination of mud and water left very little to his imagination.

"It's okay," she said with a strange little catch in her voice. "The door was unlocked. I'm sure it'll be fine." She swung her head around as another crack of thunder shook the building's foundation. "Goodness, will you look at that?"

His heart hammering with a potent mixture of adrenaline, fear, pain, and red-blooded arousal, Jake looked out the apartment-wide triple row of roll-out windows. Above the trees he could see the storm moving over the town like an invading army. The wind howled, and whipped his hair like a desert sandstorm. A brilliant bolt of lightning ripped across the churning charcoal sky, its accompanying thunderclap loud enough to have grown men calling out for mama. He'd seen it happen more than once in the service.

"Incredible, isn't it?"

She didn't sound the least bit fazed. Jake looked down at her and felt something inside him break loose. He took in the soaked, muddy clothes that outlined her every sweet curve and a fierce heat engulfed him as he remembered in agonizing detail the feel of her body pressed against his. He burned everywhere with the need to feel her in his arms again. To keep her there until neither of them cared about anything but the way they'd made each other feel in Pittsburgh.

"Where did you learn to love storms so much?" he breathed, trying desperately to focus on something else.

Her gaze lifted from his mouth to his eyes. "From you."

Jake closed his eyes as the memories tumbled through his mind, painfully vivid memories of storms they'd shared as kids. His body throbbed as he recalled sitting on his back porch, pulling her between his legs and wrapping his arms around her from behind, keeping her close and warm and safe. He'd damn near gone crazy with wanting her once she'd started to fill out, but he'd treasured those stolen moments of shared closeness too much to risk losing her trust by touching her sexually.

And now...?

"Jake?"

Caught between the past and the present, he opened his eyes and looked down at Rebecca, knowing he was in no condition to start something that could only end in disaster. With a monumental effort at self-control, he shook his head and started to turn away, but Rebecca's unexpected sob stopped him cold.

"Oh, God, Jake, no...please...don't do this to me again."

The raw pain in her voice ripped him apart. Cursing himself all over again for having hurt her eight years ago, for not letting her go when she'd bolted from the house in self-defense tonight, he turned to face her. Turned to take her in his arms and, once and for all, apologize for every rotten thing he'd done to her...

Then get the hell out of her life.

But Rebecca had stepped back, well out of his reach...and looked totally appalled by what she'd just said. What she'd just let slip. "I'm sorry. I didn't mean that the way it came out."

Jake stared into her eyes and knew she was lying. The need was still there. Need and an unmistakable desire. For him. Horror swamped him as he realized Rebecca still wanted him. Mind, heart, body and soul. Physically responding to his touch was one thing, but the need in her eyes, this silent demand for him to give her something he was incapable of giving, was sheer torture.

"Why, Rebecca? Why are you still in Warner? Why do you still want *me*?"

She jolted as if he'd slapped her. "I don't."

"The hell you don't. It's written all over your face."

"You're wrong. I just want some answers from you."

Jake doubted it. But he'd play her game. He wasn't in the mood for the truth tonight anyway. "What kind of answers?"

"I want to know why you left me without a word."

Jake closed his eyes and swore, then looked past her shoulder, calling himself every kind of fool for not leaving her alone when he'd had the chance. *You knew it would come to this, Donovan. You knew.*

"Rebecca. Your windows are still open."

This time she swore, surprising him. Rebecca and swearing didn't go together in his mind. Rain blasted into the kitchen as she pushed past him to close the windows over the sink. Jake turned and rolled shut the windows on his side of the room. That done, he tried to calm his roiling emotions by concentrating on the changes in the apartment. The kitchen had new appliances, and the dining and living room areas were an unfamiliar mix of white wicker and dark wood. The wood, obviously old and lovingly preserved, reminded Jake of Rebecca's bedroom as a girl. And of the bedroom set he was now using.

Jake wondered if she'd kept her old room or moved into her mother's, then shoved his thoughts in another direction. This was not the time to be thinking about Rebecca and bedrooms. His body still ached from the unmet need of his earlier arousal. His emotions still recoiled from the question she'd asked.

To apologize was one thing, but to explain would mean exposing himself, and that he couldn't afford to do. If Rebecca had any idea of how much he cared, he'd never leave Warner again.

He turned back to the kitchen and noticed her mopping up the counters. He grabbed a towel from the couch, and moved to help her by soaking up the muddy puddles on the floor. His hip screamed in protest, but he didn't care. It got his mind off other things.

Apparently Rebecca enjoyed her work with the children at the library if the number of art projects she'd brought home with her was any clue. Tossing the first soaked towel into the empty kitchen sink, Jake glanced at the colorful paintings and craft projects that decorated the refrigerator door. He returned to the couch for another towel and noticed the crude ceramic handprint bowl on the coffee table. A battered Raggedy Ann peered up at him from beside the pile of folded towels.

Rebecca disappeared down the hall, probably to close the bedroom windows. Jake finished mopping up the main living area, then stood and took a look around, grateful his emotions were beginning to settle down. Except for the white wicker, the place was pure Rebecca, all the way down to the recent copies of *Antiques*, *Town and Country*, and *Country Victorian* on the coffee table.

Seemed her dreams hadn't changed all that much. She was still into antiques and upscale living.

So what was she doing here in Warner? And what did it have to do with *him*?

Jake's gaze shifted to the ceramic handprint bowl next to the magazines, then lifted to the battered Raggedy Ann doll on the couch.

She had a child.

"No."

The word escaped him in fervent denial. He stood there for a long moment, stunned to the core, feeling fresh waves of shock and disbelief roll through him as intensely as the storm that raged outside.

Then Jake did what he did best.

He bolted.

Chapter Four

Tuesday morning found Rebecca in her office, grumbling over the library budget proposal spread across her desk. Each year it was the same old story. The community's response to the programs the library had introduced during the year was more than positive, but the town council—its chairman in particular—didn't want to pay for them.

This year she had the added challenge of how to fund the upcoming building expansion, as well. The money to add on the new rooms had already been raised through tireless community efforts, but she'd need new equipment, furniture, books, etc. to fill the new space. The council apparently expected her to pull the money out of thin air.

Then there was her other problem. Jake. He'd vanished while she was closing the windows in Katie's bedroom. Once she'd recovered from her stunned disbelief, she'd decided she couldn't blame him.

She'd wanted him. In the middle of the storm. In the middle of her living room floor. And Jake had realized it. She'd seen the shock in his eyes, heard the disbelief in his voice.

She'd been pretty shocked herself. Getting involved with Jake again hadn't been part of the plan. Even now, recalling the unmistakable desperation in her voice when she'd begged him not to do this to her again made her burn with embarrassment.

She'd just have to get over it. She'd done it before, she could do it again. So what if she'd humiliated herself in front of the man Sunday night? She wasn't the important one here anymore, Katie was. And Katie deserved the chance to know her father. Just as Jake deserved to know about Katie.

But if simply letting Jake know she wanted him made him feel as trapped as he'd suddenly looked, what would telling him he was a father do?

The telephone on her desk rang. Irritated by the interruption, Rebecca answered it abruptly.

"Having a bad day?"

"Jake?"

"Got it in one, considering this is the first time we've ever talked on the phone."

Jake was calling her? Rebecca closed her eyes and slumped back in her chair, feeling ridiculously weak with relief. Maybe she *wouldn't* have to chase him down again.

"I'm calling to apologize for Sunday night." Jake said. "I, uh, shouldn't have left without saying goodbye."

"Oh." Her spirits soared, then sank. "I see." Was he saying goodbye *now*? Leaving town? Because of her?

"Guess I've kind of made a habit of it. Cutting out on you like that."

"Yeah, well, I've kind of gotten used to it." Rebecca winced even before the words were out. Here the man was apologizing and she was rubbing it in his face. Way to go, Becca.

Silence, then: "Guess I deserved that."

Rebecca couldn't agree, or disagree, without making things worse. "So, how much longer do you think you'll be in town?" she asked as casually as she could. Might as well spare herself the suspense.

A pause, as if he might be trying to gauge the reason behind her question. "Long enough. I found the stash of bills you left inside the bible on my dresser."

"Oh, I forgot about that. That wasn't my money, Jake. It was already there."

"You're kidding. It couldn't have been Mickey's—he wouldn't have opened a bible if his life depended on it."

"Maybe that's why your mother put it in there."

"My mother?" Jake seemed stunned.

"It was her bible, wasn't it?"

"Well, yeah, but...oh, wow."

Silence reigned, while Jake apparently digested this new information, and Rebecca considered the image of Jake actually opening the bible in search of guidance after their emotionally tumultuous encounter Sunday night.

Was it possible he'd found some faith in prison?

On the other end of the line, Jake cleared his throat. "Anyway, I stocked up on food yesterday. Started scraping the house, too."

"I know. I heard you." She'd spent *her* Monday afternoon sitting by the pool, listening to him scrape, and driving herself crazy. She knew what she had to do, but her fears and insecurities had kept her too paralyzed to even take the first step.

"I thought you were at work."

"The library is closed on Mondays."

"Oh." He sounded confused. "You didn't come over."

He'd actually expected her to show up? Apparently her humiliating revelation Sunday night hadn't repelled him as much as she'd thought.

Ignoring the implications of *that*, Rebecca vowed not to let her emotions get in the way of telling him about Katie again. God was giving her another chance. She wouldn't mess up this time. She swiveled her desk chair so that it faced away from her office door for privacy and lowered her voice. "To tell the truth, my muscles were a little sore. I also had some work to do. It's budget time." Not that she'd been able to concentrate for anything, knowing he was just on the other side of the hedge.

"Does that mean you won't be interested in stopping by to help paint?"

"Tonight?"

"Whenever. It's going to take a couple of coats."

God was definitely giving her another chance. Rebecca laughed in gratitude and sheer relief. Maybe they could work their way through this mess like the friends they had once been after all. Like responsible adults. "Count me in. I've got some laundry to finish up at Aunt Martha's, but I can be at your place by seven."

Still feeling blessed, she swung her chair back around and hung up the phone. Avery Dillenger, reigning chairman of the town council, all but glared at her from her office doorway.

Rebecca's smile fell. "Avery. What can I do for you?"

"Was that Donovan?"

Taking in Avery's Italian suit, salon-styled hair and classically handsome features, Rebecca could see why, at age thirty-two, some considered him the town's most eligible bachelor. Registering his superior expression and contemptuous tone of voice, she knew why others disagreed.

"Jake?" she asked coolly. "Yes, it was. He got home on Thursday night."

"So I heard. You're seeing him again?"

"Seeing him *again*? Jake and I were never a couple, Avery. We're friends."

"You expect me to believe that? You never laughed like that around me."

Not for the first time, Rebecca regretted having briefly dated Avery during her first summer back in Warner. She'd finally accepted his third or fourth invitation to dinner in a moment of weakness after Katie's fifth birthday—the fifth birthday she'd had to celebrate without a father.

But things hadn't worked out with Avery—on any level—so as gracefully as she could, Rebecca had stopped seeing him.

Avery hadn't taken her rejection well. That fall he'd been installed as council chairman—and her boss on paper. In reality, she reported to the entire council. But for the past two years, Avery had made it known he claimed a special interest in his library director. He seemed to take perverse pleasure in making her job as difficult as possible.

"Why are you here, Avery? Is there a problem with the library?"

His lips tightened in a way she knew well. Avery Dillenger didn't like being challenged. By anyone. "The council's going to want to take a look at your proposed budget at the next meeting," he said with unnecessary authority.

"I'm aware of that. I've been working on it for the past two weeks."

"We're also going to address the subject of whether to renew your contract at the end of the fiscal year."

She smiled blandly. "The council does that every September, Avery. It's part of the budget approval process. What's different about this year?"

"The company you keep."

"Excuse me?"

"You know who I'm talking about. The man's a convicted killer. We don't need him around frightening our women and children."

"He's not some kind of escaped wild animal, Avery."

"What do you think prison is, Rebecca? Summer camp? Donovan's been living with animals for eight years. He's got no chance of fitting into a quiet family community like Warner."

"Just where do you suggest he go?"

"I don't care, as long as it's not here. As council chairman, I have to look at the whole picture. Weighing the impulses of one man against the safety of an entire town—"

"You make it sound like Jake's going to snap out and go on some kind of rampage."

"From what I hear, he's done it before. Can you say he won't do it again? Do you know him well enough to guarantee it?"

"I'm not responsible for Jacob Donovan, Avery."

"Maybe not, but as our library director, you're responsible to the citizens of this community. If they don't feel safe coming here, we'll have to find someone for the job who inspires their trust."

Rebecca went cold inside, then hot. The supercilious bastard. He was actually putting her on notice. "If you're finished, Avery," she said icily, "I have work to do."

"I'm merely pointing out what you're up against, Rebecca. It's not only me who's wondering."

"Wondering *what*?" If Jake was going to start killing people in their sleep? People couldn't be that paranoid, could they?

"Think about it, Rebecca. He killed a woman in a sexually motivated crime."

"I refuse to believe that."

"You're saying twelve jurors and a judge were wrong?"

"I'm saying the evidence against Jake was circumstantial at best." The paper had said Jake allegedly strangled the woman in her bed when she'd changed her mind about having sex with him. Rebecca routed the ugly images from her mind. Jake resorting to murder when a woman said no? Totally ludicrous. "The Jacob Donovan I know would never have been capable of such a heinous crime," she added without any hint of uncertainty.

"The Jacob Donovan you knew, Rebecca," Avery corrected arrogantly. "Past tense. You have no idea what the man is capable of now. Has he told you about prison? The things he saw and did there?" He drew the question out as if the subject gave him a secret thrill. Rebecca suppressed a shudder at the thought. "Think about it, Rebecca. Think about what else he's keeping from you. You might have been friends as kids, but you haven't got a clue as to how his mind works now. If I were you, I'd watch my back."

"Jake wouldn't hurt me, Avery."

"From what I understand, he already has," Avery said smugly.

Rebecca's stomach took a header, and she mentally cursed the town gossips, but kept her expression bland and pointedly picked up her report. "If you're finished fishing?"

Dillenger's smile fell. "See you at the next council meeting, Ms. Reed. Make sure your figures add up."

****

Rebecca's unsettling exchange with Avery practically consumed her thoughts for the rest of the afternoon. By the time she left work, she'd revived her determination to get a few answers from Jake. The man owed her.

She stepped into his yard and spotted him immersed in painting the east side of the house. He'd chosen white to cover the weatherbeaten gray. She recalled throwing the suggestion at him in the heat of anger. Seeing he'd taken her up on it softened her mood somewhat. She took a moment to gather her courage, and couldn't help but notice the changes in him over the past four days.

He looked healthier, heartier...and sexier than ever in a faded pair of denim cutoffs and new Nikes. The muscles in his tanned back and arms rippled like water as he moved the brush up and down the side of the house in smooth, even strokes. He bent to catch a spot he'd missed on the lower part of the house and Rebecca caught a glimpse of pale white skin as his shorts slipped down the small of his back. He wasn't wearing underwear.

Heat suffused her. A vivid memory of pale pink sunlight filtering into her college apartment bedroom as she drank in the sight of Jacob Donovan, gloriously naked and sleeping in her bed at last, filled Rebecca with such need she nearly groaned.

God. The memories were so sharp. So painful. How could she get him to open up about that night, when *she* couldn't even think about it without hurting?

More important, how was she going to get him to talk to her about what had happened afterward?

Suddenly feeling hurt and inadequate and insecure all over again, Rebecca double-checked her outfit. The old blue T-shirt she'd put on had seemed a bit snug, so she'd deliberately covered it with an equally old checked cotton shirt. Nobody could accuse her of trying to put the moves on him in either of those, or the faded cutoffs she wore, but the pie in her hands, well that was a different matter.

That was bribery, plain and simple.

She needed to spend some time with Jake and food offerings seemed to be her best bet so far. After all, he'd invited her back to help him some more—which he wouldn't have done the week before.

Pasting a confident smile on her face, she approached him from behind. He'd stopped painting and was intently scraping trim from the dining room windowsill.

She tapped him on the shoulder. "Hey, Donovan, look—"

The next thing she knew she was back first against the house, a steely forearm pressing into her windpipe, a heavy knee between her legs. A look of black ice filled Jake's eyes, striking terror deep in Rebecca's soul. She lifted her hands in self-defense, but before she could grab Jake's arm to try to pull it away, he stepped back as if she'd scalded him.

"Jesus, Rebecca. I'm sorry. Are you okay?"

"I...I...don't know." Feeling dazed and disoriented, Rebecca started to look at Jake, then changed her mind, unwilling to face that horrible blackness in his eyes again. She glanced away in confusion, and spotted the shattered red raspberry pie, its sticky filling spattered obscenely across the side of Jake's freshly painted white house. A wave of dizziness washed over her and her knees started to buckle. "Jake, I..."

He swore and caught her before she hit the ground. Her heart still racing, she found herself torn between wanting to pull away and wanting to lean into his warm strength as he carried her into the house.

Jake wouldn't hurt her. What had just happened between them was a mistake. An ugly, horrible, *explainable* mistake. It had to be. He'd scared the snot out of her, but he hadn't hurt her. As soon as he'd recognized her, he'd stopped whatever it was he was about to do to her.

With trembling arms, he sat her down on the living room couch. "Rebecca? Are you all right?"

She tried to speak, but couldn't. Her mind kept returning to the horrible darkness in his eyes. The astonishing strength and speed with which he'd pinned her to the house.

Jake went down on one knee. "Rebecca?"

She blinked, then realized she'd never seen him look so pale, or uncertain of himself. Clearly, he was as shaken as she was by what had just happened. "I'm...fine," she managed to croak. Something wasn't working right in her throat. "Fine." She shuddered in an involuntary spasm of relief, and spotted paint on the couch seat. "I'm getting paint on your couch."

"Forget the couch, Rebecca, it's you I'm worried about. Are you okay?"

She took a moment to remove her outer shirt, grateful for the distraction. Jake took it from her, folded the paint stains inside, then laid it aside. "I'll buy you a new one."

"No. You don't have to. Really. It's old, and I was...I was planning on getting paint stains on it anyway."

"I'm sorry, Rebecca. I wasn't expecting you so soon."

Confused, she looked at her watch. It was seven on the dot. Jake's gaze followed hers.

"Wow. Is it that late already? I must have lost track of time."

34

He squeezed her hands once and stood. "I'll get you some water. Here," he said, returning half a minute later to where Rebecca sat on the couch, still fighting the adrenaline shakes. Awkwardly he handed over the glass. His hands seemed to be shaking as well.

Rebecca closed her eyes and took one small sip of water, then another. "So..." she began awkwardly. "Where did you learn how to do that?"

"In the army."

"I thought you were a mechanic."

"Mechanic, driver, and unofficial body guard for—"

"The General, I remember. You'd gone someplace and couldn't tell me where you were. You took a bullet in the hip and saved his life."

"Yeah, well, the training he sent me for saved mine."

"In the army, or in prison?"

"Both. Listen, Rebecca, I'm really sorry. I'm still not used to being out."

"No. I…I should have realized."

"Realized what? That I'd attack you?"

"It was self-defense, Jake."

His expression hardened. "Not this time."

Rebecca let the subject drop, unwilling to ask if he'd been attacked from behind in prison. Surely no one could live in such a hellish place for eight years without being taken unawares at least once.

"How does your throat feel?"

She managed a reassuring smile. "Fine." It was true. He hadn't hurt her, just scared her. She studied his face, and tried to reconcile his gentle care and concern with the lethal moves he'd used on her earlier. It had happened so fast, she couldn't even remember him moving. All she knew was that in the split second before he'd recognized her, she'd been convinced she was a goner.

Avery's warning that afternoon came to mind, and for the first time since she'd known Jake, Rebecca had to ask herself who *was* the real Jacob Donovan? Regret and remorse filled his dark eyes as he seemed to read the question in hers, and suddenly she knew. Jake's years in the army had trained him to kill, but Jacob Donovan was no killer. Beneath his combat training was a complex man with a conscience who suffered just as she would if she'd inadvertently caused an innocent creature pain.

"I'm sorry, Rebecca. So sorry."

She reached out to touch his face. "It's all right, Jake. Really.

35

I'm okay now."

"Maybe you should see a doctor."

"For what? I lost my voice for a couple of minutes, but that was from fright, not because you hurt me in any way."

He looked into her eyes for what seemed like forever. "Nothing happened, Jake. Really." She touched his warm cheek, feeling closer to him than she ever had, yet farther apart. This was her Jake, but she was only now realizing there were parts of his life he would never share with her, parts of him she would never be given the chance to try to understand. The idea saddened her more than she would have thought possible, given the dark days of anger and bitterness she'd had to fight off over the years.

But now, all she felt was regret. Regret, and the need to feel his lips on hers again.

Without thinking twice, she leaned forward to kiss him.

Jake pulled back abruptly, leaving her feeling stung to her soul. "I'll see you home now," he said roughly, not meeting her eyes.

She accepted his cool, impersonal hand up from the couch, and reminded herself she should have known better.

Jacob Donovan had never wanted her, and never would.

****

Jake sat alone in the dark, a pale sliver of moonlight illuminating the dishes he hadn't bothered to clean up after he'd walked Rebecca home. At his elbow sat a forgotten cup of coffee, black and stone cold.

He'd spent the hours since he'd left her thinking about Rebecca. She'd always had more compassion than anyone he'd ever known, but tonight she'd transcended compassion into...what? He'd never forget the deep well of understanding in her eyes, or the gentleness of her touch as she'd forgiven him for, at the very least, scaring her half to death.

She'd forgiven him for so much. But Jake couldn't forgive himself. Not for not leaving her alone in the first place, and not for exposing her to the beast he battled inside himself daily. It took every ounce of control he had to walk around Warner pretending he was as normal as the next man. Every time he left the house, he could feel the eyes boring into his back, waiting and watching and wondering what he was going to do next.

Wondering if he was going to snap out again, like he had on that poor, innocent woman in Wyoming.

His prosecutor had been so convincing. She'd gotten ahold of

Jake's juvenile record, and while it wasn't admissible in court, she'd still managed to use it to plant seeds about him as a hot-tempered man recently injured in a military skirmish, quite possibly suffering from PTSD. The experts she'd brought in had convinced the jury it was more than possible he'd had some kind of combat flashback while he was in bed with Christine, and gone ballistic on her. They hadn't been convincing enough to net him a not guilty by reason of temporary insanity, but they'd kept him from serving life without parole, much to his pretty young prosecutor's disappointment.

Then, in that hellhole she'd sent him to, Jake had scared himself with how close he'd come to being the killer everyone thought he was. The beast inside was why he'd been denied parole for two years after he'd been eligible. That and the programs he'd had to complete. Anger management, batterer's group, victim awareness, half a dozen courses in all. He'd learned right away that until he'd satisfied their requirements, jumped through all their hoops, they weren't going to let him out of that place. Never mind that their courses had done nothing to tame the beast inside him. Nothing at all.

And now, tonight, he'd almost unleashed it on Rebecca.

The fear in her eyes would haunt him forever. Just thinking about what could have happened…

Swearing fluently, Jake pushed away from the table. He stood and scrubbed his hands over his face. The kitchen clock said it was three in the morning. He stepped onto the back porch and took in a deep draft of cool night air. The sight of Rebecca's apartment didn't help. A light shone in the rear left bedroom, the one that overlooked the pool, the one that had been her bedroom as a girl.

The thought that Rebecca was still awake, alone and quite possibly in pain, drove him off the porch and into the shadows. But instead of moving forward, toward Rebecca and the light, Jake turned away, toward the shadows of his silent street. By the time he reached the end of his dirt and gravel drive, he was jogging, by the end of his street, he was running. At the first intersection he hung a right, not knowing or caring where he was headed.

All he knew was he had to keep moving or he'd explode.

He ran until the pain in his hip felt like it would kill him, then ran some more. Sweat streamed down his face and soaked his black T-shirt as he pushed himself through the chilly August pre-dawn, determined to outrun his demons.

At the east edge of town, half delirious from pain and

exhaustion, he stopped in the shadows of the old railway station to catch his breath. Moments later a late model Lincoln Town Car with tinted windows cruised into the neighborhood. Jake's instincts went on full alert as it passed him as softly as a whisper, then turned left in front of the boarded-up train station.

The Lincoln eased to a stop at the T-shaped intersection a block away. The back door opened and a boy who couldn't be more than ten or twelve emerged. He hit the pavement and didn't stop moving, running away from the Lincoln as fast as he could.

The Lincoln left as quietly as it had appeared, turning around in the middle of the street and gliding toward Glenhill, where Jake would bet his black soul one of three or more garage doors waited to soundlessly slide open as the long black Town Car rolled up the curving drive.

As he watched the car's tail lights disappear, Jake couldn't help but wonder who in rich man's land was playing with kids from the wrong side of the tracks in the dead of night.

Chapter Five

Rebecca was putting on her Coral Kiss lipstick the following morning when someone knocked on her apartment door. She opened it to find Jake standing there, holding her restored ceramic pie plate in his big hands. A closer look showed more than a dozen spidery cracks.

"I thought I'd bring this back."

Rebecca stared, floored by the image of him searching out all the pieces of a nine-ninety-nine ceramic pie plate, in the dark, no less—then painstakingly cleaning them and gluing them back together. Maybe he thought it was an antique?

"You can't talk?"

She lifted her gaze at his sharp question. "Of course I can talk. I'm just..." she nodded at the pie plate. "Overwhelmed. That must have taken you forever."

Jake shrugged, looking away as he handed the plate over, but not before she caught the embarrassed relief in his eyes. Apparently he was still hung up on the idea he'd physically hurt her last night. She accepted the plate and invited him inside. He stepped across the threshold as if entering the gallows.

Rebecca turned to set the pie plate on the kitchen table and surreptitiously blew out a long breath, knowing she had her work cut out for her. Last night Jake had left her at her door with another quiet apology for his behavior. Too emotionally drained to argue, she'd simply nodded her acceptance and said goodnight. The strain of it all had given her a massive headache.

But this morning her head was clear. She'd spent the better part of the night thinking about what she wanted from Jacob Donovan, and it was way past time she told him.

"You on your way to work?" he asked.

"Yes. I've got a budget proposal meeting in..." she glanced at her watch and frowned. Eight-forty already. "Twenty minutes." She met Jake's eyes. "How did you sleep?"

"I didn't."

So Jake was still harder on himself than anyone else could be. Clearly, whatever demons drove him these days were all but eating him alive. The day they'd seeded the lawn, she'd watched him practically push himself into heat exhaustion, stopping only when she shoved a cool drink into his hands. As for last night...God Himself could have shown up in the room and it wouldn't have convinced Jake he'd made an honest mistake.

"I see," she said, refusing to let her emotions get in the way again. Because once she got past this particular hurdle, they still needed to talk about Katie. She'd be home Friday.

"I'm sorry," Jake said again.

"I'm all right," Rebecca said, keeping her voice as calm and neutral as she could. "I should have warned you I was behind you."

"I could have hurt you, Rebecca. Badly."

"I'm aware of that. But you didn't. Now let it go."

He studied her face, then her throat. Rebecca realized he was looking for bruises. There weren't any—not even a hint of any. She'd checked and double checked herself, even though he'd barely touched her. It was the look in his eyes that had scared her.

Apparently satisfied he'd left no marks on her, Jake stepped back and reached for the door. "I'll get out of your way, then. I just wanted to make sure you were okay."

Sure. As long as he didn't count the body slam he'd given her heart when he'd rejected her kiss last night.

"I'm fine."

"I'm glad. Goodbye, Rebecca."

And with that, he was gone. Rebecca stared at her empty doorway, feeling rejected and hurt all over again. Damn the man, she thought, as an oppressive wave of heat and humidity rolled into the apartment in his wake. This time he wasn't coming back. Rebecca knew it in her bones. She scooped up her purse and briefcase, and charged out the door after him. "Jake. Wait."

At the foot of the stairs he stopped, caught in mid-flight. His dismayed expression made it clear he'd hoped for a clean getaway. She willed her heart to stop its wild, fearful hammering, locked her eyes on his and descended the steps, suddenly glad she'd taken extra time with her hair and make-up today. She knew her coral suit was one of her most flattering. She needed that to muster her courage as she joined him on the concrete drive. "We need to talk."

He eyed her warily. "About what?"

About our daughter. She licked her suddenly parched lips, and swallowed, hard. She couldn't do it. Not here. Not now. She was due at work in less than fifteen minutes. She couldn't simply drop the bomb that that Jake was a father and go to her budget meeting. "About...about us."

His features hardened. "There is no us, Rebecca."

Her temper flashed, shunting her fear aside. "How can you say that? We were friends, Jake. We were—"

"Lovers?" Hard black eyes bored into angry blue ones for a turbulent moment before he looked away. "Don't remind me."

Stung pride stiffened her spine, put acid in her voice. "I'm sorry you find the memory so unpleasant."

He jerked his head back around. "Rebecca, that's not—"

"Don't try to spare my feelings now, Jake. God knows you haven't yet."

He looked as if she'd slapped him. A dull red flush crept up his face, and she realized he was hanging on to his control by a thread. Rebecca set her briefcase down and crossed her arms, meeting him glare for glare. She'd never get a better chance to push him over the edge. "I'm waiting, Jake."

Resentment flared in his eyes, but when he spoke, it was in even, measured beats. "I left, Rebecca, because of you. Because that was exactly what I was trying to do—spare *your* feelings." His voice deepened a notch, roughened. "Because I thought things would be less complicated for you with me out of the picture."

She kept her arms crossed, refusing to be moved by the grudging admission. Refusing to acknowledge the spark of hope that ignited in her heart. "Less complicated for me, or for you?"

"For you, of course! Damn it, Rebecca—"

"And now?" she cut in ruthlessly.

He gave her another long, hard stare, clearly battling his emotions, then looked away. "And now it's not an issue any more. You're here and I'm leaving."

Her arms came uncrossed. She wanted to hit him. "Why do you keep *saying* that?"

"Because it's true! I *am* leaving, Rebecca. Just as soon as I can."

"*Why?*"

"You have to ask? Have you forgotten the reason I had to leave Warner in the first place?" His angry vehemence couldn't help but make her wonder if he was trying to convince her or himself. "I was considered a menace to society then, Rebecca. Who knows what the town considers me now."

"What difference does it make? Why do you let what a bunch of narrow-minded bigots *might* think bother you?"

"Rebecca, we're not talking about a minor youthful

indiscretion or two here. Warner's finest are convinced they have a *bona fide* killer in their midst."

She looked at him for a long, considering moment. "So stay and prove them wrong."

"Are you kidding?"

Rebecca stood there, secure in her convictions regarding Jake's innocence, despite his statement to the contrary the other night. Yesterday Jake had proven beyond a doubt that even in the grip of blind rage, he was incapable of hurting her physically, or— and she would stake her life on it—any woman.

Even now, she was doing her best to rattle his cage and he was fighting back tooth and nail—with self-control.

"We can work things out, Jake," she said softly, relenting. "I know it. If you'd just stay in Warner."

Jake's anger deflated like a balloon with a fast leak. She looked so brave standing toe-to-toe with him in her suit that matched her lipstick. Brave and strong and beautiful. He'd insulted her, abandoned her, damn near bruised her, and still she hung on. Looking up at him with those clear, trusting blue eyes, holding out an olive branch he desperately wanted to accept.

"I can't, Rebecca," he said, his voice harsh with regret. *I can't do that to you.*

Her eyes searched his, too keenly for comfort. He held his ground, but knew he'd lost the battle when she said gently, "You're never going to find what you need anywhere else, Jake."

He sneered in sheer self-defense. "And just how the hell would *you* know what I need?"

She flinched, and Jake felt as if he'd kicked a kitten.

"I guess I don't," she said with enough quiet dignity to shame him for the rest of his life. Turning away, she started for her car. As he watched her walk away, head held high, slender back rigidly straight, everything in Jake ached to follow her and apologize. To tell her she was wrong. To tell her he knew he was being a bastard, and why.

Didn't she understand that if he stayed, he'd only let her down again and again? He couldn't give her what she wanted. Couldn't be what she wanted. He didn't have it in him to be that good.

Hadn't he already proven that, over and over again, with his family?

****

"Mom, can Jenna and I go swimming?"

Rebecca looked up from the budget proposal she was trying in vain to proof-read at the kitchen table and smiled, grateful for the interruption. She couldn't focus. Hadn't been able to concentrate on much of anything, in fact, since her daughter and aunt had returned last night. All she could think about was Jake didn't want her, and she hadn't told him he had a daughter.

But she couldn't keep Katie under lock and key because of her own failings. She hadn't heard from Jake since their stalemate Wednesday morning. No surprises there. He'd made himself more than clear concerning any kind of relationship between the two of them. There wasn't going to be one. Knowing about Katie wasn't going to change that.

"Sure, honey, just let me put this budget stuff away and get changed. Why don't you run over and get Jenna, and I'll meet you down by the pool?"

Katie left, and Rebecca closed her eyes, then breathed deeply in a hopeless effort to reclaim the sense of peace she'd prided herself on before Jake's return. It refused to come.

Rebecca knew why. As long as Jake didn't know about Katie, Rebecca was living a lie.

Maybe she could send Katie over to Jenna's for a couple of hours after dinner. Then beard the lion in his den and tell him everything. Get it all out.

Half an hour later, Rebecca was parked in a lounge chair with her favorite Barbara Delinsky, trying her best to relax while the girls splashed and squealed in the pool. Reaching for her glass of lemonade on the table beside her, she looked up from her book and nearly had heart failure.

Jake stood on her side of the hedge, hands on his hips, watching his daughter and her best friend play in the pool.

In that instant, Rebecca knew why she'd sidestepped every chance she'd had to tell Jake about Katie. She was terrified. Soul deep terrified. Not of Jake but of what he would do when he found out Katie was his.

Rebecca knew all too well how much it hurt to be rejected by the people she'd wanted most to love her. Both her parents had rejected her, and so had Jake. She had no reason to expect him to welcome her child into his life, and Rebecca couldn't stand the thought of Jake rejecting Katie the way she'd been rejected. She'd rather die than have her innocent little girl subjected to that kind of pain.

Jake spotted her glued to the lounge chair. He approached

slowly, as if torn between returning home without speaking and attempting civility. He nodded politely. "Afternoon, Rebecca."

She nodded in return, unable to find her voice. He looked rough and rumpled, and sexier than sin in his faded denim cut-offs and Nikes. Her heart squeezed painfully.

Be careful what you wish for, she thought. She'd wished for another chance with Jake, and now...

"I heard the noise. Thought maybe I should check it out."

"I see," she finally managed.

Jake looked down at her and suppressed a weary sigh. So she was still pissed at him. He didn't blame her. But he couldn't take his eyes off of her, either. She was stunning in white. Her strapless one-piece suit showed off her slender arms and endless legs to perfection. Not to mention her tan. With her hair swept up in some kind of bun, her shoulders practically begged him to lean over and take a taste. He shifted uncomfortably as his mind moved on to the possibilities of this new sun-goddess image of Rebecca appearing in future fantasies.

"I got a job," he heard himself say, then felt stupid. Like he was trying to impress her. Which he wasn't.

Rebecca blinked and stared. "What did you say?"

Jake wished he'd had the good sense to stay on his side of the hedge. But no, he'd heard the girls laughing and just had to come and see who might belong to that ceramic hand print bowl. Idiot. "I got a job. I'll be working at Feeney's again, starting Tuesday.

Rebecca slowly set her book aside and gave him her full attention. As she straightened, the two wide crisscrossing bands of snug white material cupping her breasts snared *his* attention. He shoved his hands deep into his front pockets, ripping one of them in the process.

"Feeney's?" Rebecca echoed in obvious amazement. "You're kidding. What shift?"

"Morning. Six to three, six days a week, with Mondays off."

He ground his back teeth in a fruitless effort to contain his body's response to her nearness, then looked away, at the girls still splashing in the pool. Something seemed strangely familiar about the red-headed one. Was she Rebecca's? He looked back at Rebecca, and knew he couldn't ask. Not yet.

Coward.

"Ought to make my parole officer happy, anyway. The extra money won't hurt, either, considering what needs to be done on the house."

"Before you sell it, you mean," she said slowly, carefully.

So that was it. She was wondering if he'd changed his mind about staying in Warner. His erection deflated at the thought. "The job's temporary, Rebecca," he said tiredly. "Until his regular mechanic gets back. He was called out of town on family business and Feeney promised to hold his job, but he's getting swamped, so he asked me to fill in for a while." He looked over at the pool again, then crossed his arms over his chest.

In the silence that followed, Jake realized Rebecca had gone very still. She, too, was looking at the girls. Jake took a deep breath, and knew he couldn't put off knowing any longer. "So, who are the kids? They look like they're having a blast."

Rebecca closed her eyes, seemed to take her own deep breath, then said in a strangely subdued voice, "Jenna lives two doors down the street. The blonde." She paused, then rose to stand beside him, her expression determined. "The redhead is my daughter...Katie. She's been in Erie with Aunt Martha."

Jake felt his heart stop at the word "daughter." With a calm he was far from feeling, he watched Katie jump into the pool holding hands with Jenna. Finally, he looked back at Rebecca. So it was true. She was a mother. He let his gaze travel the length of her from head to toe, then back again, before he spoke. He never would have guessed. "I wondered when you would tell me."

"You *knew*?"

Katie and Jenna chose that moment to scramble out of the pool and join them. "Hi, I'm Katie. This is my best friend, Jenna."

Jake faced the girls with a comfortable smile. "Hello, Katie, Jenna. I'm Jake. I..." He trailed off, blinking in stark disbelief at the small, heart-shaped birthmark just above Katie's right ankle. Suddenly his confidence evaporated, and he felt weak all over.

"Rebecca? What's that on Katie's ankle?"

Rebecca frowned, used to surprised looks when it came to Katie's birthmark. From a distance it looked like a tattoo. Rebecca couldn't count the number of people who had commented on it, most of them taking it upon themselves to let her know they thought Katie much too young for tattoos. But the intensity of Jake's reaction alarmed her.

"Jake, are you all right? You look pale."

"It's my birthmark," Katie said. "Mom says I've been kissed by an angel."

"I see," Jake finally said, seeming dazed. "Well, I'm Jake, and I...live over there," he said, hiking a thumb over his shoulder.

"On the other side of the hedge."

"I know. Mom's been waiting forever for you to get here."

He looked at Rebecca, and suddenly she knew something was wrong. Very wrong. His eyes had filled with pain, as if he'd suffered a serious physical blow.

"Were you really in prison?" Jenna asked.

Jake seemed jolted by the question. He blinked and turned back to Jenna, drew a deep breath and said with shaky dignity, "Yes, I was. For eight years."

"Wow. That's a long time," Katie said, her eyes wide with fascination. "Longer than my whole life. What was it like?"

"Katie..." Rebecca began.

"I saw a prison once, when we went to Buffalo to see my grandma," Jenna offered. "We passed it on the road. There was a big fence around it, with lots of round barbed wire at the top, and a bunch of people standing around inside wearing orange. Were you one of them?"

"Ah, no. I was in Wyoming. And it's called razor wire."

"Oh, that's right. I forgot," Jenna said blithely. Obviously the girls had been talking. Either that, or Jenna had overheard someone—her parents, most likely—discussing Jake's return. Her curiosity about him clearly satisfied, Jenna turned to Katie. "C'mon, Katie, let's dive for rings."

The two girls returned to the pool, secure in their innocence. Jake lifted his gaze to the sky, took one deep breath, then another, his big hands flexing on his hips.

"So..." he said unexpectedly, in a tight voice Rebecca barely recognized, "...you made up with good old Mitch after all."

"Who?" Rebecca frowned, confused.

"Mitchell. Mitchell Kane."

"Mitchell?" What was he talking about?

"Yes, Mitchell," Jake said slowly, evenly, his eyes black as coal, and now, surprisingly angry. Angry? About Mitchell? But she hadn't seen, hadn't even thought of him in years. "The rich law student fiancé who was pushing you to take your relationship to the next level. Obviously, he succeeded."

"What?" Rebecca realized what he was saying and stared at him in disbelief. Her anger rose so fast it shocked even her. "Why you sorry son of a—"

"Ah, ah, ah." Jake held up a finger. "We have an audience, remember?"

Rebecca clamped her mouth shut, fuming. Jake's eyes bored

into hers for so long she was sure he could see every last ounce of resentment, anger and bitterness she'd felt toward him over the past eight years. She didn't care. If Jake could believe she'd sleep with Mitchell Kane after sleeping with him, he deserved her anger.

Abruptly Jake broke eye contact. Running a hand through his hair, he exhaled slowly, heavily.

"I'm sorry," he said. "I shouldn't have done that."

Rebecca simply stood there, vibrating with suppressed fury. "You think she's *Mitchell's*?"

"Let's just say I had hopes."

Her disbelief and anger rolled into contempt. "You're disgusting."

"Believe me, Becca. You can't call me anything I haven't called myself since I realized it was a possibility. She *is* mine, isn't she?"

Rebecca blinked, realizing he'd actually been searching for an out by bringing up Mitchell. Her contempt rose to new heights. She lifted her chin, no longer the least bit afraid to tell him the truth. "Yes, Jake, she's yours." There. Deal with *that*, you sorry bastard.

He looked over at the pool. "The girls are coming back. I need to get out of here."

"That's right, Jake. Run again."

"I'm not running, Becca. Damn it, I need some time!"

Rebecca gritted her teeth. "We need to talk about this."

"Not now," he insisted, his voice low and barely contained. "Not here."

"When, then?"

"I don't know."

Too much time, and he might bolt again. How well she knew him. "Tuesday night, then. You can come over for dinner and a swim."

He looked back at her, no doubt wondering if she was sane. Half-wondering the same, she chose to ignore his look. "I can't do it any sooner. We have plans tonight, tomorrow we're working at the church festival, and Monday night I'm speaking at a Kiwanis meeting. Unless, of course, you'd like to join us."

"At a Kiwanis meeting? Get real, Rebecca."

"At the church festival. It lasts all day, but I'm sure I can get away for—"

"Mom, we're going to go up and get a snack, okay?"

"All right, honey. You know where everything is."

"I didn't go to those church things before," Jake practically growled beside her. "I'm sure as hell not going to start going now."

Rebecca swung around to meet his gaze. "But you need to spend some time with her, Jake."

"Are you nuts?" he asked in outright disbelief. "I'm supposed to step in and do the dad thing, eight years later, and in front of the whole damned town? Show them what a model citizen I've become? Show them how *rehabilitated* I am? I don't think so." He looked away, angrily swiping a hand down his face. "Jesus, Rebecca, even *I* didn't deserve this."

Neither of them said anything for a long moment.

"I'm sorry," Rebecca finally offered, quietly. "I should have told you sooner."

"When's her birthday," Jake asked, just as quietly, apparently backing off on his own anger. "I don't doubt she's mine. I just want to know."

"The thirty-first of July."

It fit. Perfectly. Jake closed his eyes against the disgrace of what he'd done. He'd never meant to hurt her. He could imagine all too well what she'd suffered these past eight years, coming back to Warner as an unwed mother after having spent every day of her childhood living down her own mother's reputation for promiscuity.

"All right," he heard himself say wearily, suddenly feeling bone deep exhausted. He, Jacob Donovan, had an eight-year-old daughter. One who bore the Dillenger family birthmark. A Dillenger. He needed a drink. Make that a whole frigging bottle. "I'll come to dinner on Tuesday." Meeting Rebecca's eyes, he deliberately made his own hard, hoping it would help him get his point across. He wasn't ready to be a father. Not now. Not ever. "But that's all."

Chapter Six

Jake was sure he'd lost his mind. Somewhere in the heart of the night, with only his demons to keep him company, he'd finally wrapped his mind around the fact that he was a father.

He had a daughter. A bright, sunny, red-headed little girl named Katie.

Now, barely twelve hours later, a l Jake could think about was seeing her again. He'd be damned if he'd wait until Tuesday evening, when Rebecca had time to fit him into her social schedule.

A *daughter*.

Jake wanted to see her again today. Right now.

Fifteen minutes later, he walked the fringes of the church festival Rebecca had mentioned, hoping to catch a glimpse of his own flesh and blood. Rebecca had said she and Katie would be working at the festival together. Whether that meant at a game booth, a ticket or concession stand, the hay ride, or any of the dozens of children's activities he'd already passed once, Jake had no idea. He hadn't spotted either of them yet…but knew *he'd* been spotted and sized up time and time again.

He gritted his teeth against the burning, bitter feeling of being watched as closely and warily as some sort of predator who shouldn't be out by day, and pretended to ignore the alarmed looks, the sharp gasps of surprise and fear, the long, open stares and not-so-hushed whispers. If it hadn't hurt so much, he would have laughed at the obvious attempts to steer clear of him, as if at any moment he might reach for the nearest woman, throw her to the ground and try to have sex with her on the spot.

Then whip out a knife and stab her to death if she resisted.

In that moment, feeling like a pariah surrounded by a church yard full of *normal* families, Jake felt a consuming hatred wash over him in a way he never had before. But his hatred wasn't directed at any of the people around him, or the ambitious young prosecutor who had put him away. It was at himself, for letting her. At the time, he hadn't cared what happened to him, hadn't felt he had anything to fight for.

Now he knew differently.

And it hurt. More than he would have dreamed possible. All he could think about now was how much different his life might have been if he hadn't run away from Rebecca that last time.

A loud burst of laughter to his left seared his brain, and Jake spotted Rebecca. She stood at the head of the line in front of the dunking booth, warming up her throwing arm. In cuffed denim shorts and a blindingly white T-shirt with bright red lettering on the back, her hair swept up into one of those carelessly put together styles that looked sexy without trying to, she looked as young, carefree and as vibrant as the fourth of July.

Certainly not like she'd lost any sleep over what she'd done to him. What she'd kept from him for over eight years.

Carefully she took aim, preparing to throw a ball at a ruby red clown nose painted on a wall fifty feet away. In a deep, amused voice clearly meant to heckle, the sitting duck on a mechanized diving board suspended over a big, chest-high barrel of water spoke up, and stopped Rebecca short. She turned to the heckler slowly, arched a delicate eyebrow and said something that caused a wide wave of laughter to ripple through the group. She then turned back to the clown face, threw the ball, and missed.

The man called out to her again, this time in amusement. Jake scowled at her heckler, and was surprised to recognize Sheriff Sutter. The same sheriff who'd paid him a visit after Jake's trip to the town library. A man well versed in the art of intimidation.

Rebecca didn't look the least bit intimidated. Ignoring her completely dry heckler, she warmed up again and let fly.

Close, but not close enough. The crowd groaned in commiseration while the sheriff hooted. Apparently, according to the hand-written poster board beside the dunking booth that announced who would be there at what time of day—the sheriff's half hour was almost up and he hadn't been dunked yet.

Jake's fingers itched for a ball as Rebecca lined up her third and last shot. Sutter's deep, confident drawl challenged her over the heads of the crowd, but she ignored him, frowning in obvious concentration.

The ball missed the clown's nose by a mile.

The crowd groaned again, this time in disappointment. Grinning like a monkey, Sutter started to leave the platform. Rebecca checked her watch and ordered him to stay put. He still had two minutes to go.

Clearly more than willing to continue the game, the sheriff

played to the crowd and stayed put. Rebecca handed a dollar to the dunking booth attendant and bought three more tries.

Sutter started heckling again. Rebecca turned to face him, cast him a surprisingly smug smile, then whipped back around, threw the ball and hit the target head on.

Jake couldn't tell who was more surprised—himself, the crowd, or the soaked sheriff—who'd gone down so fast he hadn't been able to land on his feet in the chest-high water. In response to all the laughter and ribbing, he slicked his hair back, climbed back onto the platform—then grinned widely and continued his heckling. Calling Rebecca's dead on shot a lucky throw, he challenged her to dunk him again.

She did, not once but twice, earning the approval of everyone in the crowd, including Jake, and, much to his annoyance, Sheriff Sutter. As the crowd wandered off and the soaked sheriff stepped down to make way for the tax collector, Jake felt as he always had at these family-oriented things—like an outsider looking in. When Sutter smiled warmly at Rebecca and moved to shake her hand in congratulations, Jake turned and walked away, unable to stand his feelings of isolation.

But neither could he bring himself to leave the festival. He hadn't seen Katie yet.

A few minutes later he spotted her at the bean bag toss booth with her little friend Jenna. Neither girl was looking his way, so Jake used a nearby tree for cover as he watched his daughter from afar, and drank in the details of the beautiful child he and Rebecca had created that night in Pittsburgh.

She threw like her mama, dead on, and Jake wondered if she played ball, wondered if Rebecca had developed such good aim practicing throws with her daughter. God knew she'd never thrown balls as a kid. Neither had he. He'd been too busy throwing punches.

Katie threw again, and regret ripped through Jake at the idea that if he hadn't been such a coward, it could have been him throwing balls with his daughter in the evenings instead of Rebecca, or better yet, the three of them, playing ball together. Being a family.

Katie's turn at the bean bag toss ended, and as she collected her prize, a small stuffed panda bear and twin to the one Jenna carried, Jake debated whether to keep following Katie or go home and get some sleep. God knew he hadn't gotten any the night before. Without making any conscious decision, he found himself tailing Katie to another booth, then another, and another, until she and Jenna skipped up to the funnel cakes concession stand—where Rebecca was now working—side by side with Sheriff Sutter.

Jake couldn't miss the love shining in Rebecca's eyes when she spotted Katie. Laughing, she admired Katie's prize and showed it to Sutter, who smiled warmly at the two girls, then apparently offered to treat them to funnel cakes. He reached into his wallet, took out some money and handed it to Rebecca, then turned and handed each of the girls a funnel cake. They beamed their thanks at him and dug in.

Suddenly Jake noticed Sutter's and Rebecca's white T-shirts matched. The bright red lettering on each read Re-Elect Sutter for Sheriff.

Never mind he'd already seen the same shirt on a couple dozen other people at the festival, seeing it on Rebecca did something strange to Jake's insides. This was worse than his darkest moments in prison, where he'd imagined Rebecca living in luxury with that creep Kane. Instead, while he'd been off doing time, she'd been right here in Warner, raising their child and getting chummy with the local law. How chummy Jake had no idea, but if the look in Sutter's eyes was any indication, the good sheriff wouldn't say no to a little mattress dancing with the town's library director.

The thought of Rebecca and Katie living with another man, of Katie being raised by another man, especially a small-town cop like the kind that had run him out of town, like the kind that had ruled his days and nights in Wyoming, curdled Jake's stomach.

Jake wasn't sure how long he stood there, staring, but long enough to snag Sutter's attention. Sutter's eyes narrowed sharply as he spotted Jake, but a band of customers arrived to interrupt Sutter's cold stare. Jake knew he should leave, but couldn't pull himself away from the sight of Rebecca, laughing and smiling as she took money and handed out funnel cakes, seemingly oblivious to the amount of body contact she was having with Sutter. The booth was small, and Sutter no lightweight. At least six-two and two-ten, he practically dwarfed Rebecca as they maneuvered around the booth, bumping hips and arms and exchanging small smiles of.

What? Polite apology? Sexual awareness?

Jake ground his molars at the thought. Rebecca didn't look like she was sexually aware of the tall lawman sharing the booth with her, but Sutter looked plenty aware of her. Jake's fists clenched at his sides just as Rebecca looked up, right into his eyes. Hers widened in surprise, and then she seemed to pale. Sutter touched her arm and said something to her, which drew her gaze from Jake's to his. She looked up at Sutter and shook her head. He shot Jake a hard look, his expression leaving no mistake as to his meaning. Sutter cared about Rebecca, and didn't like the idea of Jake bothering her.

Apparently Rebecca hadn't told Sutter about Katie. Then again, maybe she had.

Jake turned away in disgust and walked off, unwilling to risk any kind of confrontation over something he still needed to come to terms with himself. He'd seen what he'd come to see. Seen more than enough. It was time to move on.

****

Rebecca watched Jake leave, her heart still caught in her throat. She'd been so surprised to see him. To look up and find him watching her. The worst part of it had been his expression. He'd looked so hurt, so angry, and so very, very alone. She could only imagine what went through his mind, seeing her work side by side with Bob, wearing her Re-Elect Sutter shirt. She wondered why he'd come, then wished she were free to go after him.

"You okay, Rebecca?"

She looked up at Bob, knew the concern in his deep brown eyes was genuine. They'd been friends since the week she'd moved back to Warner. He'd stopped by to introduce himself and made her feel welcome on the spot. Not to mention safe. Since then, they'd sat next to each other often at community events, and had had some dealings with each other over vandalism at the library. But he'd never asked her out.

Suddenly, Rebecca was glad he hadn't.

"Fine. Just thinking, that's all."

"Anything I can help with?"

"No." She smiled to soften the refusal. "But thanks for asking."

"I take it you were surprised to see Donovan here."

"I was. I..." she looked up at Bob, and wondered how much he knew about her relationship with Jake. He'd only lived in Warner the past six years, but gossip was gossip, and with Jake back...

"Has he been bothering you? I know he lives right behind you and Katie."

"No. Of course not." Rebecca swallowed, wondering what to

say. "Bob, Jake and I are...we're friends."

His eyes narrowed sharply. "Are you sure that's a good idea?"

"We grew up together. At one time we were...close."

Bob's surprise deepened. "I see." He studied her face for a long moment. Tonelessly he added, "And you're hoping to recapture that...closeness now that he's back in town."

"I didn't say that."

"You don't have to. It's written all over your face."

Rebecca didn't know what to say. So she said nothing and hoped she wasn't blushing.

Bob looked away, planted his large fists on his hips, then sighed heavily. "Be careful, Rebecca. I know you think you know what you're doing, but..."

"He's innocent, Bob. I know it. I'd stake my life on it."

He looked down at her, his expression unreadable. "I believe you would. But his rap sheet tells a different story. I can't ignore it, Rebecca, for you or for anyone else. It's my job to keep men like Donovan in line. I hope you understand."

"Jake's not going to give you any trouble. He's leaving Warner as soon as he sells his house."

"Is that what he's telling you?"

"What do you mean?"

"From the looks of things, he wasn't too happy about seeing you with me."

"He doesn't trust the law, Bob. It hasn't treated him well."

"It's not my badge he has a problem with, although I'm sure it doesn't help that I'm a cop."

"What are you talking about?"

Bob looked into her eyes, searching for something Rebecca had no idea how to give him. Finally, with another heartfelt sigh, he smiled and said, "Forget it. Occupational hazard, second guessing everyone I meet. Let's see how it plays."

****

Jake woke up at twilight. He lifted his head from the red and white star-patterned quilt Rebecca had made, the quilt that still smelled faintly of strawberries, and thought he heard a vehicle pull in at her place. Funny, how quickly he'd tuned into the sound of her little Focus coming and going. But this didn't sound like a five-year- old Focus in need of a tune-up at all.

Curiosity drew him off the bed and into the back bedroom from which he could see Rebecca's apartment. Normally he

54

avoided the back rooms for that very reason, but there was something strangely familiar about the low rumbling of the engine in her driveway.

A police cruiser. No wonder he recognized the sound. Jake's mouth tightened into a grim line as he spotted the rear fender of a cop car poking out from behind the six-foot hedge that separated his yard from Rebecca's pool. She'd apparently gotten a ride home from the festival with her good buddy Sutter.

Jake turned away from the window, unwilling to sink to spying on Rebecca. He wondered if Sutter was the reason she'd been unavailable for dinner last night. Then wondered what she'd have to say about the sheriff on Tuesday night.

If he could wait that long.

****

"You haven't been the same since you saw Donovan at the festival, Rebecca."

Rebecca looked over at Bob. He stared out the front window of the cruiser, at the swimming pool where Jake had learned he was Katie's father. Had it been only yesterday?

Why had he come to the festival? To see her? To see Katie?

"I know. I just didn't expect him to show up there. Jake's never been family oriented. I know I invited him to come—"

"You invited him there?"

"Well, yes. Sort of."

"What do you mean, sort of?"

Rebecca hesitated. "It's complicated."

Bob turned off the ignition and settled deeper into his seat, then stretched one arm out on the seat back between them. "I'm off duty. I've got all night."

Rebecca smiled, touched by the offer. But Katie was over at Aunt Martha's, waiting to be picked up, and Rebecca needed a shower. She felt hot and sticky and ached all over. Not to mention smelling like a gallon of funnel-cake grease. Bob had to be feeling and smelling the same. "I didn't accept your offer of a ride home so I could dump my personal problems on you."

"I'm a good listener."

"I know. I just don't feel it would be right to talk to you about Jake."

"Because I'm a cop?"

She shook her head. "Because Jake is Jake."

Bob looked out the front window again, then back at Rebecca. "I hope you know what you're doing, Rebecca."

She couldn't help her wry smile. "Actually, I haven't got a clue."

He swung his head around, eyes narrowed. "What in the hell is that supposed to mean?"

He looked more than a little concerned. Rebecca shook her head, painfully aware of how little he had to worry about. "He doesn't want anything to do with me, Bob. He never has."

"Wrong on both counts. Didn't you notice the way he looks at you? He wants you, Rebecca. And unless I miss my guess, after today, he's either going to make his move or get the hell out of town."

"How can you say that?"

"Easy. I'm a man." His smile was self-deprecating when he added quietly, "Something I haven't been successful at getting you to notice. Now I think I know why."

Rebecca was glad Bob couldn't see her flush of embarrassment. Bob was attracted to her? And she'd never picked up on it. Lord, she was in worse shape than she thought. Robert Sutter was a very attractive man. "I'm sorry, Bob. I had no idea."

"I'll survive. Just know I'm here for you if you need me."

He made no move to touch her, to make her feel awkward in any way. "You're a good friend, Bob."

"Be careful, Rebecca. I'd hate to see you get hurt."

She nodded. "Thanks. And thanks for the ride." Aunt Martha and Katie had left hours earlier in Rebecca's Focus.

"Thanks for staying late to help me clean up. And thanks for filling in for the no-shows at the last minute. Especially after putting your own time in at the cotton candy booth. I never could have handled that funnel cake booth alone for three hours."

She smiled. "Glad to be of help. See you around."

His answering smile was both a promise and a warning. "Count on it."

Jake's Return

Chapter Seven

Tuesday night Katie opened the door with a big smile that nailed Jake right in the heart. "Hi. Mom's still getting dressed. Can I get you some iced tea?"

"Sure. Thanks." Jake stepped into the apartment and surveyed it with fresh eyes. He now recognized the battered Raggedy Ann doll as Katie's. The drawings on the fridge were his daughter's as well, not gifts from the children Rebecca read stories to on Thursday afternoons at the library, as he'd first thought.

"Hi, Jake. Sorry I'm late. I got tied up at work."

Rebecca entered the room looking cool and beautiful in navy blue shorts and a navy and white scoop-necked T-shirt. Her smile was polite, her eyes wary. Jake sipped his tea and wondered what else she had to be nervous about. If she could keep a secret like Katie from him, what else was she capable of hiding? A cozy relationship with the Sheriff?

"No problem," he said, inclining his head coolly.

Rebecca's smile slipped. Jake wondered again why he'd agreed to this farce of a dinner. This wasn't about getting to know his daughter and both he and Rebecca knew it. She'd had eight years to tell him he was a father, and after what he'd seen yesterday, neither she nor Katie needed him around to play the role of family man. Not with Sutter waiting in the wings.

"Well," Rebecca said with an obviously forced smile, "Dinner will be ready in a jif. Katie, would you finish setting the table?" She brushed past Jake, leaving the faint scent of strawberries in her wake. Jake closed his eyes and swore silently as his body responded like it always did. Whatever else they did or didn't have between them, they would always have this. He would never be able to be in a room with her without wanting her.

Somehow Jake managed to down some barbequed chicken, baked beans and corn on the cob. He even managed to laugh a couple of times, thanks to Katie's lively stories about her trip to Erie. But after about ten minutes of after dinner conversation, Rebecca excused Katie to go and change into her bathing suit, leaving them alone.

Jake stood to help gather the dirty dishes and wondered if this was supposed to be his opening to ask whatever questions he might have. He followed Rebecca to the kitchen counter and watched her fill the sink with sudsy water. As she reached to turn off the water, her shirt neckline shifted, exposing a familiar-looking silver heart on a silver chain. Jake blinked, then looked again.

It was the heart he'd given her on her sixteenth birthday. The night before he'd left for the army. The night he'd run from her for the very first time.

The night he'd kissed her for the very first time.

"So," he asked with a calm he didn't even come close to feeling. "What happens now?"

She looked up, clearly startled by his voice, or maybe his directness. "I'm...I'm not really sure."

Great. "Why did you wait so long to tell me about her?" Might as well take the bull by the horns.

"Ready, Mom. I got the towels. Three of them." Katie emerged from a bedroom in a pink and black bathing suit and carrying three big green bath towels.

"Thank you." Rebecca smiled and slid the last of the dishes into the soapy water. "But I'm not sure Jake plans to stay for a swim." She scanned his black t-shirt and faded denims and lifted a questioning eyebrow.

He shrugged. "It was either this or cut-offs."'

"Cut-offs would have been fine. We're pretty casual around here. You're welcome to go home and change."

Was she inviting him to return for more stalling, or just to swim? Didn't matter. He remembered how she'd looked in her white bathing suit, and found himself nodding. "Thanks."

Rebecca left the dishes to soak and he followed them down to the pool, where Katie wasted no time jumping in. Rebecca stood at the deep end of the small, rectangular pool, her arms tightly crossed beneath her breasts, her attention focused on Katie. She looked as tense as could be, and Jake decided to wait until they were truly alone again to ask any more questions. He wanted her undivided attention for the answers. Saying he'd be back in a few, he took off.

Rebecca watched him round the hedge, knowing she was in trouble. Jake had given her no clue as to his thoughts during dinner, but his eyes, oh, they'd told her plenty. He was hurting and confused, and trying very hard not to be angry with her, when he had every right to be.

She'd known this wouldn't be easy, not with Katie around, but she'd hoped they could at least discuss their daughter quietly, rationally. It didn't seem likely, given the unmistakable edge in Jake's voice every time he brought it up.

Idly, she reached up to rub the silver heart he'd given her so long ago between her thumb and forefinger, the way she often had when thinking of Jake. She hadn't worn it in years, for that very reason. But tonight she'd been looking for connections, not this cold distance he was hell bent on keeping between them.

"Aren't you going in?"

Rebecca jumped at the sound of Jake's voice next to her ear. How long had she been standing there, lost in thought? Her breath caught as she realized he'd left everything but his cut-offs behind. Oh no. A half-naked Jake was not conducive to discussing anything rationally. To talking, period.

"Sure." She turned away, peeled off her shorts and shirt, and slid out of her sandals. Beneath her clothes, she'd worn her black lap-swimming suit. Behind her, she could feel Jake slip into a panther-like alertness that did nothing to ease her already escalating pulse rate at the idea of him watching her undress, however innocently. She dropped her shorts, shirt and towel on a lounge chair and headed for the diving board. Without looking back at Jake, she stepped onto the board, paused to collect herself, then executed a surprisingly flawless dive, considering how rattled she felt.

The water felt frigid against her flushed skin. Brisk. Stimulating. She came up for air at the shallow end, and slicked her hair back, to find Jake still watching her.

Lord. How was she supposed to breathe, much less think, with him looking like sin defined and scowling down at her like some dark-eyed warrior from the past? Had she truly done the right thing, keeping Katie a secret all these years? Or had she done it to protect *herself*?

"Coming in?"

"Right behind you."

He followed her example and made a graceful arc off the diving board, then joined her in the shallow end. Watching his muscles bunch and ripple as he came up for air and slicked his own hair back made her feel hot and flushed all over again.

His eyes locked onto hers and turned dark as coal. She shivered in a purely elemental response. He smiled an almost predatory smile.

"Mom! How about a game of keep away?"

She looked over to where Katie stood in the water watching them, holding a beach ball and wearing a half-confused, half-hopeful expression.

"Sounds good," Jake said. "I'll take the deep end."

Half an hour later, Rebecca called an end to the game when she realized Katie spent very little time holding the ball. Her usually very competitive and agile daughter had managed to mis-throw the beach ball more times than she had all summer, leading Jake and Rebecca to bump bodies with unnerving frequency as they scrambled to keep the ball away from each other.

Rebecca's budding suspicions about her daughter went into full bloom when Katie pulled herself out of the pool and announced she needed to call Jenna. Before Rebecca could even consider what to do next, Katie was gone and Jake was closing in on her like a shark.

He broke through the surface three feet away from the corner she'd retreated to, to catch her breath. He flashed her a killer smile, then glided closer, still smiling. "Alone at last."

Her arms resting on the decking behind her, Rebecca realized she was trapped.

"Not that I'm complaining," Jake said, still smiling. "I haven't had that much fun in years."

The almost speculative look in his eyes told Rebecca his mood might have improved during the game, but he hadn't been any more oblivious to the amount of body contact they'd made during the game than she had. The knowledge sent a fresh current of awareness humming through her veins.

Jake leaned his head back and looked up at the stars. "God, this water feels great. Brings back a lot of memories."

Rebecca sent him a droll look, all too aware she'd had nothing to do with those memories. Many a night she'd heard muffled giggles and quiet splashes in the dark pool after midnight, and had known it was Jake and his on again, off again girlfriend Mimi Modano. They'd come by when her mother was out, and Aunt Martha was asleep.

He caught her expression, and smiled a slow, knowing smile. "So tell me," he said, as he edged closer and sent her pulse rate soaring. "Were you ever jealous of Mimi?"

"No. At the time I was disgusted." And heartsick.

"Why?"

"She couldn't keep her hands off of you."

His smile turned fondly reminiscent. "I remember."

"I believe that's why you dated her."

"We never dated, Becca, we just…"

"I know what you did with her, Jake."

"Good. Then this won't come as a surprise." The next thing she knew, he'd braced his arms on either side of her and was kissing her. Gently, tenderly, with sweetness and finesse. No other part of their bodies touched as he made love to her mouth with an erotic thoroughness that rocked her senses. Rebecca considered lowering her arms from the decking, then realized if she did, she'd either have to hold onto Jake or go under.

Either way, she was sunk.

Long moments later, Jake pulled back, leaving Rebecca feeling dazed and disoriented. "I've missed you, Becca."

She didn't say anything. When he leaned back to see her expression, she stared at him, totally confused. "What do you want from me, Jake?"

"More of this." His mouth found hers again and without thinking, she reached for him, reached for the dream she'd denied herself for what suddenly felt like every day for the past eighteen years. Jake groaned and deepened the kiss, adding a note of pure possessiveness. Rebecca wrapped her legs around his waist in response, with no thought for anything beyond the moment.

And what a delicious moment it was. Supporting them with one hand on the edge of the pool, Jake slid his free hand between them to palm a full, aching breast. Rebecca moaned, just as the floodlight at the top of the stairs to the apartment flashed on. A split-second later the storm door opened and shut.

"Mom?" Katie called uncertainly.

Rebecca released Jake so fast she went under. He caught her beneath her arms, but not before she got a snootful of water. She came up sputtering and coughing and feeling like an absolute idiot.

"Mom? You okay?" Katie asked, running down the stairs.

"She'll be fine, Katie," Jake quickly reassured her over his shoulder as he discreetly straightened the top of Rebecca's bathing suit. "She just, ah, swallowed some water." His voice sounded rough as gravel.

Katie came to a halt on the decking beside them. "Jenna's mom's on the phone. She wants to talk to you."

Her eyes still watering, Rebecca looked up at her daughter in bleary confusion. "Right now?" She'd only met the woman once or twice. She'd found Mrs. Mueller to be on the self-righteous side, but nothing she couldn't handle in small doses.

"Why don't you tell Jenna's mom that your mom will call her back in a few minutes?" Jake suggested, guessing Rebecca needed some time to pull herself together.

Katie's small voice sounded strangely ominous as she held out the phone. "I don't think she wants to wait that long."

Jake and Rebecca exchanged puzzled looks. He climbed out of the pool, then reached out to give her a hand up. "You okay?" he asked, as he handed her a towel.

She scrubbed at her face. Her nose and throat burned. "No, I've apparently lost my mind." What was she thinking, wrapping her legs around Jake's waist in full view of her daughter?

"Want me to wait around?"

She looked at him then, and knew what he was asking. She also knew she wasn't ready to discuss what had just happened, nor was she emotionally prepared to discuss their daughter. Not anymore.

"I don't think so. It's late and...I need to help Katie get ready for bed."

Jake lifted an eyebrow, but was kind enough not to point out that Katie seemed more than capable of getting herself ready for bed. "Thanks for dinner, then. And the swim. I enjoyed myself." He turned and tousled Katie's hair. "G'night, Peanut. Guess it's time for me to go. See you around."

"See you," Rebecca managed past the lump of emotion in her throat at the tenderness in Jake's voice toward Katie, then turned to climb the steps to her apartment. Once inside, Katie vanished while Rebecca put the receiver to her ear. "Hello?"

"I understand you're entertaining that...that *convict* tonight. Jenna tells me he came over for dinner and a swim."

Rebecca's stomach took a header. Just what she needed right now. With an effort, she kept her voice calm. "Jake's no longer in prison, Mrs. Mueller. He's out on parole."

"I don't care what he is. I refuse to allow my daughter to continue playing with yours as long as that man is around. You ought to be ashamed of yourself, exposing your daughter to such blatant vulgarity."

"Excuse me? Mrs. Mueller, what are you...?"

"Do you deny you were kissing that man in the swimming pool?"

Rebecca stared at her telephone receiver in shock. Were her neighbors *watching* her?

"I picked up the telephone and distinctly heard your daughter saying to mine, "Oh, my God, Jenna. They're kissing in the pool. *French* kissing."

Rebecca's cheeks flamed. "Mrs. Mueller. I...I don't know what to say."

"I do. From now on, I forbid Jenna to have anything to do with you or your daughter. Once word gets out you're having an affair with that...that *murderer*, I don't think any *decent* mother in Warner will allow her children anywhere near you."

"Now wait a minute. I'm not having an affair with Jake. We were just—" Kissing our brains out in the pool, in front of our seven-year-old daughter.

"I'm reporting this to the town council, Ms. Reed."

Rebecca saw where this was headed. Right into Avery Dillenger's waiting lap. "Fine," she said in a calm, clipped voice that barely belied her fury. "You do that. Thank you for calling, Mrs. Mueller. It's been enlightening."

She hung up the phone and scanned the dark apartment. Katie hadn't turned on any lights. She wandered into the bedroom to place the phone on the recharger, looked out the window and saw that the deep end of the pool was shadowed by the garage, but in clear view of the window next to her bed. Obviously her daughter had known what she was doing all along, had fully intended to watch her and Jake from the window. At least the pool lights hadn't been on. Katie would have gotten quite an eyeful if that had been the case.

"Are you mad at me, Mom?"

She turned to find Katie anxiously watching her from the doorway. "No, sweetheart, of course not." She switched on her bedside lamp. "Mrs. Mueller shouldn't have been listening in on your conversation, and Jake and I shouldn't have been...getting so friendly in the pool."

"You like him, don't you?"

"Of course I do, Katie. We grew up together."

"Did you kiss a lot then, too?"

"No. We were never...we were friends."

And what were they now? Rebecca had no idea. But she knew what people thought of Jake.

"Katie, I'm going to change, and then we need to talk, okay?" Five minutes later, Rebecca beckoned her still uncertain daughter to join her on the living room couch. As she wrapped a reassuring arm around Katie's shoulders, Rebecca wished she didn't have to have this conversation. Wished she'd kept her hands and mouth and legs to herself tonight. "Honey, Mrs. Mueller isn't going to let Jenna play with you anymore."

Katie's eyes widened in stunned disbelief. "What did I do?"

"You didn't do anything, sweetheart. Mrs. Mueller doesn't approve of us spending time with Jake."

"Because he was in prison?"

"Yes. For murder." She hadn't gone into details before, because she wasn't sure what Jenna might have told her, but it was obvious Mrs. Mueller thought she knew what Jake had done.

Katie's eyes rounded. "You mean he killed somebody?"

Rebecca closed her eyes. The very thought pierced her heart. But she knew it wasn't true. It couldn't be. The man who had kissed her so gently in the pool tonight and called her daughter "Peanut" couldn't possibly be a killer. "The jury convicted him, yes. But I don't believe he's guilty."

"Because he's your friend?"

"Because I know Jake, and I know he would never hurt another human being unless it was in self-defense."

"Why doesn't Jenna's mom know that?"

"Because she doesn't know Jake. She's never met him."

"Then how can she say he's bad?"

"She's probably heard a lot about him from other people in town. People who knew Jake when he was younger."

"Was he bad then?"

"It probably seemed like it. Jake was pretty wild, and he liked to see what he could get away with. But deep down, no, Jake wasn't bad. He just..." Needed someone to love him. "Needed a friend."

"So what are we going to do?"

"I don't know. What do you want to do?"

"You mean if we stop seeing Jake, Mrs. Mueller will let Jenna play with me again?"

Rebecca doubted it, but she refused to paint the situation entirely black. "It's possible. But I can't promise you anything. She seems pretty upset. Maybe in time she'll see things differently." She paused, her heart aching for all of them. "And maybe she won't."

Katie considered this, then said quietly. "Then I guess I'll have to see Jenna at school."

Rebecca's eyes misted with tears of pride. "Sweetheart, I'm afraid school's not going to be as easy as it was last year."

"I know that, Mom. I'll be in second grade instead of first."

"That's not what I mean. There are other parents in Warner who feel the same way about Jake that Jenna's mom does. Parents who won't want their children playing with you because they think Jake will hurt them."

"That's so stupid, Mom."

"I know, sweetheart. But life doesn't always make sense."

"It's a good thing Jake has us then. I mean, without us, he wouldn't have anybody, right?"

Rebecca's heart nearly broke. She wondered if she was doing the right thing, dragging her seven-year-old daughter into such a miasma of public rejection. But Jake had been cheated out of so much already. He deserved a chance to get to know Katie. Katie deserved to spend some time with her father before he left town again.

Smiling grimly, Rebecca kissed her daughter's hair. Her sweet, funny, compassionate daughter, who was about to learn how cruel and unforgiving the world could be.

"Right. Without us, Jake wouldn't have anybody."

Chapter Eight

Jake looked out from under the hood of the sheriff's Blazer and up at the sky for the umpteenth time in the last hour. The wind was picking up and he didn't like the looks of those dark clouds moving in from the east. Once before, when he was stationed in Kansas, he'd seen angry clouds like that, and was lucky he'd lived to remember it. It hadn't rained in Warner since the day he and Rebecca had seeded his yard, nearly two weeks ago. The storm brewing today had all the makings of a twister. No doubt they needed the rain, but not at that price.

He turned back to his work and thought of Rebecca, getting ready for her Thursday afternoon story hour at the library. Thought of the high, cathedral ceiling, the floor-to-ceiling windows in the north and south walls, the rows of heavy bookcases in between. He wondered where Katie was, who watched his daughter while Rebecca worked.

His daughter. The idea of it still boggled his mind.

The service bell rang as Avery Dillenger pulled up to the service pump in a long black Lincoln. Feeney had left to run some errands, so Jake was alone. He wiped his hands on a rag, and prepared to face one of his least favorite people. "Fill 'er up?" Jake asked.

"Check the oil, too."

Jake went through the motions, knowing full well the oil tank would be full. With six car dealerships to choose from, Avery Dillenger rarely drove a car that had more than a thousand miles on it.

"Where's Feeney?"

Jake ached to say he'd stuffed him in the drink cooler. "Had some errands to take care of." He didn't offer to relay a message.

"I'm surprised he left you alone with the cash register."

Jake kept washing the Town Car's tinted windows.

"How long are you planning on keeping up this honest citizen charade, Donovan?"

Jake didn't answer. All he could think about was seeing a long dark car like Dillenger's quietly dropping off a young boy in the middle of the night. He felt sick inside just thinking about it. But that kind of car could have belonged to any number of people who lived in Glenhill.

"You may have a half-senile old coot like Feeney fooled, but I know better," Dillenger was saying. "You're nothing more than a no-good lazy drifter. No morals, no goals, no ambition. Look at you, still pumping gas for minimum wage at the same place you worked as a teenager. I wouldn't be surprised if you've scared off half of Feeney's customers since you started 'working' here."

"If you're done, Dillenger, that'll be thirty dollars." As Jake had expected, all the gas tank had needed was to be topped off.

"I find your attitude offensive, Donovan. How can you justify destroying Feeney's livelihood to satisfy your own agenda?"

This, from the man who'd been badgering Feeney to sell him the station for the past five years, so he could raze it and build a mega-dealership. Feeney had told Jake that ten years ago, Dillenger had picked up the bankrupt Chevy dealership for a song. Since then he'd gotten it in his head to become the car king of northwestern Pennsylvania, and managed to buy out or bankrupt all of his local competition. Now he wanted to consolidate. Feeney had also told Jake that Dillenger already owned the four lots behind the service station. All he needed was the land the station sat on, the pinnacle of the triangle, to make the package complete.

But Feeney wasn't selling. The station had been in his family for generations and he owned it free and clear. He also felt he had a moral obligation to keep Dillenger from buying it just so he could crown himself king. "You'll have to talk to Feeney about that, Dillenger. I just pump gas."

Why the man didn't have someone at one of his dealerships fill up his cars, Jake didn't know. He couldn't believe Dillenger kept coming to Feeney's just to harass him. They might be second cousins, but Dillenger had never made any attempt to seek him out before—quite the opposite.

As usual, Dillenger took his sweet time removing his gold money clip from his trouser pocket and peeling off one of more hundreds than Jake cared to think about. Dillenger smiled as he handed it over. "I think this will cover it."

Jake gritted his teeth. Since one of Feeney's errands was the bank, Jake had just turned over the roll of bills he usually had in his pocket. All he had left were a few fives and a couple tens. "I'll have to get change." He turned and headed for the cash register.

"Oh, that's handy," Dillenger said, and followed Jake into the office. Once there, Dillenger looked the place over as if he already owned it, and didn't care for the sight of his cousin from the wrong side of the tracks on his property. He smiled another insincere smile and helped himself to a bottle of Dr. Pepper from an old time drink cooler while Jake made change at the equally antique cash register. Dillenger watched him like a hawk, and Jake had to suppress a laugh. Did Dillenger really think he'd slip a twenty in his pocket without someone there to look over his shoulder? Jake made sure to take out an extra dollar for the pop.

"Holy shit," Dillenger said suddenly.

Jake looked up to see an enormous black funnel cloud bearing down on the town. He slammed the cash register shut and hurdled the counter, shoving Dillenger's change into his midsection as he ran past him. Ignoring Dillenger's startled, "Hey!" Jake bolted for the door, and Rebecca's library.

Dillenger followed him outside, still swearing in amazed disbelief. He stopped halfway to his car, Dr. Pepper in hand, and gaped at the churning sky.

"For God's sake, Dillenger," Jake shouted from the street, "Get out of the open!"

Dillenger seemed to come to, and disappeared into one of the service bays. Jake figured if he had any brains, he'd hide in the employee restroom at the back of the garage. Meanwhile, Jake struggled to reach the library, two blocks away. If Rebecca didn't know what was coming down, she'd need help.

The wind howled like a banshee around him, the force of it slamming him into a telephone pole shoulder first. His shirt ripped as he pulled away from the pole and street debris flew like confetti as he blindly fought his way up the block. A bicycle rack crashed through a storefront across the street. Hail the size of golf balls pelted his head, shoulders and back. By the time he reached the library, Jake felt like a freight train was at his heels. He forced the front door open against the wind and dived inside the building just as a deafening explosion broke loose behind him. Rolling to his feet, he stood there and panted as if he'd run a three-minute mile. A dozen strangers stared back at him in a state of general shock. Rebecca stood ashen-faced before a seated circle of children.

"Move!" He bellowed. "Away from the bookcases! Under the tables! Now!"

Everyone scrambled for cover. Jake hurdled tables and chairs to reached Rebecca's side in seconds. Scooping up a child with each arm, he deposited them under the nearest of half a dozen tables. "Becca! We need to get these kids under cover!"

She grabbed two of the smallest children. The older ones seemed to catch on and suddenly the floor crawled with shrieking pre-schoolers. Unearthly lightning flashed continually as Jake and Rebecca herded the children to safety. Yellow, blue, green, purple—the sky erupted in a lethal kaleidoscope of color as Jake snagged the stragglers. One boy broke free and bolted for the bookcases just as the south windows blew out with a thunderous crash.

Jake swore and tackled the sobbing boy, coming down hard. Pain ripped through his left shoulder as he hauled the now screaming kid under the nearest table. The bookcases toppled like dominoes, crushing anything in between. Adults screamed, children howled. Wind and rain and glass swept through the library with an unholy vengeance. The north window shattered as what looked like the town Christmas tree flew into it from a block away.

It was over as quickly as it had begun. After several excruciatingly long minutes, Jake lifted his head to the sound of eerie silence inside the library, a steady downpour outside. People cowered everywhere, imprisoned by shock and deadly shards of glass. The boy beneath him was still.

"Jake?"

"I'm all right, Becca. How about you?" He looked over to where she sat beneath a table, her arms filled with shell-shocked children. Her hair was half down, her pantyhose shredded and legs bleeding. "You all right?"

"I think so. Jake. The children."

He eased to his feet. His legs felt like marshmallows. His right hip and left shoulder burned. The boy he'd thrown himself on top of moaned and stirred. Other children began crying for their mamas. Warner was one of the few towns in the country where children were considered safe. Everyone knew Rebecca ran a tight ship, so most mothers were comfortable using her weekly story hour to run errands. Jake looked around. Apparently today no mothers were there. Yet. He had no doubt those who could, would arrive soon. He looked at the boy. Hey, buddy. You all right?"

"My arm. It hurts."

Jake did a quick field exam. "It's probably broken, but we won't know for sure until the medics come. Anything else hurt?"

"No."

"What's your name?"

"Bryan Modano."

Modano? Mimi's kid? Or maybe her brother's. "Can you sit up, Bryan?"

"I think so."

Jake helped the boy sit up. "You still okay?"

"Yeah. Just scared."

Jake smiled. "So was I Bryan, so was I. But you're gonna be okay now. We all are." He looked around and saw most of the painted cinderblock wall that led to the restrooms had remained intact. "I'm going to carry you over to that yellow wall by the restrooms, okay?"

He lifted the boy into his arms, then turned to Rebecca. "Sit tight. When I get back, we'll move the rest of you away from this glass. I'll carry the kids over. We can wait for the rescue crews by the back door."

One of Rebecca's clerks—the short, pudgy one who'd gone white that first day he'd come to find Rebecca—was already making her way toward the restrooms. "I'll wait here and keep the children quiet."

"Thank you, Eunice," Rebecca said, and rose to her feet. Jake watched her stand and look down at the blood on her legs, and the blue suit that matched her eyes. "It looks like we'll need to do some first aid. Eunice, would you see if the water in the restrooms is still running? Is everyone else all right?" she called out to the room in general. No one answered in the negative. "Good," she said, and continued organizing things, speaking to people by name.

Impressed as hell, Jake made his way over to the painted cinderblock hall and settled Bryan against the bright yellow wall. The other adults started moving toward each other, while Jake kept his focus on Rebecca and the children. He lifted the first whimpering toddler from Rebecca's arms and carried the little girl to where Eunice waited with a first-aid kit. He was surprised by how trustingly the child wrapped her short, chubby arms around his neck, how warm and sturdy she felt in his arms, how protective she made him feel, simply by being there. It was the first time he'd had anything to do with children, and he felt more than awkward, but somehow he managed, talking, soothing, occasionally even smiling and stroking a small head of cornsilk-soft hair.

A few minutes later, they had all ten children lined up against the wall. Some mouthed lollipops Eunice had found, some looked at picture books, but most watched every move Jake made with big, big eyes. He smiled back at them, threw a wink or two their way, then looked around for Rebecca. Like the trooper she was, she'd picked her way across the deadly sea of glass and debris to join the children on her own. There was no doubt in his mind that these children felt completely safe in Rebecca's care.

He spotted her as she left the restroom with a little girl, looking calm and in control. A quick scan of the wrecked library confirmed his work there was done. "Rebecca. I've got to get back to Feeney's."

"Wait, Jake. You're bleeding."

"I am?" No wonder the kids were staring at him. He looked at his ripped shirt and shoulder. It hurt like a SOB, but... "I'll be okay."

"Maybe you should wait for the rescue team."

"Nah. You guys need them more than me. Besides..."

"I need you to look for Katie, Jake."

"Katie?" Jake's stomach sank to his toes. "Katie?" he repeated, suddenly feeling both winded and stupid. He'd been so wrapped up with the kids, he hadn't spared a thought for his own child. Guilt engulfed him, making him feel like a complete failure as a father. Here Rebecca must've been going out of her mind with worry while she'd forced herself to stay focused on making sure everyone in the library was safe. "Where is she?"

"I have no idea. Aunt Martha was watching her, but they could be anywhere. That's why I need you to find her. Make sure they're okay. They stopped by this morning and were on their way home when the storm hit, but...but..." Her eyes suddenly filled with tears, and he realized she was starting to lose it. "Oh, God, Jake, if anything's happened to them..."

"Shhhh," he heard himself soothing as he reached out to her for the first time that day. As he brushed back a strand of hair that had fallen free of her loose bun, Jake battled a sudden need to pull her close and never let her go. "I'm sure she's fine. Everything's going to be all right." He'd see to it. If he had to scour the entire town on foot, he'd see to it.

"But what if she's not, Jake? What if she needs me?"

Me, not us. Jake realized what she'd said about the same time he realized he was stroking Rebecca's hair. He pulled his hand back and focused on beating back his own churning emotions. Fear for Katie, hurt that Rebecca would cut him out like that, guilt that she even felt the need to, and regret for all the mistakes he'd made with her. "Jake?"

"I'll find her, Rebecca. I'll find her and bring her to you."

She seemed to sag in relief. "Thank you," she breathed. "I

need to know she's okay, but I can't...I can't leave here right now."

"I understand. I'm on my way."

He turned as the first rescue crew arrived, on their heels the first frantic mother, sobbing her children's names. With something fast approaching awe, Jake watched Rebecca step back and pull herself together, squelch her equally desperate fear for her own daughter, and turn to reassure the wild-eyed woman that her children were alive and well.

It was true. It was also a miracle, Jake thought, as he scanned the shattered remains of what had less than thirty minutes before been a beautiful building. For the most part, the children seemed to have suffered only minor cuts and bruises. Bryan's broken arm appeared to be the only exception.

He was on his way out the door when he overheard someone call Rebecca's name. He turned back in time to hear a medic telling her Katie had been taken to the hospital.

"I recognized her lying on a gurney in the hall. I don't know what's wrong with her but I thought you'd want to know."

Jake stilled as he watched Rebecca take the news like a body blow.

"You want a ride to the hospital?" the medic asked her.

"I...can't. I can't go right now," he heard her say in a high, strained voice that told him she wished with all her heart she could go. "Jake?" His heart stopped as she looked around uncertainly, no doubt sure he'd already left. Her expression of relief when she spotted him moving toward her barely had time to register before she called out to him, "Jake! Katie's at the hospital. Can you go?"

He pulled up short and swallowed. Hard. "Of course."

****

Forty minutes later, Jake strode through the halls of the community hospital, determined to search every last room in the place if he had to. Between fighting off frantic relatives and fielding non-stop calls, the admitting personnel had been too busy to help him find Katie. They probably wouldn't have let him see her anyway, not in the shape he was in. He ignored the startled looks and offended stares he caught as he poked his head in each room. He was on a mission and didn't care who he upset.

He found her on the third floor, at the end of the hall. "Katie?"

She looked up from her bed and saw him in the doorway, and broke into the most beautiful smile he'd ever seen. His legs went weak and he nearly fell to his knees in relief and gratitude on the spot.

"Jake! You're okay! I'm so glad. Where's Mom?" She looked past him hopefully, then back at him uncertainly. "Isn't she with you?"

"She's...she's at the library," he said, trying his best to stay upright as he stepped into the room. "Taking care of things there." He watched her budding fear shift into confusion. "She's fine. She asked me to come and make sure you were okay."

If she was disappointed, she hid it well. "You'll never believe what happened. I got hit on the head when a tree limb smacked into me. I was in the front yard, trying to make it back to the apartment. It knocked me out and I've got a con...concussion, but the doctor said I should be fine."

"Where's your Aunt Martha?" He looked around, as if she might materialize at any moment.

"She left as soon as she knew I was going to be all right, to go to the Red Cross office. She said she wanted to help."

That fit right in with what Jake remembered about Rebecca's aunt. Always first in line to help those in need. "I guess I should get back to your mom, then. Let her know you're okay."

"Oh." Katie looked crestfallen.

Jake stepped forward in concern. "What's the matter?"

"Nothing. I just...I just really don't want to be alone right now."

His heart melted. "I understand, Peanut," he said, and came the rest of the way into the room. "I'll stay as long as you want me to. Just let me see if I can find a way to get a message to your mother."

"Omigod, Jake, you're bleeding."

Surreptitiously he latched onto the side railing of Katie's bed for support and struggled for a smile. "I know." His back and legs suddenly hurt like a sonofagun. Not to mention his hip and shoulder. "I probably got cut. There was glass all over the library. I just need to clean up a bit."

"The bathroom's over there," she pointed out helpfully, clearly not at all certain he was telling the truth.

"Thanks. I think."

"Jake?" He turned to see Rebecca standing in the doorway, and wondered how she'd gotten there so fast. Then again, someone probably would have told her right away where Katie was. She looked as dirty and disheveled as before, but as beautiful as ever. All he could think about was how relieved he was that all of them were alive and together. Suddenly he wondered why she was frowning so hard. "Are you all right?"

"Fine. Maybe a little tired, but..." A wave of warmth and dizziness washed over him.

"More like exhausted. Maybe you should sit down."

"Did everyone get out of the library all right?"

She stepped into the room, her eyes soft with unexpected pride. "Yes, they did. Thanks to you."

His grip on the bed railing tightened. "I didn't do anything. You're the one who—"

"Jake? Are you...? *Jake*!"

The last thing he heard before everything went black was Katie's scream, and Rebecca shouting for a doctor.

****

Jake awoke to find himself lying on his stomach on a hard, sterile-smelling bed. His thighs and back felt like they were on fire. His right hip and left shoulder throbbed. He tried to move and groaned immediately.

"Welcome back."

"Rebecca?" Jake turned his head to find a nicely curved hip at eye level. She stood beside the bed, which he realized in embarrassment was the hospital bed next to Katie's. His daughter looked over at him from her bed, her expression an odd mixture of hope and worry.

"You okay, Jake?" she asked.

"Yeah. I'm fine. Just give me a minute." He moved a leg. Jesus, where were his clothes?

Rebecca was still wearing her bloody cornflower blue suit, so he couldn't have been out that long. What the hell happened to him? He tried to roll over, but couldn't quite get his limbs to cooperate.

"I wouldn't try that just yet if I were you," he heard Rebecca say as a fresh surge of pain swirled through his body. "You had about two dozen shards of glass embedded in your backside," she added, her voice noticeably neutral, "and you bruised your left shoulder, probably when you tackled Bryan."

Jake thought he remembered something about hitting a telephone pole, too, but his brain didn't seem to be firing on all cylinders yet. "Where are my clothes?"

"What's left of them is in the closet. They cut your shirt off, but I managed to stop them before they did the same to your pants."

74

"Thanks. What happened?"

"You passed out. Since the bed was vacant, they just pulled the curtain around you and treated you here."

How humiliating. "So when can I get out of here?"

"Any time you're ready to have me look you over and pronounce you good to go, Mr. Donovan," a pleasant female voice offered from the doorway. "We need your bed now that you're awake."

At that, Jake gritted his teeth and forced himself to push up, roll over and sit up, the pain be damned. Smiling her approval and appreciation, a young, pretty blonde doctor moved to the foot of his bed. She picked up his chart, and offered Rebecca a more apologetic smile. "Katie's, too, I'm afraid. You're free to take her home, Ms. Reed. Just follow my instructions regarding the concussion and she should be fine."

Twenty minutes later Jake had his torn and bloody jeans back on and was being discharged over Rebecca's protests that he needed more time to recover his equilibrium. Since Rebecca's car was still at the library, and neither of the town's two taxis were available, the three of them had no choice but to head for home on foot. Within minutes, though, town council member Matthew Hannan, whose two young daughters had been in the library that afternoon, stopped to offer them a ride.

"The girls are fine," he said when Rebecca asked. "I took them home and came back with the four-wheeler to help with rescue efforts."

The trip seemed to take forever, the town a tortured landscape of naked tree trunks, twisted metal, and scattered debris. Occasionally they got out of the car to help blocked motorists move obstacles the storm had swept into the still-wet streets. Jake kept an eye out for Rebecca, and Rebecca kept a worried eye on Jake, but knew doing his share was as important to him as doing hers was to her. Both of them insisted Katie stay in the car.

No one in town seemed to have escaped some sort of damage. A horrifically high number of homes and businesses had been demolished. By the time the four-wheeler pulled up in front of Aunt Martha's Dutch colonial, Rebecca considered herself braced for anything.

Except the total destruction of her home.

Rebecca stared, unable to grasp what she saw. Her garage apartment no longer existed. In its place stood a huge pile of rubble. The nightgown she'd taken off that morning hung from a splintered elm tree, fluttering like a novelty flag in the evening breeze. Katie's Raggedy Ann doll lay atop Rebecca's bedroom dresser, which appeared to be intact, despite having fallen from the second floor. A lone corner of the first floor garage wall still stood, but beyond that, her home was gone.

"Rebecca, I'm so sorry," Matthew Hannon said from the seat in front of her.

"Oh...my...God."

"Mom? What are we going to do now?" A wide-eyed Katie asked from beside Rebecca in the back seat, her voice sounding very small and frightened.

"Is there somewhere else I can take you?"

Rebecca looked at Katie, then at Jake, sitting silently in the front passenger seat, then at Matthew Hannon. "Take us?"

"To stay. Until you can."

"Until we can what?" Rebecca asked numbly. *Get this awful mess cleaned up? Rebuild? Find somewhere to else live—along with more than half the families in Warner?* "I mean, no. I'm sure my aunt..." She looked over at her aunt's house and saw the west corner had been sheared off, leaving a gaping hole in the upstairs guest room and the living room where Aunt Martha had so proudly displayed her precious collection of red depression glass. "Oh no," she cried softly. "It's gone. It's...all gone. All that beautiful glass."

A long silence followed, interrupted only by Jake's quiet, "You and Katie are welcome to stay at my house."

She blinked at him in confusion. "Your house?"

"It's still standing, from what I can see, so it can't be in that bad a shape."

Rebecca looked past her aunt's rubble-filled pool and over the hedge to where Jake's freshly painted white house did indeed look as if it still stood intact. The second floor windows were blown out, but at least they were still windows.

Matthew Hannon's cell phone rang. His wife wanted to know when he was coming home. Rebecca realized she was keeping him from his family. "I'm sorry. Thanks for the ride, Matt."

He half-turned in his seat, to address both Rebecca and Katie. "Listen, I hate leaving you guys here like this, but..."

"I understand. We'll be fine. Really."

"You sure?"

"I'll take care of them, Hannon."

He looked at Jake, who met his gaze unflinchingly. A moment later, he nodded, seeming satisfied. He grabbed a note pad from the dash and wrote two numbers on it, then ripped the page off and handed it to Rebecca. "Here's our home number and my cell number. If you need anything, just give us a call." He looked at Jake. "Same goes."

Jake simply nodded.

Matt half-turned to look at Rebecca again. "You want me to drive you around the block?" He meant drop her off at Jake's.

"No." Determinedly, Rebecca opened her door. "I want to check on my aunt. Thank you again, Matt."

He looked from Rebecca to Jake, then back to Rebecca. "Thank you. Both of you. I don't know what I'd do without my little girls."

****

Aunt Martha wasn't home. She'd left a note on the kitchen counter, inviting Rebecca and Katie to stay in her sewing room. Looking at Katie and Jake, who'd followed her into the house, Rebecca said to Katie, "Aunt Martha has offered to take us in, Katie. We can sleep in her sewing room. What do you think?"

She'd always tried to give Katie as much say as possible regarding the decisions that affected their lives, and today was no exception. Rebecca believed that, like adults, children needed to feel they had some control over their lives to be happy. And at that moment, Rebecca would have done just about anything to keep Katie happy. Once her daughter realized what they'd lost...

"Jake said we could stay with him."

Rebecca turned to Jake, who suddenly looked as if he were on trial and she was about to pass judgment. "I know, and I'm grateful, but I'm not sure that's the best alternative. Jake is leaving again, and he wants to sell—"

"I've got the room," Jake interrupted. "You could each have your own bedroom if you wanted to."

There was no hint of emotion in his voice, one way or another, but Rebecca knew Jake enough to know if he didn't want her and Katie there, he wouldn't have offered. Her heart jumped at the chance, but her mind held back. People were already talking.

What would happen if she and Katie moved in with Jake? How would it affect Katie in the long run? What would Aunt Martha say? Rebecca adored her aunt and under different circumstances would have loved to stay with her, but this was Jake. Offering her and Katie shelter in his home.

Katie. His daughter.

Rebecca was sure he wouldn't invite anyone else to stay with

77

him if she turned him down. By accepting his offer, she would leave her aunt free to offer her sewing room to someone else in need. She would also give Jake and Katie the perfect opportunity to get to know each other the way they were meant to know each other. As father and daughter.

And what about her? What did *she* want?

Rebecca wanted to stay with Jake. She wanted Jake, period. She always had. She'd lost almost everything else in her life. She wasn't going to lose either Jake or Katie if she could help it. Somehow she'd find a way to make all of this work out

She looked Jake in the eye. "All right. We'll do it. '

Chapter Nine

"Good, the electricity and water are still running," Jake said, testing each as they entered his house through the kitchen door. "You and Katie can have my bed for tonight. I'll sleep on the couch. Tomorrow we'll see about digging through those boxes downstairs for linens in the other rooms. I just need a few minutes to clean up the glass and put something over the windows." He looked at Rebecca, who couldn't seem to pull her thoughts together. "Hey, you okay?"

"I don't know," she said honestly. "I'm not sure it's sunk in yet. I mean, I may have just picked my way past that huge pile of rubble out there, but..."

Jake's expression softened, and for a heartbeat it looked like he might pull her into his arms. Instead, he smiled gently and said, "You've had a heck of a day, Becca. A heck of a shock." Rebecca realized he was watching his language for Katie's sake, and was touched. But when his right hand came up to curl a stray tendril of hair behind her ear, Rebecca had to fight herself not to sway towards the comfort she knew he could bring her. That wasn't what this was about. This was about Jake and Katie spending time together. "Why don't you take a hot bath and relax?" Jake suggested softly. "Katie and I can throw something together for dinner."

"Sure, Mom. Just leave everything to Jake and me."

She looked from one to the other. The excitement that bubbled in her daughter's eyes told Rebecca that Katie, too, still hadn't absorbed the fact that her home had been destroyed. Clearly, Katie was dealing with it by considering it all one big adventure. Starring her new hero. Her father.

Rebecca sighed, too weary to think anymore. She managed a grateful smile. "Thank you. I'll see you guys later."

"I'll get you something to wear in a minute," Jake called after her, reminding Rebecca she didn't even have a change of clothes—for herself or for Katie. Her suit was ruined. She'd never get the bloodstains out. Maybe in the morning they could salvage some things from the rubble.

Nearly an hour later, she left the bathroom wearing one of Jake's black T-shirts and a pair of damp, but freshly rinsed panties. It was either that or go without.

She slowed to a halt at the foot of the staircase Katie was sound asleep on the living room couch, one slender arm wrapped around the Raggedy Ann doll Jake had apparently rescued. Fighting tears, Rebecca kissed her daughter's forehead and thanked God again for sparing both Katie and Jake.

Jake was heating canned soup and making peanut butter sandwiches. "She conked out on me ten minutes after you went upstairs," he said as Rebecca entered the kitchen. "I threw her doll in the dryer for a while, long enough to get the worst of the wet out of it, anyway."

Tears threatened again at the image of Jake slipping the treasured doll into her sleeping daughter's arms. Rebecca blinked rapidly. "Is she okay?"

"She says she is. Just a little tired."

"Maybe I should call the doctor."

"Maybe you should *listen* to the doctor," Jake said, not unkindly. "Katie needs rest. Unless she develops a fever or starts acting weird, she's probably fine." He smiled, reminding her of the countless times he'd reassured her when they were kids, usually after a test she'd been convinced she'd messed up on.

But this was no simple test. This was their daughter they were talking about.

Jake's smile faded as he realized the enormity of the responsibility he'd undertaken. Katie and Rebecca living under his roof, under his protection. His child and his...his what?

Better to focus on his child for now. "Relax, Rebecca. I've had concussions. You'll get through this one just fine. Both of you."

To keep from touching her, he turned back to his peanut butter sandwiches, then stilled as a thought struck him. He was going to have to be able to provide a hell of a lot more than peanut butter sandwiches for them. How was he going to manage that?

"Here. Let me do that. You must be exhausted."

Rebecca stepped up to the counter beside him, her arm brushing his as she reached for the peanut butter knife. Jake snatched it up and moved to the side, putting some space between them. "I'm fine."

Stubbornly, he refused to give up the knife, refused to relinquish what little control he still had over his life. "I'd rather you rested. You're the one who's had the bad day."

"And you're the one who bled all over the library then passed out at the hospital. Come on, Jake. Really. The bath worked wonders. But you haven't stopped moving all afternoon—with the exception of your twenty-minute nap at the hospital."

"Was that all it was?"

"Yeah." She smiled. "So c'mon, Donovan, give me a break, here." She pulled out a kitchen chair. "You need a rest and I need something to do to keep my mind off of...you know...out there," she nodded her head in the direction of where her apartment had been. "Besides, it won't kill you to let someone else take care of you for a little while."

"All right." Gingerly, Jake lowered himself into the chair she'd pulled out for him. Covering the windows with plastic while Rebecca was in the tub had all but sapped the last of his strength. "Thanks. I was getting a little bushed."

"I'm amazed you're still alive," she murmured, and proceeded to finish making supper.

Afterward, they did the dishes together. As they entered the living room, Jake insisted on carrying Katie upstairs. After he'd placed her on the bed, he opened a dresser drawer and pulled out a black T-shirt and a pair of cotton camouflage drawstring pants. He offered Rebecca the T-shirt for Katie to sleep in, kept the pants for himself, then excused himself to wash up while Rebecca dressed Katie for bed.

He emerged from the bathroom in time to see Rebecca gently tuck the groggy seven-year-old in, then patiently wake her daughter to ask the questions the doctor had told her to ask. Regret coursed through him, strong and sharp, at seeing mother and daughter talk quietly like they must have for thousands of bedtimes over the years. He backed away from the door and went downstairs.

Half an hour later he heard Rebecca's soft footfalls coming down the stairs. He stood at the kitchen sink, where he'd been watching the full moon rise, and swore softly. He'd hoped to avoid talking to Rebecca again tonight. His back, shoulder and hip hurt like hell and he felt too exhausted and raw for company.

"She asleep?" he asked when Rebecca entered the kitchen.

She paused in the doorway, frowning at his bare chest. Jake realized he hadn't given a second thought to putting on a shirt. Rebecca had seen him shirtless thousands of times.

But that was before they'd started sharing space. Looking at her legs, the long, slender legs he'd done his best to ignore during dinner, Jake could see this was going to be a problem.

Rebecca swallowed and cleared her throat. She looked very young and vulnerable with no make-up and her hair down around her shoulders. "Yes. She's asleep."

"Any problems?"

"No. Before she drifted off, she wanted to make sure I wouldn't worry about replacing our things. She's just glad we're all safe." Her eyes filled with a soft, maternal pride, and Jake knew he'd made the biggest mistake of his life, inviting Rebecca and Katie to stay with him. How was he supposed to get through the next few weeks, knowing the two things he wanted most in life were right under his roof and he could never have them? "She's incredible, isn't she?"

Damn. She was getting all misty-eyed again, and this time Jake wasn't sure she'd be able to win out over the tears. It had amazed—and relieved—him that she'd managed to hold it together this long. He tried to muster a smile of his own, and wished she'd go back upstairs to leave him alone with his aches and pains and mountain of regrets. "She sure is. Smart and strong and brave and beautiful. Just like her mama."

Rebecca moved to the table, where she unnecessarily rearranged the salt and pepper shakers. "She also said to be sure and tell you thanks for letting us stay here, and for coming to the hospital to find her." She looked up at him, her eyes clear and direct. "She sees you as her hero, Jake."

Jake closed his eyes as a fresh wave of guilt swept through him. "I don't want to hear this, Rebecca. You know as well as I do I'm nobody's hero."

"You saved our lives at the library."

"I did what I had to. And that's what I'm doing with you and Katie."

"You mean...you wouldn't have offered to let us stay with you if...?"

"If Katie wasn't mine? No. I wouldn't. Your aunt has more than enough room to keep you."

"What if I'd denied Katie was yours?"

"Then we both would have known you were lying."

"How so? She doesn't look anything like you."

"She doesn't have to. She has the Dillenger family birthmark. I've got one just like it. Inherited from my mother. Hers was on her left shoulder."

Rebecca frowned. "But I've never seen..."

"Mine's on my pelvis." Jake touched his right side. "Just to the right of my family jewels."

Rebecca's gaze dropped to the drawstring pants Jake had no intention of removing as long as Rebecca was within fifty yards of him. Almost immediately, she looked back up at his face, hers flushing. "Oh," she said. "Oh."

"Yeah, oh."

Suddenly her eyes narrowed. "Why didn't you tell me?"

Jake saw a fight coming and welcomed it. Bone-tired, hurting like a sonofagun and hungry for something he was never going to have, his voice took on an edge he didn't want to have to use on her, but knew he'd have to, to keep her at a distance. No telling what he'd end up saying, or promising, if she started crying again. "Seems to me that question ought to belong to me," he said, crossing his arms over his chest. "If I recall correctly, in fifteen letters you never once mentioned you were pregnant with my child."

Rebecca stared at him as her initial surprise changed into something darker. "So you did get them."

"Of course I did." Memorized every last one of them, too. He locked his gaze on hers. "Why didn't you tell me, Becca?"

He'd expected her to flinch. Instead, a visible calm seemed to settle over her, unsettling Jake more than he would ever let on. "I was waiting."

"For what?"

"You."

"Oh, give me a break."

"I was! I came to Wyoming, Jake. I caught a ride to Denver with another student who was going home for Thanksgiving break, and caught a bus from there. I came to see you at the Laramie county jail. But you hadn't put any names on your visitor's list, so they wouldn't let me past the check-in desk."

Jake stared, reeling. "You didn't."

"I did. I stayed overnight and took a bus back to school. Maybe I should've stuck around for a few days, written a letter to see if you'd be willing to see me. But I was scared and almost broke and if I stayed, I didn't know how I was going to get back home."

Jake's mind spun back in time as he realized she was telling the truth. "So that's what they meant. They told me I'd had a visitor, a young, pretty, female visitor, but I thought they were yanking my chain again." He frowned, narrowing his eyes. "What do you mean you took a bus home? What happened to the student you caught a ride out there with?"

"We didn't get along."

Jake's mind leapt to the worst case scenario. Rebecca alone, him in jail. "Did he hurt you?"

"No, but I wasn't going to get into a car with him again."

Jake's guilt morphed into anger as he thought of the danger she'd put herself in for him, the vulnerability she'd suffered because of him. Eight long years of it. "For God's sake, Rebecca, what were you thinking?"

"You don't want to know, Jake, you really don't."

"You should have told me about her."

"What difference would it have made?"

"What difference would it have made? What *difference* would it have made? For one, I would have—"

Fought like hell to get out of there. To come back to you. If I'd thought for one minute that you wanted a life with me instead of that rich dude you were planning to marry...

Jake's thoughts slammed into him so hard all he could do was clench his fists against the pain and stare at her in stunned disbelief. He couldn't tell her that. If he told her that, he'd never leave Warner. "I...I would have sent you money or something," he ended lamely.

"Money?" Rebecca repeated icily. "For what?"

"For support, Rebecca," he answered wearily. "What do you think?"

She stared at him, long and hard. "You would have sent me guilt money?"

"No! You had to know I...I cared about you, Rebecca."

She snorted. "I should hope so. We were friends, Jake. For six years I was your best buddy. The one you turned to when you were feeling lost or lonely or in need of some undemanding company."

"I know."

"So what possessed you to take off that morning?"

Jake's defenses locked into place so hard and fast he couldn't have fought them if he wanted to. He shook his head, unwilling to give her the answer she needed. To do so would mean giving up what precious little freedom he still had.

He spoke quietly, doing what he could to soften the blow. "I'm sorry, Rebecca. I can't answer that."

Jake's Return

"I deserve an answer, Jake. I'm not the one who got myself locked up for sleeping with another woman two weeks later."

Jake stared at her, and realized with no small amount of amazement that she was more upset about the bedding part than the murder. "I didn't go to prison for sleeping with her, Rebecca. I went to prison for murder."

"Did you? Think about it, Jake. We both know you didn't kill her. Which means the only thing you're guilty of is being in the wrong bed at the wrong time. Did she have a boyfriend?"

"Well, yeah, but..."

"My point, exactly. After all, who knows your game plan when it comes to women better than I do? If they're already taken, so much the better. If not, never promise them anything, and when the pressure starts, get the hell out of Dodge."

"Now wait a minute, I never—"

But Rebecca was on a roll. She'd waited eight years for this conversation and she wasn't about to let go of it now. "Suddenly I was just one of the bunch, wasn't I? The only one who was available the night you got out of the army, looking for some company. And since I was engaged to someone else, there were no entanglements to worry about. I was spoken for. You could ride off in the morning with a clear conscience." She glared at him, letting him see how angry she was, even now, after all these years. "Fifteen letters, Jake. Fifteen. Not once did you write back. Not once did you think to ask how I was doing, if my plans had changed, if you might have left a souvenir behind when you slunk out of my life."

Jake winced. She was dead wrong about most of it, but beneath her anger she had a point. "I was wrong to leave without saying goodbye," he said. "I was wrong to take you to bed. I was wrong for not answering your letters. But you've got to know I would have answered if I'd known about Katie."

"Which was exactly why I *didn't* tell you about her," Rebecca snapped. "I wanted you to write back because you cared about *me*, not because you thought it was 'the right thing to do.'"

"You're kidding."

"Call it stupid, call it selfish, call it impossibly idealistic if you want to, but yes, I wanted you to admit you had feelings for *me* before I told you about the baby." She looked at him, apparently running out of steam. "But you never did, so here we are."

Neither of them said anything for a while. The silence was

crushing as Rebecca went back to rearranging the salt and pepper shakers. The phone rang and Jake looked over at it in relief.

"I'm sorry to disturb you, Jacob, but might I speak with Rebecca? I got her note, but wanted to make sure she and Katie were all right."

"It's your aunt."

Jake left the room. He and Rebecca weren't going to get anything resolved tonight about Katie or anything else. He'd never seen Rebecca lose her temper before, never imagined she could blow like that.

Unfortunately, the sight of her angry only strengthened her appeal for him. She was kind of wild and sexy when she was mad. Face flushed, hair loose, blue eyes flashing fire.

He sank onto the living room couch, shook his head, then dropped it into his hands. This was never going to work.

"Maybe you should take her up on her offer after all," he said when he heard Rebecca enter the room.

"Not tonight. Katie needs her rest."

Jake lifted his head, which was beginning to throb. Rebecca looked like she wanted to argue some more, but the time for talking was over. He'd probably said more in the past half hour than he had in a year in prison. "I'll see you in the morning."

She said nothing, simply crossed the room and went quietly up the staircase. Jake wondered if he would have preferred it if she'd stomped. Obviously he'd hit his head when he'd passed out at the hospital. Left his common sense lying somewhere on the floor. He listened to the floorboards squeak as Rebecca entered his bedroom. The room she'd filled with her own furniture. Furniture that, from the looks of it, was all she had left.

Jake tried to take that into account. The woman had just lost almost everything she owned. She had a right to be upset.

Someone knocked on his front door. A man Jake vaguely recognized from the library that afternoon stood on his doorstep. "Mr. Donovan? My name is Whitney Moog. I'm a reporter with the Forest County Register."

"We're not in Forest County."

"I know, but I was in town today doing research, and this goes beyond local news. I wonder if I might ask you a few questions about your heroic rescue at the library this afternoon for a story I'm writing."

Jake closed his eyes and pinched the bridge of his nose as his headache shifted into high gear. The last thing he needed was some reporter poking around in his life. "I just did what I had to do. Nothing special."

"On the contrary, Mr. Donovan. You saved the lives of two dozen people, including ten children and the mayor's grandson. You're a convicted murderer, recently paroled from prison, and a decorated war hero. I'd say that adds up to quite an interesting story. Now, I realize it's late, but..."

He trailed off and Jake turned to see Rebecca standing midway up the staircase, one hand on the banister. She'd put on a pair of cotton camo pants to cover her legs, but it was obvious she was wearing his clothes.

And he wasn't wearing enough.

The reporter cleared his throat. "Hello, Rebecca."

"Whitney."

He turned back to Jake. "So tell me, Mr. Donovan, what exactly is your relationship with Ms. Reed? Can you tell me how long the two of you have been—*hey*!"

Jake shoved the screen door open so fast he nearly knocked the reporter back into his home county. "Listen, buddy, I don't care if you work for White House Press Corps. You write anything even *remotely* unflattering about Ms. Reed and you're dead meat."

"I...I was going to say friends."

"That's right. We're friends. She's staying here tonight because her apartment was wiped out this afternoon. She and her daughter will be bunking here until they can find somewhere else to live. But you're not even going to say that much about her. You're not going to say anything about her at all. Got it?"

The reporter looked at Rebecca, still frozen on the stairs, then back at Jake. Meeting Jake's rock-hard expression, honed to perfection in prison, he nodded once, then backed away slowly. "Got it."

Chapter Ten

"Good Morning."

Jake looked over his shoulder from where he was frying bacon at the kitchen stove. The dark circles under Rebecca's eyes matched his own. He'd spent most of the night lying awake, listening to the alarm clock go off upstairs, reminding Rebecca to wake Katie and ask her the simple questions the doctor had told Rebecca to ask.

Each time, Jake's first instinct had been to climb the stairs and listen in, to reassure himself that his daughter was all right. Instead, he'd stayed on the couch, knowing he didn't have the right to look in on them—to horn in on their relationship. He'd given that up the moment he'd walked out on Rebecca eight years ago.

As he'd listened with a longing more painful than any he'd known to the soft murmur of their voices above him, Jake couldn't help but wonder how many other sleepless nights Rebecca had spent caring for their daughter while he'd been behind bars. Couldn't help but wonder what might have happened if he'd been man enough to stick around and stand up for what he wanted after their night together in Pittsburgh.

Rebecca was right. He might not be guilty of murder, but he was sure as hell guilty of slinking out of her life without so much as a thank you or goodbye.

But as for the rest of it—his reasons for seeking her out that night in Pittsburgh, his reasons for sleeping with her, his reasons for leaving her—she couldn't be more wrong about those.

"Morning. How's Katie?"

"Doing well. She should be all right. She wanted to sleep in a little longer."

"Eggs?"

"That would be nice. Thank you."

He turned back to the stove, his emotions still raw and churning. Even pale and exhausted and stiffly polite, Rebecca was everything he'd ever wanted to wake up to. "Since we're running low on just about everything, I'll have to make a grocery store run today. It's still standing, but there won't be much left on the shelves by now. Half the town's been destroyed, and the other half's scrambling for what's left."

Behind him, Rebecca closed her eyes in stark relief. At least he hadn't suggested she and Katie move out again. She'd spent half the night terrified that, once he'd had time to mull over the bitter things she'd said, the subject of her finding different living arrangements would be first on his list today.

So far so good. Still, she couldn't deny the chill in the air. She shivered and rubbed her arms. "I need to go over to the apartment this morning and look for clothes."

"Already taken care of. They're in the dryer."

"Oh. Thank you."

Jake removed the bacon from the heat, set the strips aside to drain and turned his attention toward making their eggs. Rebecca got the plates out and set the table. "What are you going to do?" she asked midway through the strained silence of their meal. "About Katie."

"You mean am I going to petition for custody?"

Rebecca dropped her fork, jolted to the core. "Of course not." She'd never even *considered* that possibility.

Jake sat back and lowered his own fork, eyeing her with speculative interest. "Does that mean you don't think I would, or you don't think I have a snowball's chance of winning?"

Rebecca scrambled for a response that wouldn't betray the depth of her astonishment...or fear. "You can't be serious."

"The jury's still out on that one."

His gaze didn't waver. Rebecca's appetite vanished at the thought of Jake trying to take Katie away from her. At the ugliness that could erupt during such a court battle. At the lives that would be shattered.

"After all," Jake continued calmly, "You *were* planning to tell me about her, so I'm assuming that means you'd hoped I'd take a more active role in her life. Otherwise, why bother telling me?"

Rebecca stared. Of course she'd wanted Jake to accept their daughter, to take an active role in Katie's life, but suddenly she realized she'd wanted it on *her* terms. Terms that involved Jake settling down, staying in Warner, building a family with herself and Katie—and any other children they might have.

Which was something Jake had never once—not even as a teenager—shown the slightest interest in doing—with her or with anyone else.

Now he obviously had his own ideas about his relationship with Katie. Rebecca swallowed the cold lump of fear in her throat and forced herself to meet his unflinching gaze.

"Jake, can't we be reasonable about this?"

"I am being reasonable. Since I don't plan to stay in Warner, at a minimum, we're going to need to consider some kind of visitation agreement. After all, Katie and I have a lot of time to make up for."

Slowly, Rebecca shook her head. "No. You can't do this. You can't just drop back into my life and try to take Katie away from me."

"It's not like I knew she existed before now, Rebecca."

"You can't have her, Jake."

"Then what do you want from me? Money?"

"Of course not! I'm perfectly capable of taking care of Katie financially."

"A fact I'm all too aware of," Jake muttered in disgust, looking away for a moment, then turning his sharp gaze back on her. "So what did you expect? I'd welcome the news with open arms and we'd suddenly turn into a happy little family?"

Rebecca flushed deeply as his words hit dead on. "God forbid," she snapped in self-defense. "We all know how allergic you are to anything that resembles a commitment."

Jake's eyes flashed, then hardened to flint. "I think I'm getting the picture. You didn't expect me to stick around once I found out."

"Have you ever given me a reason to believe otherwise?"

Jake closed his eyes briefly, but didn't take the bait. "All right. I'll ask you one more time. What do you want from me?"

"I want you to love Katie. To accept her as your own."

"But not lay any claim to her that would weaken yours."

"That's not what I—"

"Admit it, Rebecca. You're petrified at the idea of me suing for custody."

She forgot to breathe for a moment. "You're right. I am."

The pain in his eyes took her back to when they were kids, and nearly undid her. "What are you so afraid of?" he asked quietly. "That I'll hurt her?"

"No. Never. It's just that..." She paused and blinked back tears, willing herself not to break down now. But it was hard. Almost as hard as opening herself up to Jake like this. He looked so vulnerable. So alone.

But she had to remember that being alone was *his* choice, and always had been. "Everyone I've ever loved has left me, Jake. I couldn't stand to lose Katie, too. She's my life."

Was it her imagination, or did the bleakness in his eyes soften? "Do you really think any judge in his right mind would hand a seven-year-old girl to a convicted woman-killer?"

Rebecca stared, realizing he was trying to reassure her. Why, she had no idea. But sorrow filled her heart instead of relief or victory. Sorrow, and deep regret.

Jake looked at her for a long moment, then looked away, running a hand down his face. "Listen, Becca. I don't even know how long I'm going to be here or where I'm going when I leave. So why don't we just relax and leave things as they are. I'll be more than happy to accept Katie into my heart. I already have. But as for the rest...she's all yours, Rebecca. You're the one who's been there for her for the past seven years, not me. I wouldn't even know where to begin to be a father."

"Mom? Jake?" Rebecca heard footfalls on the stairs.

"In the kitchen, honey."

"Does she know?" Jake asked quietly.

"No. No one does."

Katie entered the room wearing Jake's huge black T-shirt. She spotted Jake and offered him a sweetly shy smile. "Hi, guys."

"Good morning, sleepyhead," Rebecca returned, and drew her daughter onto her lap for a morning hug. "How are you feeling?"

"Good, but...Mom? What am I supposed to wear today?"

"Jake's got some things in the dryer. But for now you can eat breakfast in that, like I am."

"Yeah," Jake drawled from across the table. "Makes you and your mom look like twins in those shirts."

Katie beamed, then stood and slid into her own seat at the table. Jake smiled and passed her the eggs and bacon. Rebecca frowned, not used to sharing her conversations with Katie. But then she noticed the quiet hunger in Jake's eyes as he watched his daughter eagerly fill her plate. His dark gray gaze all but devoured Katie's every feature and movement—much like Rebecca had done the first time she'd held her daughter. She still had moments like that when she marveled at the miracle that was her child.

And now she was Jake's child, too. Jake was right. She had cheated him out of knowing Katie. But what else could she have done? Fifteen letters she'd written to him, praying daily for an answer. A sign that he cared. A crumb to give her hope

In the end, she'd realized his silence was his answer.

And now?

He'd just agreed to continue keeping his silence.

Suddenly Rebecca realized what Jake had done. He'd played on her fear of losing Katie to get her to agree to a compromise that would leave him exactly where he wanted to be—right next to his escape hatch. By not claiming Katie legally, Jake was still free to pick up and leave Warner whenever the mood struck.

Leaning over, Rebecca finally picked up her fallen fork. Wondering if she'd ever learn, she stood and scraped her cold eggs into the trash.

After breakfast, Rebecca and Katie changed clothes and the three of them went over to Aunt Martha's to begin clean-up efforts. A neighbor came by and offered his pickup to help cart away debris. Three truckloads later, Aunt Martha called them all in for lunch at her house. Afterward, Katie fell asleep on Aunt Martha's sunroom swing, so they left her there while Jake walked to the library to retrieve Rebecca's car and go to the grocery store. Rebecca returned to Jake's to unpack what remained of her personal belongings, and wondered again if the cache of furniture she kept in storage still existed. She'd tried calling the storage facility several times, but hadn't been able to get through.

Suddenly needing to know, she called her aunt to let her know she'd be back in an hour and walked to the facility. She almost wept with relief when she saw it had survived the tornado intact. After telling the attendant she'd lost her key in the tornado, he let her into her small storage space. The minute she was alone again, she thanked God for sparing her "good" furniture. There weren't that many pieces, but she'd hand-picked each to have a special place in the home she'd planned to one day buy for herself and Katie.

Buoyed by the knowledge she hadn't lost everything, Rebecca returned to the rubble to continue sorting. It was dusk before Jake returned, looking like he never wanted to set foot in a grocery store again. Katie insisted she was starving and pounced on the four bags of groceries Jake had already set on the table, then stared in disbelief as she pulled out the contents.

"Don't complain, Peanut," Jake said, catching her horrified expression as he returned with another four bags. "I had to drive to St. Mary's to get this much. Every podunk grocery store between here and there was sold out of pretty much everything."

"But seven cans of Spam?"

"Sure. Didn't you know your mother's a whiz with Spam?"

"You are?"

"Was, Katie, was." Spam had been a mainstay in Rebecca's—and Jake's—diet as a kid. Rebecca hadn't touched it since Katie was born, though. For some reason she'd craved Spam during her pregnancy. Enough to make her never want to eat the stuff again.

"Seems to me she came in first in a regional Spam cook-off once."

Rebecca stared at Jake. "I'd forgotten all about that."

He winked at her, then smiled at her fascinated daughter. "She's just being modest. The truth is your mom's always had a knack for making something special out of the ordinary."

Dinner that night was a cultural smorgasbord—hummus, egg rolls, gyros and more. Much more. Watching Jake and Katie dare each other to sample the already prepared ethnic specialties Jake had brought home in lieu of the usual staples, Rebecca realized how predictable her life had become. As a girl, Rebecca had never known when or where, much less what, her next meal might be. Since Katie's birth, she'd sought security in the routine, raising her daughter according to what Rebecca now realized was some idealized version of how she imagined "real" families lived.

Between Katie's trip, Jake's return and the tornado, she'd been thrown off schedule, but once Katie started back to school next week, Rebecca realized she fully expected to resume her routine of spaghetti on Mondays, chicken on Tuesdays, right through to pot roast on Sunday afternoons.

Jake was the one who had yearned for new places and experiences, not she. All Rebecca had ever wanted out of life was the security of a home and family. Granted, she'd once aspired to owning an antique-filled mansion on the river, but the truth was, as long as she had Katie she could be happy anywhere.

She wished she could say the same of Jake. Watching him grin like a pirate at Katie, then pop a piece of Swiss milk chocolate into his mouth, Rebecca knew she could never keep Jake in Warner out of duty or obligation. For while her dreams had been of wealth and security, his had been of freedom and adventure. The boy she'd known had thrived on the new, the unusual, the unexpected. The man he'd become could never be happy with the simple life she'd created for herself and Katie, any more than her father had been happy living with her mother. She'd been a selfish fool to think she and Jake would be different.

"I'll get the dishes," she said, and rose from the table.

Jake reached out and caught her wrist. "Why don't you leave them for me? You haven't stopped moving all day."

The warmth of his hand flowed up her arm and into her heart, making it ache for what would never be. She avoided Jake's eyes as she gently pulled away. "It won't take but a few minutes. Why don't you and Katie play one of those board games you bought?"

He said he'd gotten them for everyone, but Rebecca suspected he'd bought them as a surreptitious gift for Katie. Rebecca's heart had twisted with regret all over again when she'd seen them. He'd missed out on so much. "Katie, why don't you pick one out?"

"All right!"

Two hours later, Jake found Rebecca in his bedroom, the room she still shared with Katie, wiping salvaged toiletry articles with a damp cloth. After finishing the dishes, she'd slipped upstairs to give Jake and Katie some time alone together. "Hi."

She turned and smiled. "Hi."

"I take it Katie's in the bathroom washing up."

"You take it right. It's past her bedtime. How'd it go?"

"She sunk all my battleships. I, for one, could have used some strategic help. That girl's ruthless when it comes to winning."

Rebecca smiled. "I know. It's scary. I'm not sure where she gets it. You never seemed that competitive, and I'm certainly not." she trailed off, feeling awkward. She'd imagined conversations like this with Jake thousands of times over the years, but now that he was here...

"I don't know," Jake mused thoughtfully. "You'd have to be pretty competitive to graduate first in your class. To sail through college with a perfect four-point-oh—at least for the first two years."

Rebecca smiled, for the first time willing to discuss the past without getting angry or defensive. "It dropped when Katie came along, but I think I ended up with a three-point-seven."

"You always were the smartest person I knew."

A hint of nostalgia entered his eyes and Rebecca recalled how, more often than not, on his way out for the evening, Jake would stop by the apartment to cadge a cookie or two and tease her about her study habits. But beneath the teasing she'd sensed his pride in her, and her dedication to making good grades had come in part from a deep-rooted desire to please him.

As she looked back now, she wondered if he'd considered himself incapable of shining academically, so had chosen to encourage her instead.

It gave her something to think about.

"So how come you're hiding out up here?" Jake asked, with the same quiet perceptiveness he'd shown when they were younger.

"The truth? I don't know what to do with myself. I'm feeling unsettled and I hate it. It reminds me of life with Chloe after…after my dad left."

Jake's expression softened. "You can't compare your life with your mother to what's happening now, Rebecca. Your home was destroyed by a tornado, not irresponsible acting out."

"I know. But being left homeless has made me realize how deeply my life is rooted in the familiar. How attached I've become to my things. We didn't have much, Jake, but what we had was special. It was part of what made the apartment a home."

Jake's smile held an unexpected hint of sadness. "Home and hearth. You haven't changed a bit, Rebecca."

Neither have you, she thought, then dismissed the bleak realization before it could ruin her evening.

"Tell me about the stuff you have in storage," he said. During dinner, she'd mentioned her visit to the storage facility, explaining there wasn't enough room in the apartment for all the furniture she'd acquired over the years, and she'd never intended to live there permanently. "You think there'd be enough room for it here?"

"Well, sure, but…?"

"If it looks anything like this bedroom set, it couldn't help but be an improvement over what's here now. Besides, you and Katie might feel more comfortable staying here surrounded by your own stuff." He met her eyes. "More settled."

Rebecca stared, touched beyond words. "Jake, I don't know what to say."

He shrugged in that way he had of pretending something didn't matter. "You don't have to move anything if you think it's going to be too much trouble to move it in and then take it out again when you find another place to stay. I just thought you might like to have the option of knowing it's okay with me."

"Thank you."

"I'll give you a hand if you need it."

"I appreciate that. I'll let you know."

Jake nodded and turned to leave.

"Jake?" She crossed the room. This would be their only chance to speak privately until tomorrow. After last night, she refused to go downstairs again once Katie went to bed. Being alone with Jake was too great a temptation. She was too attracted to him. Sooner or later she was going to have to figure out how to get past that, but for now, hiding out seemed to be her best option.

He'd paused in the hallway and was waiting. She stopped at the bedroom doorway, then cast a quick look at the bathroom door to make sure Katie wasn't on her way out. "About Katie," she whispered. "Are you planning to tell her you're her father?"

He seemed to go very still. "Why do you ask?"

"I'd like to be there if you do."

He looked at her for the longest time, saying nothing. When he spoke it was with a quiet conviction that moved Rebecca's soul. "I won't pretend to understand why you did what you did, Rebecca, or say that suddenly learning I have a seven-year-old child didn't hurt, deeply. But I won't interfere with the way you mother her. She's bright, funny, talented, and compassionate. That didn't happen on its own. You've been there for Katie from the start, guiding her and watching her grow. You know her inside and out. If you think telling her I'm her father will in any way hurt her, then I vote we never tell her. God knows I don't want to be the drag on her that Mickey was on me."

Rebecca's protest was automatic and heartfelt. "Jake..."

He shushed her with the touch of his calloused fingers on her lips. Desire stirred deep in her womb. It was all she could do not to close her eyes and lean into his light touch.

Jake cleared his throat. "Katie clearly likes having me as a friend," he said, his voice gruff. "Seems to me that's the best course to keep for now."

It had always hurt, her decision not to tell Katie who her father was, but suddenly their deception burned like acid in Rebecca's heart. Even so, she had to think about what would happen when Jake left Warner. If Katie knew Jake was her father, she'd feel abandoned when he left—and rightfully so.

Rebecca knew all too well how being left behind felt. She also knew she'd do whatever she had to, to spare her daughter that kind of pain.

"Sounds like a plan," she said quietly.

Jake turned away, never imagining that her agreement would

cut so deeply. With no small amount of surprise, he realized some insane part of him had actually hoped Rebecca would defend his right to let Katie know he was her father. Right then and there. As soon as she got out of the bathroom.

Instead, he knocked on the bathroom door to tell Katie good night and that he was going out for a run. He couldn't stand the thought of spending the rest of the evening in the same house with Rebecca, knowing how desperately—how pathetically—he wanted her. Knowing how obviously she wanted to avoid him—now that she'd let him know how she felt about letting people know that he, Jacob Donovan, was the father of her child.

But what did he expect? Rebecca had known him since he was a kid. If anyone was in a position to judge him, it was Rebecca. And if she didn't think he made the grade.

There wasn't much point in sticking around.

Chapter Eleven

Taking a coffee break at Feeney's the next morning, Jake scowled at the weekly paper's headline story. A condensed version of his life in print was not what he considered news. Nor did he care for the startlingly clear shot of himself, covered with blood, carrying Bryan Modano to safety across a sea of shattered glass. His left shoulder twitched at the memory.

Jake found it ironic to be credited with saving the life of the mayor's grandson, when twelve years ago he'd derived a defiant satisfaction from causing trouble between the mayor and his daughter. He hadn't seen Mimi yet, wasn't even sure she still lived in town, but figured he'd find out soon enough once people got a good look at his picture and realized just who had been around their nieces and nephews at the library.

He looked back at the picture of himself and Bryan. Funny, he would have thought survival would be front and center in everyone's mind at the time, not photo ops. Apparently that reporter Moog wasn't one to let a little thing like wholesale destruction get in his way. Jake skimmed the article again, relieved that Moog hadn't made any reference to the personal relationship between himself and Rebecca.

Now that was a story for the paper. Jake figured it would fit right in with the soap opera section. With a snort of disgust he set the paper aside and went back to work, happy to have something familiar and productive to lose himself in while the world went crazy around him.

Ten minutes later, Sheriff Sutter pulled up in a cruiser.

Jake's instincts went on full alert. By now, Sutter had to know Rebecca and Katie were staying with him. God knew *he'd* have something to say about it if he were in Sutter's spit-shined shoes. Especially if Sutter and Rebecca had something going.

Sutter's I've-got-your-ass-now look as he climbed out of his cruiser was all too familiar to Jake. He braced himself as an involuntary shaft of fear sliced deep into the pit of his belly. The first time he'd seen that look in a lawman's eyes, he'd lost everything dear to him, including his brand new bike and the second-hand leather jacket Rebecca had given him for his eighteenth birthday.

It took everything Jake had to keep the fear that coursed through him at bay, and focus on the engine he was rebuilding as Sutter approached Feeney and started talking.

Several long minutes later, Jake felt the hairs on the back of his neck prickle. He straightened slowly, every muscle in his body tense as Sutter strode toward him. The tall, physically fit man radiated power and authority, and that alone would normally have had Jake's back up in a flash. But the lethal look in Sutter's eyes told Jake what was going down here was personal.

Real personal.

The closer Sutter came, the louder Jake's instincts screamed at him to *run*—but his feet remained rooted to the ground. An image of Rebecca and Katie wearing matching black T-shirts—his T-shirts—at the breakfast table yesterday morning popped into his mind, and Jake suddenly knew with absolute certainty that if he ran, he'd be leaving the door wide open for Sutter to move in on Rebecca, and that was *not* an option.

Not when Jake knew Katie was his. He might not be the best candidate to raise his little girl, but the idea of Robert Sutter taking over the job was dead.

"Donovan."

Jake nodded. "Sheriff."

"Feeney tells me you were working the station alone Thursday afternoon."

Jake almost frowned. This wasn't about Rebecca? He nodded slowly. "For about an hour before the tornado hit. Why?"

"I understand you were working on my vehicle."

Jake suddenly registered that Sutter wasn't driving his Blazer, but a squad car. Ice filled his insides and he clamped down on his emotions at the memory of being arrested for Christine's murder. He'd resisted the arrest, knowing they had the wrong man. Big mistake. Shoving him into the back of the cruiser all battered and bleeding had been only the beginning of his eight-year sojourn into hell.

"Mind if I have a look around?"

"Not if Feeney doesn't mind. It's his place."

Sutter brushed past him, saying nothing. Jake fought back the memories of prison search teams and the choking resentment at having his space invaded as the sheriff took his time looking over Jake's personal workbench, where he kept the tools Feeney had loaned him until he could afford his own. But unlike the search and destroy missions his cell had been subjected to in prison, Sheriff Sutter touched nothing.

Still, Jake knew the man's sharp eyes didn't miss a thing. Sutter obviously took his job seriously, and given that there hadn't been a whisper of real trouble in Warner in years, he seemed an effective enough candidate for re-election. Jake was stunned to find himself thinking he'd rather deal with Sutter any day over the slick ex-cop from the city Dillenger was backing. Jake had met his kind many times over. All spit and polish on the outside, rotten to the core on the inside.

Knowing Sutter expected him to break the silence, Jake obliged so he could get on with his day. "What's up, Sheriff?"

Sutter turned and eyed Jake coldly, his low voice feral. "What's up is some cocky sonofabitch sliced my brake cables halfway through, and I damn near didn't make it back down from checking out Holton Hill last night."

Jake stared, unable to believe what he was hearing. Someone had sliced the sheriff's brake cables? And Sutter suspected *him*?

Suddenly Jake remembered Dillenger. Remembered leaving Dillenger at the station just before the tornado hit. Remembered sending him into the service bays for protection. Alone. Without thinking, he flashed his gaze to the cubbyhole where he'd stashed the distinctive red and black-handled boot knife he'd come across in his basement last week. A memento from his adolescence. When he'd found it, he'd smiled wryly, thinking how little he'd known about knife-fighting then. He wasn't sure why he'd brought it to Feeney's. Especially since he wasn't allowed to carry weapons.

His insides cramped as he realized it was gone.

Sutter's low voice held ugly speculation. "I'm thinking you might know a little something about who did it."

Jake looked back at Sutter, who fixed him with a hard, knowing stare. His blood ran cold as Jake pictured Avery Dillenger recognizing the knife as Jake's, smiling smugly, picking it up, then getting down on his knees in his thousand dollar Italian suit.

And cutting the sheriff's brake lines.

Christ.

No one would believe him. Least of all Robert Sutter.

Jake forced himself to meet Sutter's hard stare with one of his own. No way was he taking the rap for this one. "Sorry, Sheriff. I can't help you."

Sutter's eyes narrowed to black pinpoints of fury. Stepping

up to Jake, he warned, "I'm going to be watching you, Donovan. Every move you make. One wrong step and I'm gonna be on your ass like a tick on a dog. I don't care what kind of hero the paper is making you out to be. When I find the knife that cut my cables and your prints just happen to be on it, you're going down for good. I damn well guarantee it."

With that, he pivoted on his heel and left, leaving Jake more stunned and shaken than he'd felt in years. And that made him angry. Swearing almost non-stop, Jake spent a good fifteen minutes searching the workbench from top to bottom for his knife. He didn't find it—but he did find a half empty bottle of Dr. Pepper on the floor beneath it.

Damn it all to hell. He should have seen that one coming a mile away. Should have known there was a reason Dillenger kept coming around the station. From what Jake had heard about his power-hungry cousin since his return, there wasn't anything Avery Dillenger did without having a plan.

And most times that plan wasn't revealed until it was too late.

Jake didn't have time to keep looking for the knife as people started pouring into the station. By noon, he was feeling like he'd entered an alternate reality. Women were bringing him food, and men were treating him with a new, if grudging, respect.

Even his grandmother stopped by. She didn't speak to him. She never did. But Jake could feel her cool blue eyes watching him from the back seat of her tinted-window Bentley. The same Bentley she'd rode off in with old man Dillenger the night of Jake's mother's funeral.

No, Jake wasn't likely to forget *that* car.

To top it off, several of the parents—and grandparents—of the children he and Rebecca had rescued stopped by to thank him, including the mayor, while photographers snapped their picture and a handful of reporters tried to interview them. Refusing to have anyone intrude on his life any more than they already had, Jake left the interviews to the mayor and retreated to the service bays for the rest of the afternoon. With the same respect he'd shown for Jake as a teen, Feeney left him alone, and went about handling the gas customers with his usual flair for service with a smile.

Meanwhile, Jake counted down the minutes until he could go home to Rebecca.

Rebecca, who owed him a few answers.

But Rebecca wasn't there. Which unsettled Jake even more, since his first thought upon entering the kitchen was he'd walked into the wrong house. Holding the note Rebecca had left that said she and Katie were out shopping for clothes and wouldn't be back for dinner, he stared at the beautiful claw-footed oak table and chairs that had replaced the battered Formica and chrome set he'd grown up with. The change certainly lent his outdated kitchen a startling air of elegance, but where had it come from?

The muted bong of a clock chiming in the dining room drew Jake deeper into the house. The air smelled soothingly of lemon oil. An impressive grandfather clock graced the far wall. A matching cherry breakfront dominated the room's inside wall, the delicate china inside it convincing Jake he'd definitely entered an alternate reality this time. The house might be his, but its contents belonged in some monster house in Glenhill.

Feeling more than a little disoriented, he crossed the living room—which he noted with some relief hadn't changed—and climbed the stairs. The two smaller bedrooms were now furnished with eye-catching ensembles of polished oak and cherry.

Add that to the rosewood set in his room and it was clear that Rebecca had tucked away more that 'just a few pieces of old furniture.' He was staring at what had to be a small fortune in antiques.

"Like it?"

He spun around, startled to realize he hadn't heard Rebecca come up behind him. She stood a good four feet away, obviously having learned her lesson with the raspberry pie. The reminder filled him with renewed remorse. He hid it with a brittle smile. "I thought you were shopping with Katie."

"I changed my mind. I couldn't stand the suspense. What do you think?"

Jake didn't know what to say. "It's...incredible, Rebecca."

She smiled. "Thank you. I've put a lot of work into finding the right pieces."

"It shows." Elegance aside, there wasn't a piece that seemed out of place. "How'd you get it moved so fast?"

"I paid three college students with a truck. I. didn't want to bother you."

More likely, she didn't trust him to keep his word. That stung. But he couldn't blame her, the way he'd been running hot and cold on her lately. Jake looked into the room that had been his as a child. "Is that a sleigh bed?"

Rebecca grinned. "I found it at an estate sale and refinished it. I just had to have it."

"You've really gotten into this antiquing stuff, haven't you?"

"Sure have. And now that I'm out of a job—"

"What do you mean, you're out of a job?" Had she lost it because of him?

"Temporarily. The library can't open again until the glass has been cleaned up and the windows replaced. Since finding food and shelter for the homeless are understandably the town's priority right now, the library's been closed until further notice. Once I get my FEMA and insurance claims filed, I intend to use my time off to go shopping for Barb Peca. She owns an antique store downtown. Sells consignment pieces for me now and again."

"You deal in antiques?"

Rebecca's smile actually turned smug. Jake thought she couldn't look sexier. Smiling and sassy, a warm and genuine self-confidence shining in her eyes. "Yep. And I've gotten pretty good at it, too, if I may say so myself. I spent years haunting the auctions and estate sales, looking but not buying. No money. But then I learned the value of things, and I *found* the money. In the last three years I've picked up some beautiful bargains, refinished them, and re-sold the ones I didn't want to keep for myself through Barb."

"Why not open your own shop?"

Her smile fell as she met his eyes. "A single mother needs a regular paycheck."

Jake looked away, ashamed of himself all over again for abandoning her the way he had.

"Did you hate me?" he asked quietly, suddenly needing to know.

"The truth?"

He swallowed, knowing he wasn't going to like it. "Yeah."

"Then, yes, I hated your guts."

"I'm sorry, Rebecca. So sorry."

She reached out and took his hands, then looked him in the eye. "It wasn't a constant hatred, although in the beginning it was pretty strong and a big part of what kept me going. That and my anger and bitterness at being left alone—again. I missed you, Jake. Deeply. I was so hurt and confused and so very, very angry when you left, even more so when you refused to answer my letters. I ranted and raved and cried at the unfairness of it all more times than I care to remember. I lost count of the nights I cried myself to sleep, all the while cursing you to hell and back for not being with me when I needed you. For giving up on me and leaving me to face the hardships of parenthood alone."

"Rebecca..."

She squeezed his hands, hard. "Hear me out, Jake This needs to be said. Because you also gave me Katie, and there is no way I could ever hate you for that. She's given me so much, I haven't got the words to describe all the differences she's made in my life. All the positive changes. I thought I was pretty grown up, after having spent most of my life making the decisions and taking care of the responsibilities my mother should have been taking care of, then taking care of myself when she left.

"But having Katie taught me that taking care of yourself, even at sixteen, is child's play compared to the responsibility of weighing every decision you make, every action you take, or don't take, in light of how it could affect the life of someone who is completely dependent on you for their survival. Not to mention the responsibility of teaching that person how to get along in what can be a very harsh and unforgiving world."

Looking deep into his eyes, she smiled so serenely it took Jake's breath away. "But having Katie also taught me I was worth loving unconditionally, and that, I think, has been the greatest gift of all."

Jake didn't know how to answer such unflinching honesty. So he just stood there, feeling raw and worthless, wishing he had the courage to tell her she'd had his unconditional love from the day they'd met.

"Deep down," Rebecca said quietly, "I think I knew you had your reasons for not writing back. Ever since that day you rescued me from that group of bullies who cornered me behind the school, I've noticed you've been protective of me."

"Protective?" Jake snorted in self-disgust, using the opportunity to pull his hands free, to set her straight on what had been the most careless, thoughtless, selfish thing he'd ever done. "How protective is it to make love to a woman in this day and age without a condom? How protective is it to not even bother to ask her afterward if she might be pregnant?"

"You didn't know, Jake. I didn't tell you. I *chose* not to tell you. Don't be so hard on yourself."

He looked away, scrubbing a hand down his face. The guilt alone was enough to kill him. "Rebecca, when I think of you struggling to raise her alone—"

She caught one hand again. Firmly she clasped it between her own. "Exactly. If you *had* known about her, Jake, you wouldn't have ignored her, no matter what the circumstances. But I was young, idealistic. I wanted you to want *me*, to love *me*, before I told you about Katie." She studied their joined hands, her slender white ones dwarfed by his darker, much larger one, scarred and calloused and dirty with oil and grease stains he'd never be able to fully get rid of. "But now I think Katie deserves a chance to know her father," she said quietly. "And you deserve a chance to know her, no matter what my feelings are on the situation."

And what are your feelings? Jake wanted to ask, but was afraid to. Terrified to. Never in his life had he wanted or needed anything as much as he wanted Rebecca at that moment, and just the idea of her rejecting him when he was feeling so vulnerable was more than enough to keep him silent.

More than enough to fill him with self-loathing at the realization that he didn't even have the courage to open himself up to her after she'd been so brutally honest with him.

But he couldn't let her know how he felt. Even if he had the words, if he could somehow get them out. Telling Rebecca how he felt about her—and Katie—would trap him in Warner forever.

He couldn't deal with that. Not now. Not ever. Not with a bent-on-revenge sheriff who was convinced Jake had tried to kill him breathing down his neck, waiting for him to slip up so he could send Jake back to hell. Not with Avery Dillenger, the wealthiest and most powerful man in town, going so far as to try to kill a *cop* and frame Jake for it to get him out of town. Everybody knew they went for the death penalty on cop killers, and if they didn't, once you were inside, they'd make you wish they had.

Jake had been framed by money and power in a small town eight years ago. He might have grown up in Warner, but in the end it wouldn't make any difference. He was as much a stranger to Warner now as he'd been to that cesspool of political corruption in Wyoming. While the stench of corruption didn't hover over Warner the way it had in that courtroom in Wyoming, Warner hadn't remained untouched or unchanged in the twelve years he'd been gone. There was something fishy going on around here, something that had to do with Avery Dillenger, himself, and now Sheriff Sutter.

"Where's Katie?" Jake asked abruptly, suddenly needing to know. He hadn't realized how important it had become to him to have an idea of where she was at all times. But now that he was being targeted by Dillenger...

Rebecca released his hand, clearly trying to hide her

disappointment. Jake realized she'd probably expected some kind of response to her emotional honesty, and felt as if he'd let her down all over again. Grimly, he wondered if he was destined to disappoint her no matter what he did.

"Over at Aunt Martha's," she said quietly. "She wanted to stop in and say hello."

Jake stuffed his hands into his pockets and gave the furniture another quick look around. "So, is this everything you had in storage?"

"No. I just took a few of the pieces we could make use of right now."

He nodded toward the third bedroom, the one furnished in oak.

"I guess you and Katie will be moving out of my room."

Her response was noticeably neutral. "I thought you might be tired of sleeping on the couch."

He looked at her, and wondered how he'd gotten any sleep at all, knowing she was in the same house. "Couch is a lot better than a bed of steel."

She frowned, then looked away, as if she were either uncomfortable or embarrassed by his reference to prison. So much for that. Apparently she preferred to forget about that part of his life.

"I see," she finally said. "Well, if that's it, I guess Katie and I will be going." She turned toward the stairs. "We should be back by ten, so you'll have the place to yourself for a change."

A prospect Jake found depressing in light of his rapidly darkening mood, his chilling suspicions about Dillenger, and his renewed determination to leave town again ASAP. If Dillenger was out to get him, the last thing he needed was to spend any time alone. Alibis were hard to prove when you spent large chunks of time alone. "Feel like going out for dinner?"

Rebecca looked back at him in obvious surprise. "What about Katie?"

"I was hoping we could all go together. We could go clothes shopping afterward."

"You're sure?"

"Why wouldn't I be?"

"Well, shopping isn't something many men consider a fun way to spend an evening."

True, but it was a lot more appealing than the idea of sitting around waiting to see what Dillenger had in store for him.

Not to mention wondering if he hadn't made targets of Rebecca and Katie as well by now. Inviting them to move in with him had *not* been a good idea. Especially with these latest developments.

That settled it. Until he figured out what Dillenger was up to, and if Rebecca or Katie figured into any of his twisted plans, Jake wasn't about to let either of them go anywhere alone at night.

With an effort, he dusted off his most disarming smile. "I'm sure we'll be able to work something out."

Chapter Twelve

The college age hostess, whom Jake had never seen before, recognized him. Her startled gasp of recognition echoed through Pizza Sam's as she hurriedly led their party of three to a dimly lit corner booth. When she proceeded to mangle the evening's specials, Jake began to wonder if he'd made yet another mistake in bringing Rebecca and Katie here. It didn't help that within minutes of their arrival, two of the four closest tables cleared out. Whether it was coincidence or not, Jake tried not to notice.

Then, as a teenage waitress more flustered than their hostess served their meal, Jake overheard a big, bosomy woman complain to her companion as they passed that it wasn't right that decent folks couldn't go out for a meal anymore without worrying about who they'd run into.

Jake looked at Rebecca, who simply smiled and thanked their fumbling waitress, then took over serving the pizza. Even so, she couldn't quite hide the soft flush that colored her cheeks. Anger rose in him, swift and sure, as Jake realized Rebecca had just been snubbed—because of him.

Suddenly he realized that Katie, who had talked non-stop in the car, hadn't said a word since they'd entered the restaurant. He looked over at her, noticed her subdued expression, and recalled thinking one of the younger girls who had left almost immediately after they had arrived had looked familiar.

Jenna. Katie's little friend from the pool.

Swearing silently, and wishing himself anywhere but in Warner, Jake forced himself to eat the two slices of pizza Rebecca had served him. Keeping his anger in check with an effort, he willed himself to choke down every last bite, even though it tasted like sawdust. It didn't take long. They left the restaurant half an hour after they'd arrived, without ordering dessert or even finishing their large family pizza.

No one spoke during the five-minute drive to Warner's outdoor mall. Jake had heard at Feeney's that the tornado had spared all but the drug store at the west end of the mall, veering off to trash a trailer park instead. In grim silence, they passed the entrance to what looked like a rubble-filled dump before pulling up to the mall.

Still, Jake had to smile. Warner's Main Street Mall couldn't compare to the one in Erie, seventy-some miles away, but it did offer the essentials. The three blocks of retail storefronts that faced each other had banded together to coordinate signage and seasonal promotions, and had come a long way since Jacob Donovan had last darkened any of its doors.

The late August evening was cool, the crisp scent of fall in the air. It reminded Jake of school nights, and brought to mind memories of chilly football games, concealed whiskey and hot cheerleaders.

After their experience in the restaurant, Jake was surprised by the number of people who stopped to talk to Rebecca, most to cluck over her loss of the library and apartment. Even though Jake knew it would be futile to do so, Rebecca made no effort to hide where she was staying. This inevitably resulted in an uneasy look cast his way, followed by a forced or nervous smile—and a hasty end to the conversation.

With each skittish departure, Jake's temper rose. He was the reason people stared at them. He was the reason they cut their conversations with Rebecca short. He was the reason some people weren't speaking to her at all, and probably never would again. Jake knew it as well as he'd known his inmate number. It burned him to watch people treat Rebecca warily because of him. It burned him deeply. He wanted her, no doubt about that, but not at the cost of her standing in the community.

His anger and frustration rose another notch when he noticed the salesclerks steering a wide berth around him—and consequently Rebecca and Katie. Shoving his hands into his front pockets outside the third store, he bluntly told Rebecca it would be better for all of them if he waited for them on the sidewalk from now on.

She gave him a sharp look, then offered a cool, "You're right. It would."

She took Katie's hand and left him standing there, stunned by her agreement. In the wake of her departure he felt even more frustrated and alienated. He hadn't realized until that very moment how much he'd hoped the new, spunky Rebecca would defend his right to shop at the mall like any other law-abiding citizen in Warner.

But she didn't.

Jake stewed. So lost was he in his self-absorption that he barely noticed the giggling approach of two teenage girls. Shoving a small white paper shopping bag toward him, they blurted out a request for his autograph. As he stared at them in disbelief, Rebecca emerged from the store with her arms full of packages.

"Jake? Is something wrong?"

The girls froze as if afraid to move. As if suddenly realizing they were face-to-face with a convicted woman-killer. Jake didn't know what to do next.

"The girls were asking for my autograph," he managed quietly.

"We just thought..."

"You being a hero and all... "

"Never mind," they chorused, and bolted.

Jake watched them go, feeling very bewildered. A hero? *Him*?

Rebecca shifted, the packages in her arms rustling. To hide his sense of imbalance, Jake reached out to take the packages from her. "I'll run these out to the car."

She gave them up, but searched his face with such thoughtful intensity he wanted to throw down the packages and run. "Are you all right, Jake?"

The woman saw too much. Knew too much. She always had. "I'm fine."

He could tell she didn't believe him, but she only nodded thoughtfully. "We'll be in the toy store," she said, then went back inside the dress shop to retrieve Katie.

Feeling even more unsettled than before, Jake loaded Rebecca's packages into the trunk of her Focus, then seriously considered giving her the keys and walking home. She'd be safe enough from Dillenger here, he thought, scanning the parking lot. Both the mall and parking lot were well lit and crowded enough. God knew he hadn't had a moment's peace since they'd arrived. Rebecca seemed to know everyone in town, even if they didn't stop to speak.

He suddenly noticed people sending him quick, suspicious looks, as if he might be planning on breaking into someone's car. If he didn't get moving, someone might call his good buddy Sutter.

Good grief, he was getting paranoid, Jake thought on the way back to the mall. He spotted Rebecca and Katie outside the toy store, laughing and window-shopping while they ate matching double-dip chocolate ice cream cones. Rocky Road. It had always been Rebecca's favorite. Jake held back to watch them, to savor the sight of them side by side, their beautiful mother-daughter faces lit with excitement as they pointed out the various dolls and stuffed animals.

Suddenly all he could hear were the notes of longing and regret in their voices. His feelings of inadequacy spiraled to new heights as Jake realized his only child had lost her entire stuffed animal collection in the tornado, and there was nothing he could do to bring it back.

Nothing. He was practically broke. What money he still had he needed to continue making repairs to the house and to provide basic food and shelter for Rebecca and Katie. He'd made that clear when Rebecca had tried to give him money for groceries. Jake wasn't about to accept money from Rebecca. He hadn't contributed a penny to Katie's support in the past eight years. He'd never be able to make those years up to them, but the least he could do while his daughter and her mother were staying under his roof was feed, if not clothe them.

Katie seemed enthralled by a large, shockingly expensive polar bear with its arms wrapped lovingly around its cub. Her gaze returned to it again and again, while Rebecca gently suggested several smaller animals, subtly guiding their daughter the way she no doubt had since birth.

Ironically, she reminded Jake of his own mother then, and he wondered how his life might have turned out if she hadn't abandoned him to his father when he was Katie's age. A father who had taken great delight in reliving his own in-your-face childhood by turning his "mama's boy" into a total hellion.

Not that Jake had minded, in the beginning. After all, it had been his only way to earn Mickey's notice or approval. But when the trouble he was getting into started getting serious, and Jake realized he was being used...

Jake hadn't thought about his parents in years, but watching Rebecca mother Katie brought back memories of his own parents and what they *hadn't* given him—with unsettling clarity. Unconditional love. Served up with a heaping dose of patience, protectiveness, and kindness. No matter what he did or said or looked like. No matter what kind of mood he was in. No matter how bad he felt.

Funny, he still wanted to be loved like that. And despised himself for it, knowing he had nothing to offer in return.

"Ready to go inside?" Rebecca asked Katie, and tossed her

napkin into a nearby trashcan.

"Yep." Katie grinned in anticipation and threw her own napkin into the trash as the toy store door opened. Rebecca reached for the handle to hold it open, and then seemed to freeze as Avery Dillenger, wearing one of his fancy suits, emerged from the store. He carried two mega-size paper shopping bags, both stuffed to near overflowing with small toys.

Jake stared. Toys? Dillenger? Everyone knew Avery Dillenger lived alone in the biggest mansion in Glenhill. He didn't have any siblings or even cousins he could claim close kinship with—except Jake, and *that* relationship had never been openly acknowledged by either side of the family, even before Jake's mother's suicide.

"Rebecca. Katie. How nice to see you again."

Jake didn't miss how Katie backed up against Rebecca as she took in Dillenger's polished smile. Until then Jake had assumed his dislike of the man was personal. Now he realized he wasn't alone. Katie and Rebecca didn't much like Dillenger, either.

"Avery," Rebecca said coolly, her hands coming to rest on Katie's small shoulders.

Jake stepped out from the shadows, prompted by his own protective instincts. Dillenger looked up and their eyes met. Dillenger's gaze hardened with annoyance, then crystallized into an almost smug malice. In that instant Jake knew Dillenger had his boot knife and was holding it for a reason. Suddenly he felt as if a heavy noose had dropped around his neck.

"Donovan. I might have known you'd be lurking nearby."

"What's with the toys, Dillenger? Christmas isn't for another four months."

Dillenger smiled nastily. "Obviously you've been too wrapped up with your "houseguests" to notice there are still quite a few families stranded at the homeless shelter. I thought the children might appreciate a diversion while their parents struggle to find new homes. Not everyone was fortunate enough to be taken in by a family friend," he added with a thinly challenging look at Rebecca.

"That's very kind of you, Avery," Rebecca responded evenly. "I'm sure they'll appreciate your generosity."

"I'm sure they will," Dillenger returned blandly, then focused on Katie. She shrank closer to her mother, obviously afraid of him. Jake stepped forward, catching Dillenger's attention. He speared his cousin with his hardest look, making sure the slimy bastard understood Rebecca and Katie were off limits. If Dillenger so much as touched either of them, Jake would break the man's lily-white hands.

Dillenger leaned down to meet Katie at eye level, but kept his hands on his bags. "I understand you lost your beautiful stuffed animal collection in the tornado. I'm sorry to hear that. I know how much you loved it."

"Mama's buying me a new animal tonight. We're rebuilding."

Mama. Not Jake. Not Mom and Dad. The knowledge ripped Jake's heart apart.

"How nice, but it's going to take quite a while to replace everything you lost, isn't it?" Dillenger reached into one of his bags and pulled out one of the larger animals, a medium-size giraffe. "Here, why don't you start with this one?"

Katie looked up at her mother. She'd obviously been warned not to accept gifts from strangers. But Dillenger was no stranger, not if he'd seen Katie's stuffed animal collection.

"Really, Avery, it's not necessary," Rebecca began. "I'm sure the children at the shelter—"

"But I insist." He all but shoved the giraffe into Katie's midsection.

"Thank you," she responded politely, but without any real sincerity, hugging the giraffe protectively to her chest.

Dillenger's smile made Jake's skin crawl. "Maybe when you play with it you'll think of me, hmmm? Remember all the fun we had out on the bay." He looked up at Rebecca and Jake, then straightened. "Well, I'd better get going if I'm to make the shelter before bedtime."

"Thank you, Avery," Rebecca offered stiffly. "I'll see you at the council meeting next week."

Avery glanced at Jake, then broke into another malicious smile. "I look forward to it."

As Dillenger strode away, it was all Jake could do not to rip the damned giraffe away from Katie and stuff it in the nearest trash can. "How does Dillenger know about Katie's stuffed animal collection?" he asked in a low growl once they were in the toy store and Katie was out of earshot. Meeting Dillenger had raised Jake's hackles so much he wasn't about to leave Katie or Rebecca alone for even a minute.

"He's seen it."

Jake stared at Rebecca. "He's been in your house?"

"Once or twice. He took me out a few times."

"Dillenger?" The thought of the man in Rebecca's apartment was bad enough, but the idea of him alone with her...

She shot him a look. "You cut me out of your life, remember? Of course I tried dating."

"But *Dillenger*?" She might as well have run a stake through his heart.

"It didn't work out, Jake. There's no need to make an issue of it now."

She started to walk away, but he grabbed her arm. "Why didn't it work out?"

Rebecca's pointed glare had the same effect as throwing a bucket of cold water at him. Jake suddenly realized how close he was to making the kind of scene everyone in town expected of him, and released her. "Katie didn't like him," Rebecca said evenly, then went to rejoin Katie.

At least one of you had some sense, Jake thought hotly, following her. The idea of his daughter growing up anywhere near Avery Dillenger was enough to make Jake crazy. It wasn't until much later, after they were back at the house and Rebecca was upstairs helping Katie get ready for bed that it occurred to Jake to wonder if *Rebecca* had liked Dillenger.

Or had it been Dillenger's mansion that Rebecca had wanted? Standing in his shabby little house unexpectedly filled with beautiful antiques, Jake had no trouble imagining them gracing any of the glittering homes in Glenhill.

But Dillenger's?

"We need to talk," Jake said, as soon as they'd shut the door to Katie's room—his old room—after saying goodnight. Katie had been thrilled to move into the sleigh bed. As she'd crawled between the crisp new Barbie sheets. Rebecca had bought that evening, Jake hadn't missed that Katie had abandoned Dillenger's giraffe in favor of the smaller elephant Rebecca had bought her. The last he'd seen of it, the giraffe hadn't made it past the kitchen. Jake considered snagging it off the counter on his way out the door for his nightly run—and drop kicking it into the bay.

Rebecca had crossed her arms, and was eyeing him frostily.

"What?"

"You said we need to talk."

"We do."

She arched a cool eyebrow. "About?"

"About tonight. We can't do it again."

"Do what? Go out to dinner? Or go shopping together?"

"Pretend we're a family."

Rebecca blinked, then shot him a look of pure disbelief. Clearly, the only happy family thoughts tonight had been his. "I wasn't pretending anything of the sort."

Then why did Jake feel like he'd been on display tonight, paraded around like some tightly leashed Doberman, while Rebecca shopped for household items bound to be reported all over town? "Then why did you have to stop and talk to half the people on the street and let them know where you're staying?"

"It's hardly a secret, Jake. You know how this town is."

"You aren't going to be here that long, Rebecca."

"I'm not? Weren't you listening to those conversations, Jake? More than half the town is still homeless. Did you see the trailer park that used to be next to the mall? There must have been a hundred homes destroyed in that area alone."

"Yeah, well..."

"You invited Katie and myself into your home, Jake, for as long as we needed to stay. You also invited me to move my furniture into the house, something else that will not go unnoticed around town. I'm sorry you're having second thoughts about the situation, but the facts are that Katie and I are living here, for better or for worse, until a viable alternative presents itself. I don't see that happening any time soon, so I suggest you get used to the idea of having company."

With that, she turned and disappeared into the extra bedroom, shutting the door behind her. Obviously, she'd moved out of his bedroom, which left Jake to either sleep on the couch again or return to his bed. He chose the bed, then spent the rest of the night tossing and turning and cursing as the fresh scent of strawberries sent his mind into endless replays of his memories of Rebecca.

But not once did Jake consider moving back downstairs to find sleep.

Chapter Thirteen

"I've been thinking," Rebecca said as she handed Jake his first cup of coffee in the kitchen four mornings later. Much to Jake's surprise, she'd taken to getting up at dawn and fixing coffee, starting the morning after their less than memorable trip to the mall.

Jake wasn't about to complain. He'd always enjoyed Rebecca's company more than anyone's. But now, more than that, he enjoyed the time alone with her. He adored Katie, but there were times when he wanted Rebecca all to himself.

They rarely had more than ten minutes together before he had to leave for work, so there wasn't enough time to let his lust get the better of him. Instead he settled for simply enjoying the sight of her, dreaming endlessly of her at night, and carrying with him to work each day warm memories of sharing morning coffee with the woman he loved.

It was only at night, alone in the dark, surrounded by the strawberry-scented sheets he kept putting off washing, that he wondered how he would survive when Rebecca and Katie moved out and he left town.

Taking them with him wasn't an option. Rebecca and Katie were not his to keep. It would be years before he could support himself with any degree of comfort, much less a woman and a child.

"Jake? Are you listening?"

"I'm sorry. What were you saying?"

"Instead of going antique hunting today, I'm going to volunteer at the soup kitchen. Much as I hate to admit it, Avery Dillenger was right. I've been so wrapped up in my own problems I haven't considered how other families are coping. But now that I've submitted my FEMA and insurance claims, replaced the essentials and we're settled in here, I think it's past time to reach out."

Jake had stopped listening after the word Dillenger, his morning mood completely soured. Nothing could have reminded him more rudely that what he was thinking and feeling these days was not permanent. Quite the contrary. The thought put an edge in his voice he didn't like, but couldn't help. He still had no idea what Dillenger was up to with his boot knife, and was getting mighty tired of being Robert Sutter's prime suspect. A day didn't pass that Jake didn't spot a cruiser slide by, making no secret the police were keeping an eye on him.

"What? My fine, upstanding cousin has suddenly awakened in you a need to help your fellow man?"

Rebecca looked startled, then annoyed. "It wouldn't hurt you to try it, Jake. Maybe then people would stop looking at you like you're an axe murderer."

It was Jake's turn to blink, stunned by her calmly delivered words—words that wounded him to the core. "So," he said slowly, "You finally admit you're ashamed to be seen with me."

"Don't be ridiculous. I'm living here, and so is my child. That says a heck of a lot more about our faith and trust in you than walking down the street together. You were the one who said we couldn't have any more 'family' outings."

So that was why she'd made herself scarce in the evenings since then. One night she and Katie had gone to her aunt's for dinner while he replaced the windows the tornado had blown out, the next she'd had some sort of businesswomen's dinner to go to while he watched Katie. Last night they'd eaten dinner together, but afterward, she'd gone over to her aunt's to knit afghans or something for the church to distribute. Jake didn't see why she couldn't knit the damned things here, but at least he'd had Katie to keep him company. They'd played some street ball, then she'd sunk all his battleships—again.

"Oh. I thought you were avoiding me."

Rebecca crossed her arms over her chest and shot him an arch, "Now why would I want to do that when you're so darned pleasant to be around these days?"

"What are you talking about?"

"You. Acting like the town pariah. Aunt Martha would have loved to have you join us for dinner with the Beeson's the other night, but no, you had to take care of the windows."

"The wind was cutting through the plastic, Rebecca. I didn't want you or Katie to freeze."

"But did you have to do it at *dinner* time?"

Grudgingly, Jake recognized she had a point. "I don't even know those people," he grumbled. The Beeson's, a young family of four, had moved in with Rebecca's aunt after the tornado.

"We'll you're not likely to *get* to know them—or anyone else in town for that matter—if you continue to blow off everyone's efforts to befriend you."

"What the hell are you talking about?"

"The night we went to dinner at Pizza Sam's."

Jake stared at her, wondering if they'd been in the same restaurant. "Excuse me, Rebecca, but nobody tried to *befriend* me at Pizza Sam's."

"How could they, after you let the biggest busybody in Warner put you in a foul mood anyone could spot, then spent the rest of the night scowling like you dared anyone to speak to you. Plenty of people were willing to talk with you that night, Jake, but you refused to give them a chance."

Jake frowned hard, stunned. Was she right?

She looked at him and sighed, her anger apparently spent. "I'm sorry. I've tried to keep my mouth shut and let you work this out on your own, but as far as I can tell, you're determined to keep that huge chip you've got on your shoulder."

"Is that all you think it is? Some kind of grudge I'm holding against everybody? Have you forgotten I'm—"

"A convicted killer? How could I? You don't miss a chance to remind me—or anyone else. It's your whole attitude, Jake. The way you look, talk, walk and move. It says, 'Don't mess with me.' If you want to walk the streets of this town—or any other town—without sending people scrambling to get out of your way, you need to treat them a little nicer."

Jake couldn't believe what he was hearing. *He* needed to clean up his act? When at least one man wanted him out of town badly enough to frame him for murder? "What do you suggest I do?" he asked, fascinated that she'd obviously given this a lot of thought. Short of drinking some sort of magic formula that would turn him into the perfect gentleman, Jake had no clue as to how to accomplish this miracle Rebecca apparently expected of him.

She leaned forward, elbows on the table, clearly warming to her subject. "Try smiling for a change, Jake. Try being open instead of defensive. Try forgetting where you've been and focusing on where you're going. You'd be amazed at the difference it makes."

Jake stared at her, and wondered if she really was naive enough to believe that was all it would take. "Is that what you did?"

Her expression didn't waver. "As a matter of fact, it is. Do

118

you think it was easy, coming back to Warner as an unwed mother? After Chloe? It was what people expected of me, Jake. But I've since proven I'm not Chloe, and you can prove you're not Mickey."

"Like hell." He looked just like the old man. People weren't likely to forget that. "How?"

"By being yourself. By being the Jake I know. By not sinking to the level of people's expectations. People expect you to be surly, Jake. They expect you to lose your temper over little things and pull the kind of crazy stunts you pulled as a kid. But Mickey's not around anymore, and you're in charge of your life now. For God's sake, Jake. You're a hero. You saved the lives of ten children, whose families are extremely grateful to you, and all you can do when they try to thank you is growl at them as if they've insulted you."

Jake studied her across the table. Her soft blue robe covered her from neck to toe, but he'd long since decided it was the sexiest piece of clothing he'd seen on her. She leaned forward just then, inadvertently causing the V-neck to open a little and give him a welcome peek of smooth, tanned skin and ivory lace. He nearly groaned aloud.

"You have the power to make your life anything you want it to be, Jake," she said softly, her eyes deeply earnest. "All you have to do is try. All you have to do is open up a little."

Jake swallowed, hard. Rebecca was asking him to trust her. Being himself wasn't nearly as easy as she made it out to be. Jake didn't like himself very much, but didn't know how to be anything but what he was.

So he fell back on his usual defense, even though it didn't seem as solid as before, even in his own mind. "It's not just me I'm thinking of, Rebecca. It's you and Katie. I can't stand the idea of people looking down on either of you because of me."

"Then why did you invite us to move in with you?"

Jake ran a hand through his hair in frustration as her robe slipped again and the erotic images that consumed his nights spilled into his day. "All I could think about at the time was you had no home and I'd done nothing to help you over the past eight years," he muttered.

"So you did it out of guilt."

His gaze returned to hers. "I owed it to you, Rebecca."

She set her coffee down, but kept her fingers wrapped around the iridescent gold mug from Feeney's, her face unreadable. "Do you still want us to leave?"

The question was like a spear to the chest. "I think it would best. I won't throw you out on the street, but I can't give you what you want, what you need. Either of you."

Her fingers tightened around her mug. "And what would that be?"

"You need stability and security, Rebecca. You need a place to call home." Couldn't she see that? How he was looking out for her?

"And what about you, Jake? What do you need?"

You. Katie. "I need to move on."

She looked into her coffee, then picked up the mug and took a long swallow, keeping her eyes—and thoughts—to herself. "It always comes back to that, doesn't it?"

"You're not being realistic, Rebecca. What you're suggesting, what you're hoping will happen, is pure fantasy."

Her head came up, her eyes sparking with blue fire. "What about Katie? Is she pure fantasy, too?"

"Of course not. She's my child. A child I've only known about for eleven days. I can't support her—or you—not working at Feeney's."

"Money doesn't matter, Jake."

"And what about the kids who'll treat her like scum once they find out her dad is an ex-con? Hell, they're already treating her like a leper and school hasn't even started yet. Did you see how crushed she was when her little friend Jenna walked out of Pizza Sam's behind her parents?"

"Did you notice Jenna looked equally crushed? It's her parents causing the rift between them, not the girls."

"Maybe, but you know about peer pressure, Rebecca. You've been there. You know how much being different hurts. How can you justify putting that kind of load on a seven-year-old?"

She looked away for a moment, then sighed heavily. Jake ached to be able to give her what she wanted, but he didn't have it in him to make another person happy. To try to be what Rebecca wanted him to be, to do what she wanted him to do, to fail and see the same sad disappointment in her eyes he'd seen in his mother's eyes, day after day...

"So what do you suggest we do?" she asked quietly.

He answered before he could change his mind. "Split up as soon as we can. Once you're settled again, I can sell the house and take it from there."

She just looked at him.

"How else am I going to get any money, Rebecca? I need a fresh start."

"Where?"

"Anywhere but here, damn it! Anywhere Avery Dillenger isn't trying to send me back to prison."

"What?"

Jake swore. "I didn't want to have to say anything about it, but your good buddy Sutter stopped by the station the other day. Seems someone sliced the sheriff's brake cables while it was in the bay at Feeney's getting the alternator replaced."

Rebecca stared at him in disbelief. "He thinks it's you?"

"Who else would it be?"

"Oh, for Pete's sake. Just because you have a record doesn't mean you're guilty of every unsolved crime in the county."

"Yeah, but that's the beauty of being an ex-con. Anything goes wrong, and everyone looks your way first."

"It's not funny, Jake."

"You think I don't know that? I had access, Rebecca. And, some would say, motive. Sheriff Sutter and his deputies have been dogging me since I hit town. Who's to say it hasn't pissed me off?"

"This is exactly what I mean about sinking to the level of other people's expectations. You're better than that, and you know it."

"A leopard can't change his spots, babe, and *you* know that."

"That's Mickey talking, not you. Now what's this about Avery Dillenger trying to send you back to prison?"

Mickey talking? Jake was startled to realize she was right. How many times had he heard the old man say the exact same thing? Apparently, all these years later, he was still buying into the old man's lies. Repeating them, now.

It gave him something to think about.

"Dillenger was at the station just before the tornado hit. I left him there alone when I ran to the library."

"You think *he* cut Bob's brake cables?"

Bob. Jake met her appalled gaze, head on. "See? Who's going to believe me?"

"But...but why would he want to get rid of you?"

She seemed genuinely bewildered. "Beats the hell out of me. Unless it has something to do with you. You did say you dated."

"Briefly, Jake. Very briefly. Hardly long enough to give him any ideas about having a relationship. Besides, that was over two years ago. I've dated other men since, and he hasn't tried to run any of them out of town."

"Like *Bob*?"

She stared at him for a moment, then rolled her eyes. "No, not *Bob*. Now would you mind keeping the conversation on Avery? What makes you think he cut the cables?"

"My boot knife's missing. The one I carried before I left for the service. I found it in the basement last week and took it to Feeney's without thinking. Now it's gone. What do you want to bet it turns up again one day when I least expect it?"

Rebecca frowned, her wheels clearly moving. "You know, Jake, Robert Sutter really is a decent man. I think you should go to him with this."

"Are you nuts?" Just the thought of seeing the inside of another police station had Jake's insides churning. "You think he's going to believe me over Dillenger?"

"I don't think Bob would automatically accept whatever story Avery chose to tell him. There's been friction between the two of them in the past, and—"

"Now Dillenger's backing the city boy from Pittsburgh?"

"Exactly. Avery and Bob don't see eye to eye on a lot of issues. So what have you got to lose?"

"My freedom, for one." *You. Katie.* Jake leaned forward, his mission clear. Rebecca tended to see everyone in the most positive light possible, even scum like Dillenger, and it was clear she liked this Sutter dude. "I don't mean to burst your bubble. Becca, but Sutter's got a dark side just like the rest of us. The man wants me out of here. He doesn't think his streets are safe as long as I'm in town, and with that knife missing, I think he might be right."

Chapter Fourteen

The homeless shelter soup kitchen was big, hot, busy and noisy. Jake took in the controlled chaos, amazed at the number of people in Warner still without the means to feed themselves. Much like the victims of those killer hurricanes down south, Warner had a long way to go to recover even the basics of food and shelter for its residents.

Meanwhile the rest of the world had moved on to the next big headline.

Jake hadn't said a word since their arrival fifteen minutes ago, but if he'd given in to his gut, he'd have left fourteen and a half minutes ago. The place, which was filling up fast now that it was after four-thirty, reminded him too much of prison. The pitch of voices was higher because of the women and children, and the undercurrent of always being on the edge of violence was missing, but air of hopelessness and despair was the same, as was the smell of sweat and urine—and in this case full diapers.

But it was the feel of the place that had his stomach churning. Institutional.

Maybe you didn't spend six years working in the prison kitchen for nothing, Donovan.

Jake blinked, blindsided by the thought. Where the hell had *that* come from?

Rattled, he looked over at Rebecca and the volunteer coordinator, talking beside him. He'd called Rebecca when he'd gotten to Feeney's that morning, to ask her if she'd wait for him before going to the soup kitchen. She'd been thrilled with him until he'd told her he just wanted to check out the place before she signed on.

But in the end, much to his surprise, she'd waited.

She'd insisted on finding the volunteer coordinator right away. Turned out Rebecca knew the woman but hadn't seen her in a while. They'd done some catching up, then Becca had started asking questions about the shelter and before they knew it, they were getting the full tour.

"So where do you need us?" Jake asked abruptly, startling

123

both Rebecca and the coordinator. "The chow line?"

The coordinator lady stopped in mid-sentence, stared at him, then beamed and hustled them across the room. Within minutes, Jake found himself standing on the front line with a spoon in hand, serving up some sort of goulash. He refused to look at Rebecca, dishing up peas and carrots beside him. He wasn't going soft on her—or on Warner—he'd simply recognized a need he knew how to fill.

Their quick introductions to the regulars they'd replaced on the line had confirmed Jake's observations. Exhausted from putting out three meals a day for four times as many people as the shelter usually served, they were more than grateful for the break.

After the last dinner had been served over two hours later, Francis Xavier Cullen, the shelter's director, turned to thank Jake and Rebecca for their help and invite them to stop by again any time. After having worked side by side with the big, burly, no-bullshit black man who'd had a smile for everyone, even during the meal's busiest run, Jake was suddenly surprised to find himself shaking hands with a fellow ex-con.

"Ten years for armed robbery," Cullen said, catching the sudden awareness in Jake's eyes. It took one to know one. "A bunch of county time before that. It's no secret around here. Call me FX."

Jake looked at Rebecca, who was busy checking out the pea and carrot juice stains on her sneakers.

She'd planned this? No wonder she'd been waiting for him so nicely when he'd come home.

"Heard about you, too," Cullen was saying. "Bad rap, man. Far as I'm concerned, you've paid your debt. People want to make something of it, that's their business. Me, I got too damned many people to feed to be worrying about where people come from. Besides, it's where you're going that's important, not where you've been."

Jake and Rebecca made the five-minute trip home in silence. Jake didn't accuse her of maneuvering him into volunteering, because he'd done that all by himself. Instead, he pretended the experience hadn't fazed him a bit as he helped Rebecca put together a light supper of soup and sandwiches, offered to clean up while she spent time with Katie, then left a little earlier than usual for his nightly run.

But later that night, alone in his strawberry-scented bed, Jake relived every minute of his first real experience at helping others.

Amazingly, he'd enjoyed himself tonight at the shelter. Even managed to crack a smile or two, listening to Cullen carry on beside him in the chow line.

Maybe Cullen and Rebecca were right. Maybe it was time to give looking forward instead of backward a try.

Just the thought of it scared the hell out of him.

****

Rebecca was amazed by the change in Jake in the days that followed. He seemed more relaxed and easygoing than at any time since his return to Warner. She couldn't help but notice—and regret—how he kept himself apart from her physically and emotionally, but to Katie and the children at the shelter he gave himself unreservedly. His ideas for improving efficiency in the kitchen had FX promising to name his firstborn after Jake. It wasn't long before Rebecca found herself only one among many who looked forward to "Mr. Jake's" arrival each afternoon.

The school year started, and Rebecca fell into the comfortable routine of going antique hunting in the mornings, arriving at the soup kitchen in time to serve lunch, then slipping home for a couple of hours to take care of things there before she returned to the soup kitchen with Jake and Katie in time to serve supper.

Afterward, the three of them would go home and spend the evening together, taking turns helping Katie with any homework, then playing board games or watching rented movies. Even though he didn't touch her or make any attempt to spend time alone with her beyond their shared cup of morning coffee, Rebecca couldn't help but feel Jake was finally warming to the idea of a home and family.

Caught up in her own budding hopes, Rebecca didn't notice that Katie wasn't asking to be taken anywhere to be with her friends. At the soup kitchen Katie spent most of her time playing with the younger children, and at home...well, Rebecca assumed her daughter was enjoying Jake's company as much as she herself was. Every now and then she even caught herself feeling jealous of the seemingly unlimited time and attention Jake gave to Katie.

But other than that, life was good.

Until the letter from the town council came.

Looking stunned, Rebecca slowly handed Jake the letter she'd just opened. As he read it, Jake felt the warm sense of well-being he'd sustained in the past two weeks vanish like smoke. A slow burn began inside him as he recalled Dillenger's superior smile that afternoon at the station. Dillenger still stopped by regularly to harass him, and Jake still had no idea what Dillenger planned to do with his stolen knife, but he'd long since given up obsessing about it. In all, life had become much too sweet to waste time worrying about Avery Dillenger.

But now the bastard was starting in on Rebecca. He handed the letter back to Rebecca. "If the library lets you go, Becca, it's because of me."

She scanned the letter again. "According to this, I'm in serious and flagrant violation of the morals clause in my contract." She looked past him, her expression a mixture of confusion and disbelief. "I'd have to read my contract to find out exactly what they're talking about, but yes, I assume it has something to do with living here with you." Her eyes met his. "Avery warned me something like this could happen a month ago. I didn't believe him."

Jake said something Rebecca didn't ask him to repeat. "Have you found somewhere else to live yet?"

Her eyes widened in obvious surprise. "No..."

As in why would she have? Jake ignored his relief. Someone had to play bad cop here, and it looked like it was him. "Have you even been looking for another place?"

"Well...no...I thought we were getting along."

Except for his quietly going insane from wanting her every minute of the day and night, they were. He'd doubled his running time at night, just to keep himself out of the house until she went to bed. By the time he finally left Warner, he'd be ready to run the Boston Marathon if he wanted to.

"We are getting along, Rebecca, but that doesn't mean you can live here indefinitely."

"You still want us to leave?"

The hurt and disbelief in her voice nearly did him in. He remembered having this same discussion the night they'd gone to the mall. He'd conceded her point that night, but now it was time to face facts. No amount of time spent at the shelter was going to change how the people who ran this town thought of him, and Rebecca and Katie were going to pay the price, the longer they stayed here with him.

"My plans haven't changed, Rebecca," he said quietly, already hating himself for what he was about to say next, because it he knew was a lie. "There's nothing for me here in Warner, you know that. I'm sorry if I said or did anything to make you think otherwise."

She swallowed, hard. "I see." Looking dazed, she stared past his shoulder, clearly struggling to absorb what he'd just said. "Well...I...I guess I'd better get busy finding a new home, then."

With quiet dignity, she turned and left the kitchen. It took everything Jake had not to follow her, not to beg her to understand and forgive him for letting her down again. When he heard the first muffled sob as her bedsprings squeaked, it almost killed him. He felt lower than dirt.

Damn it. Two weeks of looking forward instead of backward and nothing had changed. He was still the same old Jake, destined to disappoint Rebecca every time. Swearing, he left the house, letting the door slam shut behind him.

He didn't make it to the soup kitchen that night, and didn't come home again until he was sure Rebecca was asleep.

****

Rebecca barely spoke to Jake in the long week that followed. Jake didn't blame her. Katie seemed to have withdrawn as well. Jake forced himself to let both of them go. He'd have to cut them loose soon anyway. He'd returned to the soup kitchen and was grateful for the distraction, but three hours of carting industrial-size pans full of steaming food to the front line each night did nothing to dim the need he felt for Rebecca when they got home afterward.

His need for her was especially intense now that he didn't have the company of her smile or conversation to cheer him. She'd stopped joining him for morning coffee. Her absence across the table had brought on such a physical ache Jake no longer drank his first cup of the day at home—although he always left a pot full for Rebecca. They weren't at war, he was simply in the doghouse and deserved it.

But God, he missed her.

Thursday night, his sixth week in Warner, Jake was downtiming in the living room after his shift at the soup kitchen, drinking a forbidden beer and watching television, when Rebecca came downstairs in heels and a knockout navy blue suit. Her red-gold hair was done up in one of her classy twists, and the double rope of pearls at her neck—probably another one of her antique finds—looked like they could have belonged to his grandmother.

The thought reminded him of the small ivory envelope Rebecca had placed on his bedroom dresser earlier in the week. The one from old lady Dillenger herself. He'd picked it up, run his fingers over the gold embossed return address on the back, then tossed it, unopened, into the wastebasket.

He had no interest in what the woman who couldn't even be bothered to say hello when she rolled through the station for gas had to say. Not after all this time, and not when he was leaving town again.

"Lookin' good, Becca. Got a date?"

"The town council meeting is tonight."

Jake sat up. "You're kidding. Tonight?" He hadn't forgotten about it, but in the past week, without Rebecca to keep him company, the days had pretty much blended into each other and he'd lost track of time. "That's where you're going? Dressed like that?"

"What's wrong with what I'm wearing?"

"You look...phenomenal."

"It's just a suit, Jake. Completely appropriate for a business meeting."

Maybe, but Jake doubted anyone else in the room would look half as good as Rebecca in 'just a suit' which, much as he hated to admit it, would probably go against her when the vote came over whether to let her keep her job.

He squelched a sigh. Either way, it wasn't going to be pretty in that town hall tonight. He downed the last of the pair of cold ones FX had slipped him in appreciation on the way out the door tonight. FX knew he wasn't allowed to drink, knew it was a parole violation, and knew if he tried buying anything at the state store it would be all over town by closing time. The first call probably would have gone to Sutter, who would have jumped at the chance to pull Jake in for a urine test.

"All right, give me a minute to get changed."

"You're going?"

"This concerns me too, Rebecca," he said, coming to his feet. "If you lose your job, it will be because of me."

"No, it'll be because Avery Dillenger wants to flex his political muscles. He's not happy with me right now."

"Right. Because of me."

She looked at him for a moment, then ceded the argument. "Then you need to shave and take a shower, Jake. You're looking a little rough."

He ran a hand across his five-o'clock shadow and nodded. "Sounds good. I'll meet you there."

****

"And last on the agenda is the matter of what do about our library, which has been boarded up since the tornado, oh, and our library director."

Rebecca gritted her teeth at the way Avery Dillenger had made her sit and wait through almost two hours of incessant bickering among the hundred or so people who had turned out for the meeting. Quite the crowd by Warner standards, but then it had been a very busy month. She tried not to react to the way he had tacked 'Oh, and our library director' on to the end of his announcement, as if she were the least of anybody's worries. She knew he'd placed the library agenda item last in an effort to intimidate her. It didn't help that he'd all but encouraged tempers to rise throughout the meeting, instead of stopping arguments when they reached the pointless stage. The tornado had left everyone's emotions close to the surface, and tonight, at this first full council meeting since the disaster, those emotions were spilling over left and right.

Apparently Avery's plan was to feed her to the sharks as a scapegoat for his failure to take care of business since the tornado. Other than buying the shelter kids a few toys, Avery Dillenger had done little besides blame FEMA for the town's lack of rebuilding progress.

She looked around, and wondered again where Jake was. Nearly two hours she'd been here, and the folding chair beside her was still empty.

Maybe he'd changed his mind. Decided it wasn't his fight after all and stayed home to finish his beer, the first she'd seen him drink since his return. The idea left her feeling more annoyed than betrayed. The betrayal had come last week, strong and deep, when he'd told her he was still leaving Warner. When he'd said there was nothing in Warner for him, and she knew it. When he'd asked her if she'd found someplace else to live.

Well, this week she had, and as soon as this farce of local government in action was over, she could focus on moving on with her life and leaving Jacob Donovan alone to deal with his.

"Ms. Reed? Are you prepared to address the council?"

Rebecca blinked, and realized Avery had chosen to recognize her at last. She stood, resisting the urge to smooth down her suit as she did so. Lifting her chin, she met Avery's eyes, and prepared to face the world the way she always had.

Alone.

Chapter Fifteen

"As I said, we'll address the issue of whether to renew Ms. Reed's employment contract before moving on to discuss the future of our library," Avery Dillenger intoned from the dais at the front of the town's fire hall. The arch look he sent Rebecca was clear. *No need to include you in any discussions about the library since you're not going to be there.*

"As some of you may be aware, like so many others in Warner, Ms. Reed tragically lost her home in the recent tornado. An unfortunate circumstance at best, especially since the library was also severely damaged that day, damaged enough that we haven't been able to spare any resources to reopen it." Rebecca noticed he wasn't able to spare any word for the families whose children had been in the library that day, children whose lives Jake had saved, either.

"I've placed this item on the agenda to discuss whether we can afford to reopen the library at this time. But before we begin any discussions, I believe it would behoove us to examine the question of whether Ms. Reed remains qualified to direct our efforts regarding the town library."

Sounds of surprise, protest, confusion and interest rippled through the crowd. Nothing a small town liked to sink its teeth into more than a scandal and everyone knew Rebecca Reed had been courting scandal since the day Jacob Donovan had rolled back into town.

Rebecca remained standing, feeling absurdly like Hester Prynne, with an A emblazoned on her forehead. But she kept her chin high, her eyes on Avery and her mouth shut, determined to let him finish speaking before she had her say. No way was she going to let him goad her into losing control in front of this crowd. Her personal reputation might be dancing on quicksand, but she refused to let the likes of Avery Dillenger question her professionalism.

"It has recently come to light that Ms. Reed has chosen to take up residence with Mr. Jacob Donovan, an unmarried prison parolee that this council considers highly dangerous to the safety and well-being of our family-values oriented town. This, in blatant violation of the morals clause in her contract." Amid another flurry of murmurs among the assembled crowd, Avery picked up a sheaf of stapled papers at his side with one hand, and slid a pair of wire-rimmed Adolpho reading glasses onto his nose with another. "It states here…"

Rebecca felt the white hot heat of remembered childhood humiliations fill her until she was so rigid she thought she might snap in two if she breathed. She barely heard the vague paragraph of boilerplate that had probably been part of every township employee's contract since the turn of the century. Instead, deliberately, she tuned Avery Dillenger's censorious voice out and focused on what the self-righteous bastard was trying to do to Jake, and to her dreams of a home and family with him.

Never mind that Jake himself wasn't helping that dream any—this attack was coming from the outside, and that she would not tolerate. Somehow, she'd find a way to expose Avery Dillenger for what he was.

But for now, for tonight, she'd confine herself to the subject at hand.

With slow deliberation, Avery set the contract aside and fixed his wire-rimmed sights on Rebecca. "Ms. Reed, can you explain this willful and deliberate violation of your contract?"

"Of course," she returned with an absolute calm that surprised even her. "After the tornado which so tragically destroyed my home," she continued in her most reasonable tone of voice, "I needed somewhere to live."

The ripple of laughter in the audience startled her, but the quiet, "Go for it, girlfriend," she overheard in its wake from somewhere behind her reminded Rebecca she wasn't without friends. In fact, she'd recognized several volunteers from the soup kitchen as she'd walked in, but she'd been too preoccupied to offer more than a quick smile or wave of greeting.

But now that she thought about it, if she had to put money on it, she'd bet she had more friends in this room than Avery Dillenger had. It was his money that gave him his power—money that hadn't done a damned thing to help anyone in the past few weeks. The thought gave her strength.

"But to be more specific, Mr. Dillenger, Mr. Donovan, whom you might recall was with me at the library when the tornado struck—since I understand he left *you* alone at Feeney's just moments earlier—"

Avery seemed to sense her renewed confidence, and moved

to try to dispel it. Leaning forward, he said into his microphone, "Excuse me, Ms. Reed, but I fail to see the relevance in that statement. If you'll confine your responses to the matter at hand, I'm sure we'll all appreciate it. It's been a very long night."

"Of course. I'm sorry," Rebecca murmured in mock contrition. "I thought you were aware that there was some trouble with the Sheriff's car afterward, and that Mr. Donovan was suspected of having tampered with it."

The crowd gave a collective gasp, and something dark and ugly flashed in Avery's eyes, but he gave no indication of his emotions as he attempted once more to verbally bring Rebecca to heel. "Ms. Reed," he said, a strong warning note in his voice. "The council fails to see how this has any bearing on this discussion."

"Then the council needs to be enlightened. Since you're calling Mr. Donovan's character into question, and, by association, mine, wouldn't this be the ideal time to clear up any misconceptions regarding either one of us, allowing *the council* to make a fully informed decision regarding the renewal of my contract?"

She had him there and he knew it. Avery Dillenger wanted everyone to believe he spoke for the entire council, but Rebecca had been at enough of these meetings to know that wasn't always the case. George Mueller she could see agreeing with Avery, if only because the man was cowed by his own wife. Mimi Modano, the council secretary, could go either way, considering her former relationship with Jake. But Matt Hannan and his brother Patrick had both been an enormous help to her and Jake in the days following the tornado. Looking at them now, sitting there on the dais, Rebecca couldn't believe the council's sentiment regarding the non-renewal of her contract was unanimous, as Avery had implied in the letter he had sent.

"May I continue?" she asked pointedly.

With a sharp look of disgust, Avery sat back and offered a deeply put upon, "Very well, you have the floor."

"Thank you. As I was saying, Mr. Donovan was also on hand when I discovered my home had been destroyed. I believe you'll find Mr. Hannan can attest to that." She nodded to Hannan, seated at Dillenger's left, and was relieved and reassured when he smiled back and said into his microphone, "Yes, ma'am, I can."

"I believe Mr. Hannan can also attest that, as any good friend and neighbor would do, Mr. Donovan immediately offered myself and my daughter *temporary* shelter in his own home, which was fortunate enough to have survived the tornado."

Hannan nodded. "That's correct."

Rebecca paused, hoping the idea of Jake as a good Samaritan would take root in at least a few of the more open minds in the room. The weighty silence as the assembled crowd waited for Dillenger's rebuttal gratified her. She didn't miss his annoyance at having it pointed out his council might not be one hundred percent behind him on this. The look he'd sent Matt Hannan for answering her questions had bordered on killing.

"I see," Avery finally said, stiffly, tightly. He shuffled his papers in front of him. "That's certainly admirable of Mr. Donovan, Ms. Reed, but isn't it true you rented your garage apartment from your aunt, who lives in the house to which the garage belonged?"

So that was where he was headed with this. "Yes, it is."

"And isn't it true that your aunt had plenty of room available in her house for you and your daughter to live in, should you have chosen to do so?"

Court TV had nothing on Avery Dillenger. Rebecca smiled, ready for him. "Of course. But our moving in with Aunt Martha would have deprived another homeless family of a place to stay. Mr. Donovan wasn't likely to offer the use of his home to anyone else in town."

"And why is that?"

"I believe you stated the council considers him highly dangerous to the safety and well-being of our town. Can you imagine anyone else accepting an offer of hospitality from him under those circumstances?"

Avery frowned, then realized she'd thrown his own words back at him. He narrowed his eyes at her in renewed challenge and asked, "Why *did* you accept Donovan's offer? Surely you don't expect the council to believe you moved in with a convicted murderer for purely altruistic reasons?"

Score one for Avery. The audience got a chuckle out of that, even if it did contain elements of nervousness. Rebecca wondered again where Jake had disappeared to, and what would happen if the town's 'convicted murderer' showed up now. It didn't matter. She'd be damned if she'd let Avery Dillenger poison the minds of everyone in the room. This was a public forum and she intended to make the most of her right to be heard.

"Of course not, Avery. I accepted Mr. Donovan's offer of hospitality because I knew my daughter and I would be perfectly safe living there."

Another murmur of response from the audience. Rebecca sensed perceptions shifting, and prayed any positive impressions she was making lingered beyond the moment.

"And just how did you know this?" Avery asked archly, clearly displeased with the direction in which she'd taken his discussion.

"Because I've known Jacob Donovan since I was ten years old, and I know he couldn't possibly be guilty of killing a woman."

Avery's eyes glittered with icy triumph, as if she'd just made a fatal mistake. "I see. So you think Mr. Donovan couldn't possibly be guilty of killing a woman. How about a man?"

Rebecca suddenly felt herself surrounded by political quicksand. She had no idea what Jake might have done in the military—or in prison for that matter—but she didn't doubt Avery Dillenger had made it his business to know.

She did the only thing she could. She punted.

"I really can't answer that, Avery, but after this farce of an inquisition, I'm sure you'd be at the top of his list."

Laugher exploded throughout the room. Whether it was from combined nervous relief or genuine mirth Rebecca couldn't say, but it gave her a few much needed moments to refocus, and left her feeling Avery Dillenger might be thinking twice about having taken her on. No doubt she'd have to pay with her job for challenging him, but right now it didn't matter. Standing her ground against the man who'd all but turned her town into his own personal fiefdom was more important. The people in town needed help and support, not these petty politics, but all Avery could see was his own agenda.

Eventually, he regained order in the room. After sending Rebecca a quelling glare obviously meant to let her and everyone else know he'd had enough of her shenanigans, he turned his attention to their audience. "Clearly, ladies and gentlemen, what we have here is an unfortunate case of the Stockholm Syndrome."

Rebecca couldn't hide her disbelief. "Oh, for Pete's sake, Avery. I'm not Jake's hostage."

He met her eyes, the icy deliberation in his letting her know he wasn't going to end this until he'd won, hands down. "Perhaps not physically, Ms. Reed, but he obviously has a great deal of control over your mind. Control that could prove quite dangerous to certain...shall we say impressionable patrons of the library—should they fall under your influence while you're so intimately involved with this man of questionable character."

"You're talking about children? You think Jake is dangerous to *children?*" Rebecca asked, incensed that anyone would *suggest* such a thing. Not to mention daring to imply she would allow Jake to abuse Katie in any way. "You're way out of line, Avery."

He sat back, and managed to look both grim and superior. "Am I? I didn't want to have to mention this publicly, but there have been several reported cases of child molestation in the area in recent weeks."

At this, an almost tangible wave of disbelief and horror swept through the room. Rebecca herself thought she might be ill at the thought of some child molester loose in Warner. But more than that, she wanted to kill Avery Dillenger for deliberately linking Jake's name with something so heinous.

"I'm afraid Sheriff Sutter has been trying to keep it quiet to disguise his own ineptitude at solving such offensive crimes during an election year, but if you don't believe me, ask him," Dillenger told the still rumbling crowd. "In fact, if I were a parent in this town, I'd demand to know what he's doing about it."

The noise in the room swelled to titanic proportions. Rebecca mentally scrambled to get her own roiling emotions under control. She'd known Avery Dillenger was slime, but this proved he was insane as well. Attacking the sheriff in public? When the man wasn't here to defend himself?

Rebecca looked around in growing confusion and concern. Where was Bob, anyway? He never missed a town meeting.

Oh, God. Was he with Jake? Had something happened and Bob arrested Jake for it? Was that why Jake wasn't here?

Avery banged his gavel to restore order in the room, then calmly refocused on Rebecca as if the past five minutes hadn't happened. For the first time that evening, Rebecca began to have grave doubts about what she was doing. The barely disguised malevolence in Avery's eyes chilled her to the bone.

He didn't just want to win, he wanted to destroy her.

"Ms. Reed? Do you have anything else to say in your defense?"

She swallowed hard and lifted her chin. If she was going to go down, she was going down fighting. "Just this. As much as you might like for it to be otherwise, Mr. Dillenger, this is no courtroom and neither I nor my morals are on trial with you serving as judge and jury. Jacob Donovan is no child molester, and you're looking at one hell of a libel suit if you plan to continue in this deliberately inflammatory vein. Just because I'm temporarily staying in the home of a single man who spent some time in prison doesn't make either of us targets for public slander. And just because you own three quarters of Warner doesn't give you the right to try to control my or anyone else in this town's behavior."

But Avery only smiled and addressed the audience with supreme confidence. "Do you hear how staunchly she defends a man convicted of murder? A man whose long list of juvenile offenses are well-known to many of you? Do you hear how firmly she denies her moral responsibilities to anyone but herself? Is this the kind of woman you want reading stories to your preschoolers? Watching over your adolescents while they research their reports at the library? A woman who openly sleeps with a man known for his violent tendencies toward women and—"

"I'm not sleeping with anybody!"

"You aren't? You're living with the man, aren't you?"

"We're sharing the same house, Avery. That's it."

"Come now, Ms. Reed. Do you really expect us to believe you're not sharing a bed, too?"

"That's enough, Dillenger."

The sharp, cold voice that cut across the room startled everyone. Rebecca whipped around to see Jake standing at the back of the room, the dark fury in his eyes focused on Avery Dillenger alone. "The lady's telling the truth. There's nothing going on in my house that could even remotely affect Rebecca Reed's abilities to run *any* organization and you know it."

Straightening slowly, Avery removed his glasses and shifted his attention to Jake, still standing at the back entrance to the fire hall. Rebecca thought he looked strong and solid, wearing his new blue flannel shirt and jeans. His broad-shoulders filled the open doorway he stood in as he faced down his nemesis.

"Mr. Donovan," Avery said blandly. "How nice of you to join us."

Nervous laughter rippled through the room as the meeting's focus shifted from the confrontation between their council chairman and library director to the cold-eyed man Avery Dillenger had defamed just minutes earlier.

Calmly, Jake approached the front of the room. Ignoring the microphone in front of Dillenger, Jake placed his hands on the table. He leaned forward and said conversationally, "And just because a woman doesn't want to sleep with you, *cousin*, that doesn't give you the right to publicly question her morals or use

136

your position as head of this council to get petty revenge."

For the first time in memory, Avery Dillenger's cool composure cracked. Stunning Rebecca, he flushed a violent shade of red. "You sorry son of a bitch," he hissed, "at least I didn't *kill* her for turning me down."

The room fell deathly silent, every word having been heard by everyone in there because of the open mikes. Jake said nothing, refusing to move a muscle until he was utterly calm again. Dillenger's glare of unadulterated hatred faded into a slow, malevolent smile as he watched Jake struggle for control. A long moment later, his emotions firmly leashed, Jake rose to his full height and said calmly, "Neither did I."

Turning his back on Dillenger, Jake sought Rebecca's gaze. "I'm sorry I'm late. Are you ready to leave?"

She stood there so long, simply staring at him, that Jake was sure she was going to reject him in front of the whole town. He'd let her down again, getting there so late.

Instead, she smiled a very slow, almost knowing smile, then said, "You, know, I think I am."

With pure womanly grace, she bent and picked up her purse, stepped out into the aisle and, shoulders straight, left the building.

Jake followed her out the door, wondering what the hell had just happened.

Chapter Sixteen

"This is stupid," Jake said forty-five minutes later, feeling scrunched in the front passenger seat of Rebecca's car.

"Oh, be quiet. I'm enjoying the view." They were parked on Holton Hill, in a prime spot for looking down at the town below. "Besides, you owe me for being so late to the meeting."

"I was worried about the beer. I didn't want to show up with alcohol on my breath."

"You're an adult, Jake. You're allowed to have a beer now and then."

"Not as long as I'm on parole."

"You're kidding."

"'Fraid not. Legally I can't have one for another seven years."

"Well, then I appreciate your concern on my account."

Jake smiled. She looked so sexy when she was trying to be all prim and proper. "And I appreciate you treating me to a DQ," he said, lifting his hot fudge sundae in salute.

Saying she wasn't ready to go home just yet, Rebecca had driven them over to the DQ, then puttered the Focus up the steep hill that overlooked the town proper and Dillenger's Bay.

Jake finished off his sundae and studied the panoramic view he'd seen regularly in his adolescent days, or rather the view he'd ignored while he focused instead on the delights of various back seats. The girls he'd been here with had always driven their daddy's cars, and it had always been their idea to come up here. Come to think of it, he'd never been here in a car of his own.

Apparently that much hadn't changed.

Nor had the space they occupied. He glanced at the cars already parked on one side, then the other, then tried not to notice how her skirt had ridden up along her thigh as Rebecca took another bite of her Peanut Buster Parfait and licked her spoon clean.

Holton Hill was for lovers. He knew it, Rebecca knew it, and so did everybody else in town.

So why were they here?

"There," she said next to him. "It's over."

He squinted into the valley and realized the lights of the fire hall had winked out, the last person having finally left the building. So that's what she was doing. Seeing how long the meeting lasted after they left. He looked at his watch. It was nearly ten o'clock. Unless he missed his guess, Sutter or one of his pals would be driving by soon to clear the place out.

Wouldn't that be a nice addition to the stories that would circulate after tonight's meeting? His mind returned to the things he'd seen and heard in the fire hall, and he had to admit it. "You were incredible back there," he said quietly.

Rebecca laughed and savored another bite of her parfait. "Me? If I was incredible, you were phenomenal. Seriously, Jake. I was so impressed. You didn't even come close to losing your temper."

He registered her delight with disbelief. "And you didn't even come close to hearing what Dillenger said, did you?"

"Who cares what he said? You didn't do it. I know it, you know it, and now everyone at the town meeting knows it."

"Rebecca, no one knows anything, and they're sure as hell not going to take my word for it. I'm Mickey Donovan's son, remember?"

She waved her spoon in dismissal. "That was then. This is now. Anybody with eyes could see Dillenger was no match for you. I couldn't believe it—Mr. Supremely Confident and Composed at All Times—nearly lost it, while you—God, Jake, you were so cool I thought I could feel the temperature in the room dip. It was like you had ice in your veins."

Jake's mood shifted, as it always did when Rebecca praised him. For some reason it made him uncomfortable. "Is that what you think?" he practically growled. "I have ice in my veins?"

Rebecca blinked, the spoon halfway to her lips. "Of course not," she said quietly. "Although we *have* been cool towards each other lately."

"You can say that again," he groused, looking out the passenger window again.

Rebecca said nothing for a moment, then: "I've been angry at you. For wanting Katie and me to move."

Jake stiffened in dread at just the thought of her leaving, but masked his fear with self-righteousness. "And now? Do you finally see I'm right?"

"No," she said almost flippantly, and dug into her parfait

139

again. "But I'm not going to let it spoil my evening." She swallowed another bite of ice cream and sighed in what sounded like simple satisfaction. "You know, I've never been here before, like this."

"Like what?" Jake grumbled, wishing they would leave.

"Alone in a car with a man who keeps sneaking peeks at my legs."

His gaze shot to hers. "Tell me that's not why you brought me here." She couldn't have. Not after that meeting.

She didn't seem the least bit surprised by his reaction as she peered into her DQ cup and scooped out another bite of parfait. "Maybe, maybe not. Probably not. You don't seem to be in the mood for it, anyway." She gave a little laugh that wasn't quite convincing. "If people only knew the truth."

Neither of them spoke for several minutes. Rebecca finished her ice cream while Jake stewed and stared out at the town he considered to be at the heart of their problems. He couldn't stay, and Rebecca wouldn't leave. Even if he wanted her to, which he did, but then again, he didn't, which confused the hell out of him.

It was easier to focus on what Rebecca wanted, which she'd made clear in a hundred different ways over the past six weeks. The woman was a part of Warner, and Warner was a part of her.

And he was part of nothing at all.

"I'm leaving, Jake," she said quietly, startling him from his morose thoughts. "Katie and I will be moving out over the weekend. I've found an apartment in town that will be available on the sixth. I put a deposit on it this morning."

He looked over at her, not quite sure how he felt about that. "You're moving out?"

"Isn't that what you wanted?"

"Hell, yeah. But..." Why did it have to hurt so much? "But what about Katie?"

"You'll still be able to see her whenever you want to. I won't deny you access."

"Where is this place?"

"Over Barb Peca's antique shop. It's a nice little place off Main. Two bedrooms and a kitchenette." She smiled ruefully. "I won't have room for my furniture again, but I'll find a place for it in time. Maybe even build a little bungalow out by the bay. I've looked at a couple of half-acre lots out there that would be pretty, but haven't been able to bring myself to make an offer on any of them before now."

140

"Why not?"

She stuffed her empty cup in the trash bag and looked him in the eye. "I guess part of me kept hoping you'd change your mind about staying in Warner." When he didn't respond, she sighed and looked away, toward Dillenger's Bay. "But last week when you told me there wasn't anything here for you, it finally hit home that you didn't want me, so—"

"Didn't want you?"

"We've been living in your house for nearly four weeks, Jake. Not once have you come anywhere near to making a pass at me. Including tonight. I'd say that means you meant what you said about not wanting to get involved with me."

She looked away again, then swallowed noticeably. "Just tell me the truth, Jake." She looked at him then, her eyes dark, solemn and completely vulnerable. "If your life hadn't taken the turn it did eight years ago, would you have considered getting involved with me?"

Jake couldn't answer. Not and keep his freedom. Not after she'd stood up in that council meeting and let everyone know she didn't care about who he might or might not have killed. He'd shown up as she was calmly explaining to Dillenger how moving in with her aunt instead of a convicted killer would have deprived another homeless family of a place to stay. Naturally, Rebecca being Rebecca, she'd been more than willing to make the sacrifice.

The woman had no idea how desperately he wanted her. None at all.

He looked at her and shook his head. No way would he give in to the nearly crushing need coursing through him at that moment. No way. Not at the price of her personal reputation, which, as far as Jake was concerned, had only skyrocketed at that farce of a meeting tonight. He'd be damned if he'd unravel any progress she might've made towards getting her life back on track by facing down Dillenger tonight.

So what the hell were they doing here? On Holton Hill?

As if reading his mind, Rebecca sighed fatalistically and started the ignition. "Forget it. You were right. This *was* a stupid idea."

Neither of them said a word all the way home. As Rebecca negotiated the familiar twists and turns of the road back to town, Jake wondered where Sutter's Blazer had left the road. That train of thought led him back to Dillenger, and Dillenger was not anyone Jake enjoyed thinking about. For some reason, finding out that Sheriff Sutter was MIA gave Jake a hinky feeling about Dillenger and his missing boot knife.

By the time he got home, Jake's mind was firmly on Dillenger and what frame of mind his cousin might be in after their showdown at the meeting. He got out of the car, and headed upstairs to get his running shoes. He needed some time to think, and it wasn't going to happen here, not with knowing Rebecca thought he didn't want her.

****

Rebecca cried in the tub. It was over. Jake didn't want her and never would. She'd told him she was moving out and he'd gone out running, just like every other night. The man couldn't stand to be alone with her. Not even on Holton Hill.

She didn't know why she'd taken him up there, other than she'd felt pretty full of herself after the meeting and had wanted to go somewhere and celebrate with her best friend.

Her best friend, who had made it clear that other than friendship she didn't appeal to him. Never had, if she got right down to it. It was a miracle they'd managed to conceive Katie with Jake so opposed to having anything to do with her.

Three strikes and you're out, girlfriend. Give it up and go home.

Wearily, she climbed out of the claw-footed tub. An hour and a half later, still unable to sleep, she put on her robe and went downstairs to heat some milk. Wanting to avoid the harsh glare of the overhead light, she worked by the light of the stove. She was still sitting at the kitchen table, finishing up the last of her milk, when Jake walked in.

He paused in the doorway. "I thought you'd be sleeping by now."

Rumpled and sweaty, he'd never looked better. "I couldn't settle in. I guess the meeting left me a little wired." She pointedly ignored their trip to Holton Hill.

Jake looked away, then back at her. "How's Katie?"

"Fine, I guess. I left her at Aunt Martha's for the night. We'd made arrangements earlier since I wasn't sure how I'd feel after the meeting. They haven't called to say anything is wrong."

Jake's heart dropped into his stomach. "Oh." Wow. They were alone. For the night. Wow. And she'd known it all along. Suddenly Holton Hill made a little more sense. Rebecca had been testing the waters, and he—he'd gone running. The grandfather clock struck two-thirty, and Jake looked into the darkness of the dining room, then checked the kitchen clock. Anywhere but at Rebecca. "Wow," he said aloud, still reeling from the implications of them being alone. "Is it that late already? Guess I'd better hit the shower."

He toed off his shoes and tried to cast her a quick smile. One meant to reassure her he wasn't really doing what it seemed like he was doing. Bolting. "Five thirty'll be here before we know it."

"Yeah," Rebecca said, with a disgusted look that let him know he wasn't fooling either of them. "I know."

****

Jake emerged from the bathroom twenty minutes later to find Rebecca's bedroom door closed. His disappointment surprised him. Apparently part of him had hoped she'd still be downstairs, willing to keep him company while he fixed himself a snack.

Yeah, right. After the way he'd stomped all over her feelings tonight?

He felt like slime, rejecting her both up on Holton Hill and here, where she'd sat at the kitchen table looking lower than he'd ever seen her, but what else could he do? Two hours of running and another of just walking and thinking, and he still had no answers.

Before he could chicken out, he knocked on her door. "Rebecca? You still awake?"

He heard the bedcovers rustle and a light click on, and tried not to think about what she was or wasn't wearing. "Just a minute."

Good. She was putting on her robe. It occurred to him he should have grabbed a T-shirt before he'd knocked, but it was too late now. He wiped his palms on his cotton drawstring pants and prepared himself to eat crow. When she opened the door, he knew she'd been crying.

"What happened?" she asked, unsuccessfully trying to stifle a sniffle. "Did Katie call?"

"No. Katie's fine. It's...it's me."

"What's wrong?"

Her immediate concern added another layer of guilt. *I want you. I need you. I can't have you and it's driving me crazy.* "I...I just wanted to apologize."

Her tears welled up again, even as her chin came up. "For what? Not wanting me?"

"For hurting you, Rebecca. Over and over again. I've never wanted to hurt you. Never. But it seems to be the thing I do best."

She didn't speak, but two fat tears rolled down her cheeks. Instinctively, Jake reached out to catch them. They damn near scalded his thumbs, but he didn't care. He was tired of keeping his distance. Tired of pretending he didn't care, when there was nothing on earth he cared about more. "I'm sorry, Becca. Really, I am. I just...can't be who you want me to be."

She pulled away and wiped at her eyes, then took a deep breath and met his gaze with the look of resolute strength he'd come to know and fear as well as cherish over the past six weeks. It was the look that told him she'd be fine when he moved on, the look that let him know that Rebecca Reed would never let life defeat her the way he'd apparently let it defeat him.

"The only person I've ever wanted you to be, Jacob Donovan," she said quietly, "is yourself."

He closed his eyes and ached to hold her just once. The pain of keeping it all inside was getting to be too much. Instead, he flexed his fists and took his own deep, shaky breath before meeting her eyes again. "I'm not sure I know who that is anymore."

The gentle touch of her hand on his face was like a cool, welcome rain on his parched soul. His mind told him to move back, move away, but his body refused to listen. Not this time. No more. Six weeks of running two hours a night or more, and none of it had done a blessed thing to blunt the knife edge of need he teetered on day in and day out.

"Then let me help you find him." She moved her hand up to smooth his still damp hair. She stroked it the way a mother would a child's, but when she raised an inquiring eyebrow Jake knew she was feeling far from maternal. "You know I can."

He heard the knowing smile in her voice and knew he was done for. It had been an eternity since he'd felt like this. Hot, needy...and safe.

But only with Rebecca.

Rebecca.

With a low, primal groan, he put his hands on either side of her face, tilted her head up, and kissed her for all he was worth.

She moaned and tunneled her fingers through his hair, holding on tight as he lifted her by the waist and backed her against the wall. Sliding his hands inside her robe, he filled them with the feel of her, small and soft and straining against him as if she were as starved for this as he was. He slid his hands over her silk-covered buttocks, wrapped them around her firm thighs, lifted her higher and rubbed himself against her soft sweetness, all the while kissing her like he hadn't kissed a woman in years.

Which he hadn't.

The thought was enough to stop him cold.

"Jake?"

The note of panic in her voice made him realize she thought he was going to back out on her—again. The thought brought a huge rush of guilt. "No, baby. No. I'm not going anywhere. I just...I just think maybe we ought to slow things down a little. I mean, we've got the whole house to ourselves, right?"

Chapter Seventeen

Free. Jake had never felt as free as he did in that big rosewood bed with Rebecca. Free to give her his heart and soul. Free to claim and worship her with his hands and lips and tongue and tell her all the things with his body he couldn't tell her with words.

Returning her kisses, he reveled in the clean, minty taste of her, the rightness of her warm, supple body as it moved against his. She smelled even better than she had in his dreams—of sexy aroused female and sweet summer strawberries. Her breasts were rounder, her curves more defined, her kisses and caresses surprisingly self-assured and sensual.

No doubt about it, in the past eight years Rebecca had matured into a phenomenal woman. Jake's blood sang with desire and appreciation as he pulled her closer, spreading his legs to allow her to nestle her hips against his.

As they rocked against each other, Jake's hands never stopped moving. Over her hair, her face, shoulders, under her soft cotton nightgown and up her hips and back, greedily he filled his hands with hot, smooth skin. He prayed he wouldn't disappoint her by going off like a rocket with a too short fuse.

"Oh, God, Becca, I don't think I'm going to be able to wait," he rasped as she pulled back to kick off her panties and slip her robe off her shoulders.

"Then don't," she breathed, and reached for him again.

He groaned and rolled her over without breaking their kiss. As her hands raced over his skin to help free him from his cotton drawstring pants, Jake realized he'd forgotten something.

"Condoms," he breathed. "Condoms, Rebecca."

"What?"

He forced himself to pull back, feeling hot and uncomfortable and disoriented. "Condoms, honey, do you have any?"

"*Me?*" Rebecca pushed up on her elbows and blinked, the soft moonlight that filtered through the side windows the perfect foil for her tousled hair and rumpled look. The wide V-neck of her navy blue nightshirt slid down to expose one creamy shoulder as she looked up at him in dazed confusion. "Why would I have condoms?"

Jake felt like an idiot. Here he was, supposedly the town sex maniac, and he didn't even carry a condom. How could he explain that there hadn't seemed to be any point to it? That he'd stood in front of that blasted rack of condoms in the grocery store in St. Mary's that day after the tornado for a full minute and a half, then turned and shoved his cart away, cursing himself for a fool for even thinking of buying the damned things?

"I wasn't exactly planning on this, Rebecca. I guess I thought by not...by not buying anything I'd be avoiding temptation."

She stared at him for what felt like forever, her expression never changing, then offered a flat, "Great."

"You want me to run out and get some?"

"In this town? Are you kidding? After tonight?"

She had a point.

"I think we'll be all right," he heard her say beside him.

"You think we'll be all right?" he repeated, confused.

She flashed him a look. "Okay, I'm sure we will. I haven't been with anyone since you, and—*what*?"

"You haven't been with anyone since me?" Jake stared, dumbfounded. "You're kidding."

"I was pregnant, Jake. And then I was—am—a single mother." That hadn't stopped her mother, but Jake knew better than to bring Chloe's name into their bed. "My period ended two days ago," she was saying. "I'm as regular as clockwork. Always have been. There's no way I could get pregnant again. Not tonight."

But Jake's mind was stuck on 'regular as clockwork and always have been.' "You mean you knew there was a good chance you would wind up pregnant last time?"

"Of course not! I wasn't thinking in those terms back then. I wasn't planning on having sex with anyone before marriage, so it wasn't on my mind at the time."

"And now?"

Surprising him, Rebecca smiled and looped her arms around his neck, pulling him back down on the strawberry-scented bed. "And now it's on my mind all the time. Come on Jake, There's just you and me and this big old bed. Let's not waste the few hours we have left."

"You're sure about this?"

She looked up at him with the most honest blue eyes he'd

ever known. "Dead sure."

It was all Jake needed to hear. He stood and dropped his pants, then helped Rebecca lose her nightshirt. They came together as smoothly, as seamlessly, as if they'd been together for years. When he entered her, Rebecca sighed as if she'd just come home, and Jake knew he had.

He gave them both some time to get used to each other, then moved inside her slowly, deliberately, determined to prolong their pleasure as long as he could. But within minutes he was nearly mindless again. "I can't hold back much longer, honey."

"Then don't," she breathed. "I'm tired of waiting."

He groaned and they came together one last time, Rebecca arching beneath him as she came, drawing his own explosive release from the depths of his soul.

Afterward, as they rested beneath his red and white star quilt, Rebecca's sweat-damp cheek nestled against his still-thumping heart, Jake feathered his fingers against her hip and marveled at the miracle that was Rebecca. How was it that only she had the power to make him feel happy, whole, sane and at peace with himself and the world?

"Jake?"

"Hmmmm?"

"What happened to your Harley?"

He stiffened involuntarily, remembering. "The police impounded it after they arrested me."

She didn't say anything for a long moment. "I'm sorry. I know how much that bike meant to you."

"Yeah, well, they had it longer than I did. After keeping it for a year, they sold it to pay the storage bill I couldn't. I wasn't working yet, and even if I had been, nineteen cents an hour doesn't allow for extras like storing motorcycles."

"I wish I'd known."

"I wish I'd told you. You could have gotten a good ten or twelve grand for it after springing it from storage. It would have bought a lot of formula and diapers."

More silence, then: "What happened in Wyoming, Jake?"

Something inside him dissolved. If Rebecca had the balls to face an entire town with her beliefs, if she had the courage to tell him she still wanted him, if she could still give herself to him so completely after everything he'd put her through, the least he owed her was the truth.

"I don't know. I was sound asleep. Passed out drunk on the

living room couch."

She looked up. "You'd been drinking?"

"Practically non-stop since I left you."

"Why?"

He forced himself to meet her troubled gaze. "Because it hurt so damned much, even then, knowing I could never be what you wanted."

She pulled away, to scoot up and sit beside him, then wrap a corner of the quilt around her like a toga. Jake missed her warmth right away. "But Jake, you never asked me what I wanted."

He sighed and rearranged himself as well. He propped the pillows against the headboard, rested his back against them, and said, "I didn't have to. I must have listened to you tell me more than a thousand times about having some big, fancy house in Glenhill and the money to go with it. For that you needed someone steady, dependable, smart and ambitious as hell. Someone with looks and money and the power to make it all happen for you. Someone like Mitchell Kane."

"You're really hung up on him, aren't you?"

"You wanted to marry him, Becca."

She snorted. "And I thank God every day that I didn't. Actually, I saw Mitchell a few more times after...well, you know. He came over the next day with a dozen roses and apologized for pressuring me to sleep with him. About a month later he proposed and I turned him down."

"Did he know you were pregnant?"

"No. But I did. I couldn't have lived with myself if I'd tricked him into believing Katie was his." She smiled ruefully. "That's when I learned money didn't mean that much to me after all.

"The last time I saw Mitchell I was eight months along and big as a whale. I won't repeat the things he said, but I knew right then and there I'd spent most of my life chasing the wrong values. Katie's arrival proved it. I'm still not sure how we made it through those first three years, Jake, but I do know I'd never been more grateful for anything in my life. But then my job at the university library was downsized, and I had to take a hard look at reality. To admit I could offer Katie a better, safer life here in Warner."

Rebecca sighed, recalling how she'd packed her bags and boarded the bus with Katie, mentally kicking and screaming all the way. The truth was, at the time, deep down Rebecca had hated the idea of returning to Warner almost as much as Jake claimed to hate being here now. The memories alone had been enough to bring back the nightmare of her childhood.

But she'd been back long enough now to see that change and acceptance were possible. It hadn't happened overnight, but eventually most people had forgotten about her past and her mother. Even if they hadn't, no one had mentioned it in years.

"Even after tonight, Jake, I'd rather live in Warner than anywhere else. At least here I know who and what I'm dealing with. In Pittsburgh, the staff at the day care center changed constantly. Sure I checked the place out thoroughly before signing Katie up, but it seemed every few weeks there was someone new watching her. In that sense, Aunt Martha alone has made moving back here worth it. She adores Katie and Katie adores her, and as long as Katie's happy, I'm happy."

"How happy are you going to be without a job?"

Rebecca shrugged. "I've got some savings set aside. I can probably work part time for Barb if things get tight. The Christmas season's coming up, and the people with money aren't going to be slowed down by any tornado." She looked at Jake. "But right now, I think I'll just...take a break. See what my options are."

Jake didn't say anything for a long time. "When did you get to be so strong?" he finally asked quietly.

"When I realized you weren't coming back."

Neither of them said anything for a while after that. Jake looked away, toward the moonlight streaming in the window, and Rebecca picked at a loose thread that dangled from the corner of the quilt. "Why did you go home with that woman?"

"Why do you think?"

She reached out and touched his arm. "The truth, Jake. We've been honest with each other tonight for the first time since we were kids. Let's not spoil it now."

He felt the gentle warmth of her hand, remembered the love they'd shared, and knew that despite himself, he wanted more of it, and her. "I went home with her because she looked like you."

Her hand curled into a fist and she pressed it against her mouth. "No."

"Nothing happened, Becca. I mean, I kissed her a few times, sure, but we never had sex. I didn't want her. She wasn't you."

Rebecca closed her eyes for a moment, then: "Why did they think you killed her?"

He shrugged with a casualness he was far from feeling. "She was all over me in the bar. We left together, arm in arm. Since there was no evidence of sexual activity on the body, the

150

prosecution said I snapped out when she changed her mind. The truth is we talked for a good hour before I passed out on the couch, stone cold drunk. I can't remember what we said exactly, she did most of the talking anyway, but I know I wasn't upset about not having sex. Not with her, anyway."

He looked away, then back at Rebecca. "She was a good woman, Becca. Good, decent, strong...like you. But this guy she was seeing, he was bad news. She'd caught him sleeping with her roommate, who she'd thrown out that week, and she was hurting bad, wanting something from this guy she was never going to get. So she decided to sleep with me to get back at him.

"After thinking about it, and I thought about it a *lot* while I was locked up, I realized anger had brought us together. We were both angry because we couldn't have what we wanted." He bowed his head and shook it wearily. She ended up dying for it, and I ended up behind bars."

Rebecca reached out and touched his hair. It took everything Jake had not to haul her into his arms again and make love to her until he forgot all about Christine, about how responsible he felt for her death.

If only he'd left her to cry in her beer alone...

"It wasn't your fault, Jake. You couldn't have known what would happen."

He shook his head, refusing Rebecca's offer of comfort. Sure, if he'd minded his own business it might have happened to the next guy who came along, but it had happened to *him*, and he felt responsible. "She was bruised and naked when they found her, which led the prosecution to their theory that I snapped out on her. It didn't help that the knife the crazy bastard used to kill her was mine. Or that I'd passed out so cold I never heard a thing, and was so hung over for days afterward that I never noticed my knife was missing. By the time I did, I wasn't interested in going back for it. I just wanted to get back to—"

You. He looked up, knowing he couldn't say it. To tell Rebecca the truth about Christine was one thing, to admit he'd been on his way back to Rebecca was another. Kane or no Kane.

"I just wanted to get back to my life."

Rebecca apparently didn't have anything to say to that.

"So what happens now?" Jake finally said. "Seems to me that earlier tonight you swore to a room full of concerned citizens that our relationship was completely hands off."

"I wasn't lying."

"And now?"

"Now it can be whatever we want it to be."

Jake exhaled sharply. "You never give up, do you?"

"Why should I spend my life dancing to everyone else's tune? I can't change the past and I certainly have no control over the future—including the outcome of the meeting—so why not just focus on living each day the best way I know how?"

"Don't you have dreams anymore, Rebecca?"

"Sure I do. But if I live for the future, I miss today. And today, believe it or not, has turned out to be pretty darn special."

Jake snorted at that. "Interesting, at least. Would you believe Feeney offered to sell me the station today? He wasn't kidding, either. He said he was thinking of retiring and wondered if I'd be interested in buying him out."

"What did you say?"

Jake hesitated, knowing he was about to disappoint her again. "I don't know, Becca. Taking on a successful business like that..."

"You'd feel trapped."

Jake closed his eyes and leaned his head back. Then stared at the ceiling. It was easier than looking into Rebecca's eyes.

"You're not even going to consider it, are you?"

"Sure, I'll consider it." He met her eyes again, needing to know she understood. "But Becca, when I got out my plan was to pick up where I left off. For most of my life I've wanted to be anywhere but here. You know that. I thought I'd come see what the place looked like, fix it up for cash, then hit the road. Now suddenly I've got you to think about, Katie, this offer from Feeney...I wasn't expecting any of this."

"So what you're saying is deep down you still want to be free."

"Can you blame me?"

Rebecca didn't answer.

"I'm sorry, Becca. If things were different—"

"What needs to be different, Jake? Katie loves you, you love her. You want me, I want you. We're already living here as a family. Why can't we just try *being* one for a while?"

"I won't destroy your life. You've already damn near lost everything you own because of me. Now your job's on the line. When are you going to realize I'm poison to you and Katie?"

She took a deep breath, and fixed him with a steady look. "When are you going to stop letting Mickey run your life?"

"Rebecca—"

Suddenly she threw off the quilt and rolled off the bed. "Oh, forget it. If you want to go on believing his garbage—*hiding* behind it, then have at it. I'm out of here."

"Rebecca. Come on, baby, it's almost dawn. There's no need to leave—"

"There's every need, Jake. If you don't want Katie and me as a family, we have no choice but to leave." She picked up her robe and nightgown. Jake didn't think he'd ever forget the picture she made, her hair wild and loose, her body flushed and naked.

Turning on her heel, she did just that. Left him sitting alone in his bed, the bed they'd just spent the best hour of his life in, wishing he knew what to say to her to make her understand.

What would happen if word got out he was buying Feeney's? What if people stopped coming and the station failed? What if he lost everything and Rebecca was blacklisted from finding another job in town? What if Katie got tired of never having friends?

Rebecca might not have noticed, But Jake had. No one came around the house, and Jake knew that before he'd come along, Katie had had friends.

What would happen if he ended back up in prison? After all, who would be the first person Sutter would come looking for if anything happened? It already had, if Dillenger was to be believed about some sicko preying on the town's children. Jake was surprised Sutter hadn't been by to question him already.

Rebecca didn't get it. Warner wasn't the place for a man like him. It never had been.

****

"Katie, honey, we need to talk," Rebecca announced quietly later that day as they shared an unusually solemn after school snack of milk and chocolate chip cookies in Jake's kitchen. Jake wouldn't be home from work for another half hour, which would give them the privacy they needed to discuss moving out before he returned and they had to leave for the soup kitchen at four.

"About what?"

Rebecca didn't like the almost sullen note Katie's voice had taken on lately, but was doing her best to try to see things from her daughter's perspective. They'd been through a lot these past four weeks, since the tornado, and things were about to get rough again.

She'd thought about Jake all morning as she baked cookies at home, then went to the soup kitchen to serve lunch. How could she find a solution that would make everyone happy? The only answer she could come up with was she and Katie would have to move.

They couldn't stay with Jake any longer, not if Rebecca wanted to maintain any semblance of pride. She was too vulnerable where Jake was concerned, and she'd be damned if she'd let him use her.

The man didn't want what she had to offer him. He'd made that clear enough. "We need to find another place to live."

That got Katie's attention. "What's wrong with here?"

"Jake wants to leave Warner, sweetheart. To do that, he needs to sell his house. To help him out, we need to move."

"He doesn't want us anymore?"

Rebecca reached out and covered Katie's hand with her own. "It's not that, sweetheart. Jake loves having you here more than anything. But he's not...he's not responsible for us, Katie. We're responsible for ourselves, just like we've always been. We can't impose on him any longer."

"Couldn't we stay until he leaves? Until he at least sells the house? I mean, it could be months, right?"

"It's not that simple." Rebecca had no choice but to tell Katie what little she could. "Jake and I...well, you might have noticed we're not getting along very well these days."

"So?"

The innocence of children. Rebecca couldn't believe how much it hurt to admit she'd failed with Jake. "Katie we don't agree on some pretty important things."

"Like what?"

Like loving each other. Like wanting to build a life together. Like wanting what's best for you. "Grown up things," Rebecca finally said. There was no way she could tell Katie the truth.

"Where will we go?"

"Barb Peca has offered to rent us an apartment over her antique shop. I've seen it. It's very nice."

"It's in town."

"Yes, just off of Main street."

"But nobody lives in town."

"Plenty of people live in town, Katie."

"Nobody we know."

She was back to being sullen again. Rebecca couldn't blame her. "You'll still see your friends at school."

"Yeah, right."

Rebecca stared, wondering what had happened to her usually sunny seven-year-old. Now that she thought about it, Katie hadn't been herself for about three weeks. Since school started. Suddenly Rebecca recalled Avery Dillenger's announcement at the meeting last night about a sexual predator on the loose in Warner. "Katie?" she ventured uneasily. "Has something happened?"

Fear flashed in her daughter's eyes, followed by a firm lifting of her chin. "Like what?"

Katie knew all about good touches and bad touches and not talking to strangers. Thanks to her own terrifying experiences with the men her mother had brought home, Rebecca had made a point of educating Katie on the subject. Surely she would have said something if someone had approached her in that way.

"Something at school," Rebecca prevaricated. She didn't want to scare Katie if she didn't have to. "Are you having any kind of trouble with your teachers?"

"No."

"At the soup kitchen, then?" Rebecca knew she hadn't watched Katie as closely as she normally did among strangers while she was busy serving, but with so many people around…

"Just forget it, Mom. There's nothing going on."

She knew Katie was lying, but she also knew to push would make Katie clam up tighter. "You'd tell me if there was, wouldn't you?"

"Yeah. Can I go now?"

Rebecca didn't know what else to say. She'd never encountered this situation before. Nor had she ever felt so scared and helpless. "Can I give you a hug, first, sweetie?"

Katie shrugged as if she didn't care one way or another. A piece of Rebecca's heart shriveled up and died. "Sure, if you want to."

Gently Rebecca pulled her small, slender daughter into her arms, and forced herself not to hold on as tightly or as desperately as she wanted to. Everything seemed to be falling apart on her...her reputation, her job, her dreams, her temporary truce with Jake…her previously unshakable relationship with Katie, who didn't resist the hug, but neither did she return it, which only cut Rebecca more deeply.

She dropped a quick, determined kiss onto her daughter's baby soft hair, released her and forced a cheery smile. "Don't worry about packing. You've been through enough these past few weeks. I'll take care of it, okay? But maybe tomorrow after school we can go to the new apartment and you can help me make a list of what we'll need to fix the place up, hmm?"

"Sure," Katie said, not meeting her eyes. "I've got homework to do."

Rebecca watched her daughter leave the room, knowing something was terribly wrong, but having no idea what, much less how to deal with it.

Chapter Eighteen

For the hundredth time, Jake cursed himself for telling Rebecca about Feeney's offer. He'd known all along he wasn't going to take it. He couldn't. To buy out Feeney he'd have to mortgage the house and take out a loan. He couldn't see either of the two banks in town giving him one.

The thought of being so deeply in debt—to anyone—for anything—left him feeling suffocated. He might not have much, but what he had he owned free and clear. There was no way he could risk his only chance of escape from Warner in a gamble like taking over Feeney's. For that, he'd have to trust the good citizens of Warner to support him.

And that was something Jacob Donovan could not do. Not when they hadn't given him an iota of support in over twenty years.

Nope. Jake didn't owe anything to anybody and that was the way he liked it.

But he also liked Rebecca's company. In fact, he yearned for it constantly now that she'd withdrawn it. The woman had clearly cut her losses and was moving on. He hadn't missed the packed boxes piling up in her room. Or her cooler than cool greeting when he'd come home from work that afternoon.

Come Tuesday, she wouldn't even be around to frost him out.

"Jake? Have you seen Katie?"

Frowning, he looked up from the soup kitchen sink where he was elbow deep in scrubbing warming pans. How *did* the woman manage to look so kissable with cheese sauce spilled down the front of her sweatsuit? "No, not since we got here."

"Are you sure?"

The note of fear in her voice revved his own instincts. One of the hot topics in the kitchen that evening had been whether Avery Dillenger's child molester claims were true or a scare tactic to get the council to see his way. Apparently it was well known around town that Dillenger believed the end justified the means.

Jake got a strange kind of satisfaction at knowing people didn't think too highly of his cousin, considering how highly

Dillenger thought of himself. What felt even more strange was the realization that no one was looking his way when they discussed Dillenger's claims.

Maybe Rebecca was right. Maybe the tide of fear his return had inspired was turning—or at least ebbing.

"It's nearly seven-thirty," Rebecca said, jolting him back to the present.

He reached for a towel to dry his hands. "Has anyone else seen her?"

"I haven't asked. I just noticed she was missing."

"I'll get someone to fill in for me here and meet you in the dining room."

He arrived a minute later to find Rebecca talking to the mother of several young children Katie usually played with.

"No one's seen her, Jake. Not since before we served dinner."

"FX mentioned seeing her outside as we were setting up."

"Do you think she might have taken a walk?" This from the young mother.

"Not without telling me where she was going," Rebecca said. "She never wanders off alone. Never."

"I'll keep asking around," Jake said. "If she doesn't show up in the next five minutes we'll start looking for her, okay?"

No one had seen Katie for hours. She'd apparently slipped away just as dinner was starting. At FX's suggestion, Rebecca went into his office to call home, but no one answered. She called Aunt Martha, and when Katie wasn't there, asked her aunt to go over to Jake's house and call her back.

Ten more agonizing minutes passed before Martha called with the news that Katie wasn't at Jake's, either. Or if she was, she wasn't answering the door. Desperately, Rebecca started to phone Katie's friends, but after receiving another self-righteous earful from Mrs. Mueller, was stunned to learn some of her daughter's other friends had been forbidden to have anything to do with Katie as well.

A call to Katie's teacher confirmed Katie had been having a rough time of it at school. As Rebecca knew all too well, kids could be viciously cruel, and her daughter had been serving as class outcast since the start of school, despite her teacher's best efforts to include her in class activities. It didn't comfort Rebecca to hear Katie continued to staunchly defend Jake in the face of her classmates' cruelties, not when she knew Katie had never breathed a word of the problems she was having to *her*. By the time she got off the phone, Rebecca was feeling hurt, betrayed, confused, angry…

And terrified for her little girl. Anyone could have her.

Within minutes Rebecca and Jake were in Rebecca's Focus, heading home first, to check for themselves. "Katie's been awful quiet, lately," Jake said from the driver's seat once they were on their way. "Maybe she needed some time to be alone."

Rebecca shook her head furiously. "No. She wouldn't just disappear without telling me. If something was bothering her, if what her teacher said is true and her friends are shunning her—"

"Shunning her?"

"It's not just Mrs. Mueller who has refused to let her daughter play with Katie. But Katie would have told me. She would have."

Jake wasn't sure how to handle Rebecca's retreat into denial. He was still reeling from the news that Katie's friends were shunning her. Why, oh why couldn't he have stayed away from her and Rebecca? Now look what he'd done. "What makes you so sure she would have told you?" he finally asked.

"We've never had secrets from each other. Never."

"What about me? We're keeping something from her about me."

Rebecca looked over at him, then shook her head again, almost violently. "That's different."

"Maybe not. Maybe she suspects something's up."

"How could she? No one knows she's yours but you and me."

"Could there be any documentation lying around that names me as her father?"

"No. Her birth certificate is in my safe deposit box."

"I still think her disappearance has something to do with me. It has to, if the kids have been giving her a hard time."

"Then why wouldn't she *tell* me?"

"Maybe she wasn't comfortable telling you." He hoped that was all it was. Because if it *was* his fault, he could probably fix it by leaving town. But if it was something else…

"I'm her mother, Jake. Who else would she go to?"

"I don't know." Jake pulled into the driveway of his dark house. "But—and please don't take this wrong, Rebecca, but you haven't been all that available to her lately."

She turned on him then, as he'd feared she would. "What do you mean I haven't been available? I've been here every night!"

"Physically, yes," Jake said in the most soothing voice he could manage under the circumstances. "Physically you've been around. But mentally? Emotionally?" He looked into her eyes, and willed her to try to understand what he was saying. "Think about it, Becca. You've had a lot on your mind lately. We all have. Katie's apparently been dealing with it by getting quieter, more withdrawn."

"Damn it, Jake, why didn't you mention this to me sooner?"

He looked at her in genuine surprise. "You're blaming *me* for not interfering in your relationship with Katie? I figured if you weren't worried, there was no need for me to be. What do I know about raising a kid? Besides, we haven't exactly been available to each other much lately, either. Unless you count last night, but…" One look at her expression, and he mentally switched gears. He took a deep breath and tried again. "Listen, Becca. I know you're scared and upset. We both are. But I can't help but think there's something more going on here than meets the eye."

"I talked to her about moving this afternoon," she finally offered, grudgingly.

"And?"

"She didn't want anything to do with me."

Jake's heart ached for her. He wondered if she had any idea how small she looked, hunched in the passenger seat, her arms wrapped around herself as she tried to deal with the pain of her daughter's rejection. It was all he could do not to reach for her and make promises he had no way to keep.

"I told her we needed to move, and she assumed you didn't want her any more."

The dull note in her voice sliced into Jake like a knife to the chest. He hadn't thought about how moving might affect Katie. All he'd worried about was getting more involved with Rebecca. Or, rather, trying not to get more involved with Rebecca.

And Rebecca knew it. "Did you tell her it wasn't true?"

"She didn't believe me, any more than…oh, never mind. Let's just get going. We're never going to find her sitting here."

"All right." Jake didn't really want to go down that road, either. "After we check the house, we can check your aunt's." Katie wasn't at either house, so while Aunt Martha waited by the phone at Jake's, Jake and Rebecca cruised every street in Warner proper, not once, but twice, Rebecca's attention never leaving the road. Jake ached for her, feeling her pain and guilt and terror as acutely as his own.

"I heard Mimi called you this afternoon," he said in a desperate bid to distract them both. It was a shame he had to find out what was going on with Rebecca from his customers at Feeney's when they were living in the same house, but that was the least of his concerns at the moment.

Rebecca glanced his way, then resumed her search. "Apparently the council voted to table the decision until the matter could be investigated further."

"Investigated? Who are they planning to investigate? You?"

"Doesn't matter. I'm not going back. If they have to deliberate on whether to allow me to keep my job based on the way I conduct my personal life, then I don't want the job. I won't be anyone's puppet, Jake."

Including his. Her message was clear. He dropped the subject. Now was not the time to get into it.

"Maybe you should start knocking on doors. She's obviously not out in the open." Or if she is, she's hiding from us, he thought, but didn't add. He didn't dare speculate on the reasons for that.

Rebecca looked surprised, and slightly offended. "You won't come with me?"

"I'd rather not. If I start showing up on doorsteps, it'll probably send the town into a panic. Besides, while you're at the front door, I can watch the shadows."

Rebecca stared at him for a long moment, but didn't argue. Retracing their path, they re-combed the town's quiet streets, Rebecca asking Jake to stop the car at every place she could think of that Katie might have gone. She knocked on doors, interrupting family meals, family fights, evening baths and television time, while Jake searched every shadow he could find. In between, they stopped people on the street. Those Rebecca didn't know, she showed Katie's first grade school picture.

Within two hours the entire town knew Katie Reed was missing.

At the very edge of town they met a woman who thought she might have seen Katie several hours earlier. "Just before dusk, I saw a girl who coulda been your daughter's age walking alone on the road that leads out of town. But then a car stopped, and she got inside."

Bone deep terror clenching her insides, Rebecca asked. "You saw her get into a car?"

The woman nodded. "Since she wasn't carrying no kind of luggage, not even a knapsack, I guessed her parents must've forgotten to pick her up somewhere and she'd started walking home."

Rebecca wasn't assuming anything of the kind. This was the first remotely viable lead they'd had, and terrifying as it was, she intended to pursue it. "What kind of car was it?"

"Oh, a nice one. One of those big luxury cars. New, I think."

"What color was it?" Jake asked tersely, thinking of the black Town Car he'd seen cruising the streets late at night, long after most of Warner had gone to sleep. The one that had dropped that young boy off near the old railroad station.

"I'm not sure. It coulda been black, maybe gray. The light wasn't so good."

"Was the driver a man or a woman?"

"I never saw the driver. But if I had to guess, I'd say it was a man."

"Why would you say that?" Rebecca asked, the growing edge of fear in her voice echoing Jake's own deepest fears.

The woman hesitated, then must have recognized Rebecca's fear. "Seems to me if the girl's mama had found her walking alone at night like that, she would have gotten out of the car and either hugged her or hit her. I know I would. Hug her, I mean. I'd be so relieved just to find her...but then those people up in Glenhill are different, aren't they?"

"Glenhill?" Jake repeated, the chill in his soul turning icy.

"They went to Glenhill?" Rebecca asked, her face pale as she looked between the woman and Jake. It was all Jake could do not to grab her and bolt for the car.

"I don't know where they went," the woman was saying, "but they turned up that way, right past Feeney's." She squinted at Jake. "Aren't you that guy's got everyone all het up? People can't decide whether you're a hero or...well, never mind. All I know is my husband thinks you're the best mechanic in three states. Said you did an amazing job on our old Mercury. He usually works on it himself, you know, but between working three jobs just to make ends meet, he couldn't find the time."

Jake remembered the car. It had been ready to fall apart. He'd been in a foul mood that day, looking for a reason to dodge customers. He'd spent the whole afternoon working the Mercury over, doing everything short of an overhaul. He hadn't billed the man for more than Feeney's original estimate to replace the carburetor, planning to pay for the difference in parts himself. But when he'd put the money on the counter, Feeney had told him to forget it. It wasn't anything Feeney himself hadn't done a few hundred times in the course of forty years.

Two weeks later, Feeney had offered to sell Jake the station. To keep him in town.

And now Jake's daughter was missing. Because he'd stayed this long. And Jake had a damned good idea of who had her.

"Let's go." He took Rebecca by the elbow and turned her toward the car. "Thank you, ma'am. If you'll excuse us..."

"I hope you find your little girl," she called after them. "Got five kids of my own, and I know how I'd feel if one of them went missing."

Jake waved an acknowledgement and hustled Rebecca back to the car. "What do you think?" he asked, as soon as they were back in the car.

"It doesn't sound like anything Katie would do, but it's the only lead we have."

"Who do you know in Glenhill who drives a new dark luxury car?"

"More than half the people in Glenhill drive dark luxury cars, Jake."

"Yeah, but who do *you* know? As in who in Glenhill would know Katie, or have any reason to stop if they saw her walking alone on the road?"

Rebecca looked at him, shaking her head. "Jake, Avery wouldn't—what possible reason could he have for taking Katie?"

Jake looked over his shoulder and shifted into reverse. "That's what we're going to find out. You said she never liked him, Becca. It's time to find out why."

As he sped toward Glenhill, Rebecca put her hand on his thigh. "Jake, wait. Let's call home first. Maybe she's come back."

Jake's every instinct screamed at him to get to Dillenger's, fast. He'd never bought Dillenger's story about buying toys for children at the shelter and hadn't seen a single one of those toys surface since. A couple of discreet fishing expeditions with FX had netted him a big zero as well.

But Rebecca was right. A quick phone call might save them a lot of trouble. Because if Dillenger did have Katie, Jake was going to have to hurt him, and badly.

"All right," he said, tires squealing as he pulled a U-turn in the middle of the road. "You can call from Feeney's."

Two minutes later, waiting impatiently while Rebecca made the call, Jake saw her shoulders slump and braced himself even before she hung up the phone. "Not a word," she said, her voice cracking as she looked up at him with big, fearful eyes. "From anyone, anywhere."

"Then buckle your seatbelt, baby."

Chapter Nineteen

"I'd like to go home now," Katie said from her seat at the far end of Avery Dillenger's dining room table.

"You would? I'm afraid that's not possible yet."

"What do you mean?"

Avery set aside his dessert spoon and leaned forward, giving the girl his full attention. "I mean, my dear Kathleen, it's not time for you to go home yet."

"My name's Katie."

"Kathleen's your given name, and I prefer to call you that."

She looked at him for a long moment, apparently having nothing to say to that. Good. He was getting tired of her questions. He preferred his guests to be quiet and compliant.

"I'm leaving," she announced suddenly, and stood.

He met her determined gaze across the length of the table, and fixed her with the look of promised retribution that had worked so well with so many others. "I don't think so, Kathleen."

She bolted.

"Kathleen!" Avery shot to his feet in annoyance as she ran out of the room, but refused to upset his digestive system by lowering himself to chasing after her. He smiled to himself. She could hide all she wanted. No one else was in the house, and there was no way out unless he deactivated the security system.

He sat back down and resumed his meal. As he ate his chocolate mousse, he ruminated over his plans for the evening. This time, he'd make sure Donovan took the fall. He smiled at his own cleverness. The bastard's knife would come in handy after all.

Having finished his dessert and coffee in peace, he rose, and, whistling, went to his security room, where he spotted the girl on one of the dozen monitors there. Stupid thing, she hadn't even made it out of the living room. She could have at least made things interesting for him by finding herself a closet to slip into. He didn't have monitors in the closets. Or in his special room downstairs. A camera, yes, but security monitors, no.

He smiled in anticipation as she rose from her hiding place behind the couch, listened for any sound of him, then began to make her way across the room, no doubt aiming for the front door.

By the time she got there, he was there to meet her.

"I'm afraid leaving is simply not an option right now, Kathleen. I still have plans for you."

She bolted again, but this time he was ready for her. He swept her back against him with one arm while he used the other to try to subdue her. "That's enough of this nonsense, Kathleen. Do you hear me?"

"No!" She increased her puny struggles, kicking and hitting like the ill-bred creature that she was.

"Stop that, you little brat," he snarled as she connected with his kneecap. "Or I'll—"

The doorbell rang.

Avery cursed succinctly. "Help! Help!" the girl screamed, before he could get a hand over her mouth. Still kicking and squirming, she bit his hand, then let out another earsplitting scream. Swearing sharply, Avery spun her around and slapped her. The idiot girl stopped screaming, but stumbled into a table holding a Ming vase filled with fresh cut flowers. As flowers and vase crashed to the marble-tiled floor, someone banged loudly on the door.

"Come on." He grabbed the girl's arm with the intention of locking her in his soundproof media room while he dealt with whatever imbecile was still banging on his door, and dragged her into the main hall. Behind him, the front door crashed open. The girl screamed again, this time even louder than before.

"Quiet, you stupid brat," Avery snarled, shaking her viciously. What the hell was happening to his evening?

"Let her go, Dillenger, or I'll kill you."

He stilled as he recognized the lethal note in Donovan's voice. Slowly, he turned and released the girl, who ran past Donovan and into her mother's waiting arms. The murderous look Rebecca sent him over the girl's head rivaled Donovan's.

Avery smiled. All might not be lost after all. "Well, well, well. What have we here?"

Rebecca ignored him, focusing on Katie. "Did he hurt you, baby? Did he hurt you?" she asked, furiously skimming her gaze over her terrified daughter for any outward sign of injury. The fresh bruise blossoming on Katie's face made Rebecca want to kill Avery Dillenger herself, but seeing to Katie came first.

Katie sniffed as tears streamed down her swelling face. "I was trying to leave, Mama, and he wouldn't let me."

166

"You sorry bastard," she heard Jake growl low in his throat. "Give me one good reason why I shouldn't beat the shit out of you right here and now."

"Jake. We've got Katie. Let's just leave."

"How long has she been here?" Jake demanded.

Dillenger shrugged. "An hour or so, two, at most."

"He wanted me to spend the night here, Mama. He wasn't going to let me leave."

Jake cursed again. Rebecca fixed her gaze, rife with anger and suspicion, on the most prominent citizen in Warner. "What's going on here, Avery?"

"Nothing devious, my dear," he returned with a patronizing smile that had Rebecca itching to slap his smarmy face. "I simply offered your daughter safe harbor for the night. When I picked her up, she didn't want to go home."

Rebecca looked down at her daughter, having a hard time believing Katie had wanted to avoid going home badly enough to get into a car with Avery Dillenger. "Katie, is this true?"

"Well, at first I didn't want to go home. But then it got late and I started missing you."

She bent to meet Katie at eye level and smoothed her daughter's hair. "Why didn't you want to come home, sweetheart?"

"I don't think that's important right now," Jake interrupted coldly. "What's important is why Dillenger here thought he could get away with bringing Katie here without your knowledge or consent, then keep her here against her will."

"You're deranged if you think I'll answer to you. On any subject."

"Then you can save your answers for the police," Rebecca said.

Dillenger's laugh was short and harsh. "I don't think so. The job of the police is to protect people like me from people like you. Not the other way around. You're not calling the police. Either of you. Rebecca because she's already in enough trouble with the town council and you, Donovan, because deep down you don't care about anyone but yourself. As soon as your parole is over, you're out of here. History. Calling the police would only make waves you can't afford to make.

"No, I should be calling the police, myself. Trespassing, breaking and entering, terroristic threats. I've got it all on tape." He nodded toward a hidden security camera. "What do you think your parole officer would say if I showed it to him?"

"Jake, I think it's time we left," Rebecca said, her arm still firmly around Katie.

"In a minute. Why don't you take Katie out to the car?"

"Jake..."

"I won't be long. Trust me."

Rebecca hesitated so long, Jake was sure she was going to refuse. To his relief, she nodded once. "Be careful." she said, before she turned away and ushered Katie out the mahogany door he'd kicked open when they'd heard their daughter's scream.

"What is it?" Dillenger snapped behind him.

Jake turned to face his nemesis. "Don't fuck with me, Dillenger. Stay the hell out of my life, and that includes Rebecca and Katie. If I hear you've bothered either of them again, I'll take care of you myself."

"Are you threatening me?"

"Take it however you want."

Dillenger's eyes glittered darkly, and he moved forward, practically daring Jake to take him down right then and there. "You'd go back to prison for them, wouldn't you?"

"In a heartbeat."

"Why? Did you enjoy being locked up that much?"

Jake knew Dillenger was messing with him again, baiting him, but Jake was thinking about the cameras. If there was any way he could turn the tables on the bastard... "You're sick, Dillenger. Really sick. Stay away from the children in this town, or you're going to find out first hand what living in a cell feels like."

"Oh, so now you think it's *me* preying on the little darlings?"

"Sutter knows, doesn't he? Is that why you tried to kill him and frame me for it?"

At that, Dillenger almost smiled. "I'm afraid I couldn't pass up the opportunity." His expression hardened. "Nor will I when it comes around again."

"Where's my knife?"

"That's for me to know and you to find out. When I'm ready to *let* you find out."

Jake let it go. He'd done all he could for now. He turned and was about to cross the threshold when Dillenger spoke in an icy voice behind him. "If you think you're going to walk away with everything that belongs to me, you've grossly underestimated me."

Slowly, Jake turned around, fully expecting to find a gun pointed at him. When he didn't, he couldn't stop an annoyed,

"What the hell are you talking about now?"

"Don't tell me you don't know she's planning to give you everything."

Jake just looked at him. What was the man talking about?

"Your grandmother. My great aunt. She's willed it all to you."

"Jesus, Dillenger, now I know you're a paranoid son of a bitch. My grandmother's not planning to give me anything different from what she's given me the past thirty years. Nothing."

"She gave you a house."

"That was my mother's house. Mickey kept it from me."

"And Amanda Dillenger bought it when she found out Princess Eileen was pregnant with her precious love child."

"Yeah, right."

"It's the truth. Your grandmother bought that house for you."

"Let it go, Dillenger. I'm nothing to your family and we all know it."

"That's where you're wrong. They all wanted you, Donovan. Desperately. Your mother, your father, your rich as sin grandparents. Don't tell me they didn't try to come and get you after your idiot of a mother killed herself. I know all about it. How your drunkard father tossed Conrad Dillenger out on his ear the night of Eileen's funeral, saying no way in hell was he going to turn his son over to some sick pervert to raise."

"What are you saying, Avery? How do you know this?"

Jake looked over his shoulder to see Rebecca had returned. She'd probably seen him start to leave, then turn around as if a gun were trained on him. A part of him wanted to kiss her for coming back, another wanted to shake her for taking such a risk with her life. For him. "Where's Katie?"

"She's fine. Curled up in a blanket and listening to the radio." Her attention returned to Dillenger. "Now what's this about the night of Jake's mother's funeral?"

"Drop it, Rebecca. It's old news," Jake warned.

"Not to me," she countered sharply. "You never told me your grandparents tried to take you from Mickey."

"They only tried once. It wasn't worth mentioning."

She glared at him. "Wasn't worth mentioning, when it was probably one of the most pivotal moments of your life?"

"What are you talking about?"

"If you'd gone home with your grandparents that night, Donovan, like you were supposed to," Dillenger sneered, "my life

169

would have turned out entirely different." His eyes filled with undiluted hatred and bored into Jake. "Because then Conrad Dillenger would have had you to play with instead of me. You have no idea how much I hate you for that, *cousin*. Because every time I tried to fight back, every time I tried to get away from the sick bastard, he'd laugh and say, 'Forget it, boy, I'm going to give it all to your cousin Jake if you don't do what I say.'

"I couldn't let that happen. It was mine." His face twisted into a dark mask of bitterness. "*Mine*. I *earned* it."

"Avery?" Rebecca interrupted gently. "Are you saying Conrad Dillenger molested you?"

"Every chance he got," Dillenger spat. "From the time I was eight until the rotten sonofabitch died when I was sixteen."

"Why...why didn't you tell anyone?"

"Who was I going to tell? My mother, whose only concern was her social calendar? My father, who was married to his law firm? Neither of them wanted to be bothered with me. They wouldn't have believed me, anyway." His gaze, still burning with hatred, flashed back to Jake. "And now she wants to give it all to him."

"Who wants to give all of what to whom, Avery?"

But Dillenger had apparently gone somewhere else in his mind, leaving the two confused and slightly shell-shocked people who stood in his cold foyer behind. "Week after week I've had to listen to her Sunday dinner prattle about how unfair life has been to her poor, neglected grandson, how she's hired private investigator after private investigator to prove he's innocent, how she plans to make amends for all the trouble he's had when she dies, how she doesn't *blame* him for not wanting to have anything to do with her. For not answering her letters."

Rebecca looked at Jake in confusion.

"My grandmother," Jake said quietly. "She wrote a few times while I was in prison. I didn't answer her."

"And you haven't been to see her since you've returned," Rebecca said, just as quietly.

"Because you know how desperately she wants to see you, don't you, Donovan?" Dillenger sneered. "You're just holding out for the big prize."

"I don't know what you're talking about."

"The hell you don't! She's leaving it all to you, you worthless bastard. The whole damned estate."

"You're not making sense, Dillenger," Jake snapped. "Come

170

on, Rebecca, let's go. The man's delusional." He stopped and turned back to Dillenger, pointed a finger. "My warning stands. You come near my girls again and I'll—"

"You delude yourself, Donovan. Rebecca and Katie aren't yours."

"Wrong again, Dillenger. Katie's mine, through and through. Come within fifty yards of her again and I will personally cut off your balls and feed them to you."

"Rebecca, can you honestly say you prefer this crass convict to me?"

"You're despicable, Avery."

"You didn't think so when we were dating. I took you out over my mother's stringent objections, you know. 'Breeding will tell,' she always said. I loved to taunt her with the idea of marrying you before she died. Chloe Reed's daughter. It would have humiliated her to the bone. Which was nothing less than she deserved, the self-centered bitch." He refocused on Rebecca. "But you slipped through my fingers, didn't you, and now you're bent on repeating your own family history." His expression hardened. "I hope what he does to you in bed is worth it, because I'm going to make sure—"

Without a sound, Jake lunged.

"Jake!" He felt Rebecca pull at him from behind, but it was too late. He'd made his move, and Dillenger was on his ass on the floor, screaming bloody murder as bright red blood gushed from his nose onto his fancy Italian suit and white marble tiles.

"Speak to her again, Dillenger, and I'll kill you. Come on, Rebecca, let's go."

Chapter Twenty

They returned to the car to find Katie feeling needy and eager to leave. Jake didn't blame her. When she asked Rebecca to sit with her in the back seat, Jake's fury increased a hundredfold. The bastard had shattered his daughter's sense of safety. It took everything he had not to go back and finish what he'd started.

As they passed Feeney's, Rebecca said, "We need to go to the police, Jake."

He looked into the rear view mirror and was surprised to see Katie already fast asleep. She looked so small and defenseless curled up against Rebecca's side, Rebecca's arm wrapped around her. Jake's stomach roiled anew with suppressed rage and revulsion at what Katie might have had to suffer at Dillenger's filthy hands. What other children in town *had* suffered.

Rebecca was right. They needed to report what they'd learned to the police. But how could he admit that just the thought of walking into a police station sent a shaft of fear so deep into his soul he wasn't sure he could actually do it?

How could he face Sutter and his crew, on their turf, knowing they suspected him of attempted murder? What if they gave him a hard time, refused to listen to what he had to say? Jake wasn't sure he'd be able to control his temper, knowing what he now knew about Dillenger. But if he lost his temper with the cops...

"He's a very sick man, Jake," Rebecca pressed when he didn't answer. "We need to stop him from hurting anyone else."

"Tell me something I don't know," he growled, showing his frustration to hide his fear. How could he make Rebecca see what they were up against? She still believed in the system that had tried its best to destroy him. He sighed heavily. "Becca, you know as well as I do the cops won't want to hear anything I have to say."

"For God's sake, Jake! He *kidnapped Katie!*" She leaned forward, her voice low with suppressed fury. "He was going to do terrible things to her, Jake. He's done terrible things to other children. My God, it was himself he was talking about at the town council meeting last night. Avery Dillenger truly believes he's impervious to the law, Jake. The Sheriff *needs* to know about this, and now."

"He already does, Becca."

"How do you know?"

"Dillenger all but admitted that was why he was trying to get rid of Sutter. Why he tried to *kill* him, Rebecca, and frame *me* for it. Do you remember that?"

"And you're going to let him get away with it?"

"I didn't say that—"

"You can't just assume this is being taken care of by someone else! This isn't something that will resolve itself in its own good time."

"All I'm saying is it's our word against Dillenger's, and Sutter already thinks I tried to kill him. What do you think our chances of going to him without proof are?"

"Finding proof isn't our job, Jake. Reporting our suspicions to the police and letting them find the proof is."

"Rebecca, that police force isn't going to find a damned thing wrong with Avery Dillenger and you know it. You said it yourself at the meeting last night. Dillenger owns most of Warner and half the people in it. Dollars to donuts you tell the wrong person in that cop shop what you heard tonight and it'll never go any farther."

"Avery Dillenger just kidnapped your daughter with the intent to molest, quite possibly rape, torture, and maybe even kill her," she said with quiet venom. "Now what are you going to do about it?"

Suddenly, Jake wondered if *this* was what being a parent was all about—setting aside his own fears and needs for the good of his child's. If so, it was a hell of a price to pay. A hell of a sacrifice to make.

But, he thought, looking at his sleeping daughter in the rear view mirror again, it was worth it—and no less than Katie deserved. He hadn't lied when he'd told Dillenger he'd go back to prison in a heartbeat for Rebecca or Katie.

"All right. We'll go see Sutter. But only Sutter."

****

They didn't make it to the station. They were half a block away when the cruiser that pulled out of the station and passed them suddenly braked and made a sharp U-turn, lights flashing as it pulled up behind them.

Jake's gut clenched, but he ignored the nearly overwhelming need to cut and run. It would be what Rebecca expected of him. Instead he pulled over and eased the Focus to a full stop. He refused to add resisting arrest to the charges piling up against him. He'd already learned that lesson, the hard way.

He also wanted to avoid waking Katie, if he could. The last thing he wanted his daughter to see was her father being led away in handcuffs.

"Jake? What's happening?"

He rolled down the driver's side window, and used the crisp September night air to help calm his rioting nerves. "We're being stopped."

"For what?"

"We'll find out soon enough."

A blinding spotlight beamed into the car. "Out of the car, Donovan, with your hands up."

"Jake, no! Wait!"

As he climbed out of the driver's seat, hands raised, Jake heard Rebecca scramble to open the back seat passenger door, and jar Katie awake in the process. He cursed under his breath, then cursed again as he realized traffic on both sides of the street had slowed to a crawl, giving everyone there a ringside seat at what had become the circus of his life.

"Hands on the roof of the car, Donovan." Without missing a beat, the deputy, Hull, spread Jake's legs, frisked and cuffed him. "Jacob Donovan, you're under arrest for—"

"Pete, stop!" Rebecca protested frantically as she sailed around the front of the car. "You don't understand—"

Jake stiffened as the second deputy, one he didn't recognize, stepped between her and her target, cutting her off. "Excuse me, Ms. Reed, we're conducting official business here. I'm afraid I'll have to ask you to step aside or—"

"I will not! Do you have any idea what we were—"

"Ms. Reed. If you don't cease and desist right now, I'm going to have to take you in for obstruction of justice."

"The hell you will!"

"Think of your daughter, ma'am."

Jake felt an unwelcome surge of gratitude to the second deputy for trying to avoid hauling Rebecca in. "Listen to him, Rebecca. Katie needs you now." Through the window he could see the poor girl huddled in the back seat of the car, looking terrified.

"Mama? What's going on?"

Jake tried for a reassuring smile, but wasn't sure he succeeded. "Everything's going to be okay, Katie," he managed to say past the huge lump of humiliation in his throat. "Just listen to your mama, okay?"

"But Jake, this is wrong!" Rebecca shrilled, peering past the deputy who blocked her way.

"Not in the eyes of the law, babe. So drop it. Now."

"Ms. Reed?" The second deputy stepped back, keeping himself between her and his partner and Jake as he held the driver's door open for her to get into her car. She sent all three men a fulminating glare before she dropped into the driver's seat with a furious thump. Meanwhile, Hull finished Mirandizing Jake.

"Where's Sheriff Sutter?" Jake heard Rebecca demand as Hull turned him toward the waiting cruiser.

"He's still out of town, ma'am."

"Does he have a number where he can be reached?"

"I'm not sure, ma'am. You'd have to check at the station."

"Believe me, Deputy Savard, I intend to."

Inside the cruiser, Jake leaned his head back against the seat and swore. He'd never seen Rebecca so militant. He was going to have to cut his avenging angel loose, before she got herself arrested right along with him.

****

"I'm telling you, Avery Dillenger is lying."

"You're saying Mr. Donovan didn't break down Mr. Dillenger's front door and assault Mr. Dillenger in his foyer, breaking his nose?"

"He was provoked!"

"That doesn't make it legal, Ms. Reed."

"What about what Avery Dillenger did to my daughter?"

"You say he kidnapped the girl—Katie is it?" he asked, and directed a kid-friendly smile at her daughter, sitting in a nearby chair, still wrapped in the blanket from the car. In her left hand she held an ice bag, which the desk sergeant had offered to help reduce the swelling on her face—after she'd returned from having someone at the station take the pictures Rebecca had insisted on.

Rebecca would have given anything to be at home with Katie right now, comforting and taking care of her daughter herself, to not have to have her baby be part of or witness to the commotion Rebecca was making—but she had to make the police see they'd arrested the wrong man.

"Yes, Katie. Kathleen Diane, but we call her Katie. He kidnapped her, then bruised and slapped her when she tried to escape. It's all right there, in my statement," she said, stabbing a finger into the document the deputy had just finished typing.

"When are you going to pick him up?"

"Why would Mr. Dillenger want to kidnap your daughter?"

"To molest her! Just like he's been molesting countless children in Warner for God knows how long."

"Do you have any proof of these accusations, or that he was planning to molest your daughter?"

"He wasn't going to let her leave the house! Isn't that proof enough?"

"I can see you're upset by all of this, Ms. Reed. Perhaps you might feel calmer if you came back in the morning."

Frustration and fury swamped Rebecca until she was afraid she couldn't speak. "No," she said evenly, precisely, holding on to what little remained of her control with an iron will, "I am not leaving. Not until Avery Dillenger is behind bars where he belongs, do you understand me?"

"I'm afraid that could take some time, Ms. Reed."

"You certainly moved fast enough when he called to report that Jake assaulted him!"

"Jake?"

"Mr. Donovan," she stabbed a finger at her statement again, the statement that the deputy himself had taken. "Mr. Jacob Donovan. Who was on his way here to report Katie's kidnapping when you arrested him."

"Ah, that Mr. Donovan."

"Yes," Rebecca confirmed through gritted teeth. "That Mr. Donovan. You certainly moved fast enough to arrest him."

"Mr. Dillenger's broken front door and nose were pretty compelling reasons to believe him."

"And my daughter's swelling face isn't?"

Deputy Savard picked up her statement and tamped the unstapled pages down, clearly preparing to end their conversation. "As I said, Ms. Reed, we'll look into the matter and—"

"When's Sheriff Sutter coming back?"

"I'm not sure, ma'am, but I'll be happy to leave a message for you."

"You do that. You ask him to call Rebecca Reed the minute he gets in. Tell him I have some information about Avery Dillenger he needs to hear. Tell him it's on tape."

"Tape? What are you talking about, Rebecca?"

She whirled around to see Bob Sutter standing in the doorway, looking as if he hadn't slept in days, and had lost a great deal of weight.

"Bob. You're back. I'm...I'm so sorry to hear about your mother. How is she?" Upon being informed the sheriff was visiting his mother who'd had a stroke in Ohio, Rebecca had declined to insist on being given the number where he could be reached.

"Better, thank you." The smile he offered was a mere shadow of his usual cheerful smile. "But it's been a rough week. Now what's this about Avery Dillenger and a tape?"

"He tried to kidnap Katie tonight. Jake and I interrupted his plans for the evening and now Jake's in jail—"

"Donovan's locked up? Here?"

"We brought him in an hour ago, sir. Trespassing, assault, terroristic threats, B & E."

"It's all on videotape, Bob. If Avery hasn't erased it, that is."

"Dillenger's got the tape?"

"He's probably got miles of tape." Rebecca looked up at the man she was convinced would be Jake's vindicator as an idea took root in her mind. "Of every child he's brought to the house," she said slowly. "I bet he would. He'd probably enjoy keeping records of his crimes, believing as he does that no mere mortal could ever punish him for them."

The sheriff turned to Hull. "Get me a warrant."

"You mean you believe me?"

"Why wouldn't I, Rebecca? You've never lied to me before. Now why don't you go home and get some sleep? I'm sure Katie would be more comfortable at home, too." He came into the room and squatted near the chair Katie was curled up in, his jaw tightening when he saw the big purple bruise forming on her face. "Dillenger did this?"

"When she tried to leave. It's all on the tape, I'm sure of it."

"You okay, sweetie?"

Katie nodded. "I want Jake."

Sutter had the grace to look abashed. "I'm afraid he's going to have to stay here a little while, pumpkin, at least until I can get all of this sorted out. In the meantime, I want you and your mom to go home and get some rest. Do you think you could do that for me?"

At Katie's silent nod, the sheriff stood. Rebecca noted again how exhausted he looked. "You look like you could use some rest yourself, Bob. I'm sorry to dump this on you the minute you get back."

He smiled wanly. "That's what I get for stopping here instead of going straight home. Don't worry about it. This could be the break we've needed to bring him in."

"Avery?"

The sheriff nodded. "I've been keeping an eye on him for several months now. Haven't been able to pin anything on him yet, but with yours and Katie's testimony—"

"Oh, thank God."

"It's a start, anyway. How about I call you in the morning, let you know what's happening? We probably won't be able to get a warrant signed for another couple of hours at least—and we'll have to wake up Judge Oates to do that."

"Oates?" Rebecca's heart dropped into the pit of her stomach. "He's the judge who sent Jake into the army. He's been friends with the Dillengers for decades."

Sutter sent her a steady look. "He's also a good man, Rebecca. A fair one. Trust me. We'll get this straightened out."

"What about Jake?"

"I'm afraid he won't be able to see the judge until Monday morning, at least. That's when he'll be arraigned. Until then, we'll have to keep him."

"But Bob, he didn't do anything any other parent—" she flashed a look at Katie, "any other decent person wouldn't have done!"

The sheriff stepped forward and placed a large, no doubt meant-to-be-soothing hand on her shoulder. "Rebecca. I said I'd do what I could. But if Donovan's guilty, he's going to have to serve the time."

She couldn't argue with the quiet steel in his voice. Rebecca recalled their conversation in the car the night he'd driven her home from the festival, and knew he was on her side, but it didn't make the waiting any easier.

"It's so unfair, Bob. He didn't do anything I wouldn't have done if I had the strength."

He released her shoulder. "Why didn't you call the police before you went to Dillenger's?"

"It happened so fast, it never occurred to us to call you. We were searching for Katie, we found out she'd gotten into a car that could have been Avery's...we just reacted."

"So you weren't even sure she was with Dillenger?"

"If you're talking about evidence, no. But gut instinct...we had to make sure, Bob. And we had to do it fast. She'd been missing for hours."

"I understand. Just be grateful Dillenger didn't press charges against you, too."

Rebecca blinked as she realized he was right. Apparently Avery thought getting Jake out of the way was all he needed to worry about. Clearly he thought Rebecca wouldn't dare take a stand against him without Jake there to fire her up.

"You'll arrest him tonight?"

"We'll go up there as soon as we get the warrant signed."

Rebecca could barely contain her gratitude. "Thank you, Bob. I told Jake we could count on you."

Sutter smiled. "You're a good woman, Rebecca. I heard what Dillenger tried to do to you at the council meeting last night." Still smiling, he reached up and gave her shoulder an encouraging squeeze. "Don't worry, we'll get him one way or another."

****

"Why did you run away, Katie?" Rebecca asked quietly, once her daughter was comfortably settled in her sleigh bed at Jake's. The question had been burning inside her ever since she'd tried to ask it at Avery's, but with everything else going on, she'd had to put her curiosity on hold. After leaving Bob Sutter, she'd brought Katie home, thanked Aunt Martha for her time and help, then kept Katie company while she took a quick bath. Katie hadn't wanted to be left alone. She then tried to ease her daughter's fears with a snack of milk and cookies and a few of her favorite bedtime stories.

It appeared to have worked. Katie seemed much more relaxed than she'd been when they'd left the police station and in the past half hour had even laughed once or twice. Rebecca was fervently grateful to have her little girl back, safe and sound, but she still needed to know why Katie had run in the first place.

"I wasn't really running away, Mom. I was just taking a walk. I wanted to be by myself, and it was too crowded and noisy at the soup kitchen."

"Why did you go so far?"

"I guess I wasn't paying attention to where I was going. Then Mr. Dillenger pulled up beside me, and..."

Rebecca suppressed a fierce shudder at the thought of Avery Dillenger stalking her daughter. "Why did you go with him, Katie?" she asked as calmly, as gently as she could.

Katie looked up at her with dark, solemn eyes, eyes that suddenly seemed much older than her seven years. "He said I looked like I needed a friend," Katie said in a small, uncertain voice. "And...well, I guess I did."

179

Rebecca's heart broke at the sound of her daughter's loneliness. "You didn't think you could talk to me or Jake?"

"Not about this." Katie picked at her new Barbie bedspread, a sure sign she wasn't comfortable with the question. "Because, well..." A brief glance in Rebecca's direction before she lowered her gaze to the bedspread again. "You're the problem."

"Me?"

Katie nodded at the bedspread, looking miserable. "The kids at school say we're living in sin."

Rebecca wanted to break furniture. She reached out and hugged her daughter instead. "Oh, baby."

"Are we, mama? Are we living in sin?"

"No! I mean...I mean...it's complicated, Katie."

Katie pulled away, sniffling as she looked up at last. "My friends don't want me to hang around with them anymore because of it, and because they think Jake killed that woman. It's like they think he's going to hurt them or something."

Rebecca had known the kids would talk, but the reality of hearing what they were saying to Katie was wrenching.

And now Jake was in jail again, for hurting someone. Never mind it was Avery Dillenger.

"We talked about this before, Katie. About how this might happen."

"Yeah, but...it's just so hard, Mom. I've still got some friends, but even they don't want to come over, and around here there's nobody to talk to play with but you guys and half the time you're ignoring each other, so..." She looked up and met Rebecca's eyes. "It's kind of hard to hang around people who don't talk to each other, Mom. I never know what to say or do."

Shame filled Rebecca for being so absorbed with her own thoughts and feelings that she hadn't noticed what a hard time Katie was having. "Oh, sweetheart, I'm so sorry. I didn't realize how much...all of this was affecting you. I thought you were happy living with Jake."

"I am. Most of the time, anyway. He's a lot of fun. I even wish—"

"Wish what, baby?"

"Forget it. It's stupid."

"Katie," Rebecca said gently, and ran a hand over her daughter's still baby-fine hair. "Nothing you could say would be stupid. You know that. No wrong answers, remember?" It was their pact. Whenever they needed to discuss something important, they would both declare, "no wrong answers" and then be free to put all their thoughts and feelings on the table without feeling stupid.

"I wish Jake was my dad."

Rebecca felt as if she'd been doused with cold water. For the longest time, all she could do was sit there, feeling heartsick and speechless. "Katie, I don't know what to say."

"I just want to be part of a real family, you know?"

"I know, sweetheart." So do I. But Jake doesn't. "I wish there was something I could do to make all of this easier on you."

"You love him, don't you, Mom?"

"Yes, I do."

"So do I." Katie smiled, and it broke Rebecca's heart to know Jake planned to abandon this child who loved him enough to want to stay with him, even in the face of her classmates' shunning. How could he throw over something so precious for something so selfish as his freedom?

What parent didn't dream of 'escaping from it all' at the end of a rough day? God knew she had, more times than she could count. But, unlike her own parents, she'd hung in there, day after day, night after lonely night, accepting the bad with the good, just doing the best job she could.

And if she could do it, Jake could damn well do it, too.

She believed in him. Katie believed in him. His boss believed in him.

What else did the man need?

Liana Laverentz

Chapter Twenty-One

Rebecca was back at the police station first thing in the morning. Even though this was her home town, and she knew most of the station personnel by sight from the library if not by name, her first few moments after she walked through the front door were unsettling. She couldn't help but remember when she'd gone to visit Jake in that jail in Wyoming, how she'd been leered at, patronized and turned away because she wasn't on his 'visitor's list'.

She squared her shoulders, smoothed her hands down her cream-colored business suit skirt, then reached into her overcoat pocket to rub her thumb against the small, unopened ivory envelope she'd placed there late last night, after finding it in Jake's wastebasket while collecting the household trash.

Reassured the letter was still there, she strode up to the desk and asked to see Jacob Donovan.

To her surprise, she was almost immediately escorted to his cell in the basement of the building. As she followed an unsmiling, unspeaking officer Savard down the steps, Rebecca's heart thumped wildly at the prospect of seeing Jake again.

At the foot of the stairs, Savard unlocked a steel door with a small mesh window at face level. "Visitor for you, Donovan," he announced, then stepped back to let her precede him.

The jail was a grim, depressing place at best. Warner didn't have a lot of crime, so Rebecca assumed the long, windowless room that contained four small, adjacent cells was more than adequate for the town's needs. Passing the first three cells, two of which contained unmade beds, she noted each held a battered sink, toilet and cot, the latter covered with dull white sheets and a green army surplus blanket. The dull gray cement floors and walls seemed clean enough—she wouldn't have expected any less from Robert Sutter—but beneath the faint smell of disinfectant, the airless room still held the entirely too distinguishable odors of alcohol, cigarette smoke, unwashed bodies, urine, and a familiar stench Rebecca associated with the flu.

She closed her eyes for a moment to adjust to the dismal feel of the place, then opened them again to face Jake. He'd risen from his seat on his cot when he realized who his visitor was and was waiting for her, his expression far from welcoming. He looked terrible, as if he hadn't slept all night.

"You can sit in this chair while you visit, ma'am, or stand if you prefer to," Savard intoned, pulling a cracked orange plastic chair over from the corner. He set the chair in front of Jake's cell. "I'll wait by the door until you're finished."

Rebecca looked at Savard in surprise. "You're staying?"

"Yes, ma'am. Regulations don't allow us to leave visitors alone with prisoners."

Prisoners. Rebecca hated the term, hated the invasion of her privacy, but knew better than to argue. Still, it made her feel unclean, as if she were a criminal. If this was the kind of environment and treatment Jake had had to endure for eight long years…

"Thank you," she murmured, her manners kicking in.

Savard nodded and left to take up a post next to the door that led upstairs.

"Hello, Jake," Rebecca said warmly, then took off her overcoat and draped in over the back of the chair.

His hard gaze roved over her suit before he asked, "They frisk you when you came in?"

She blinked, both at Jake's cold tone and the question. The idea of some stranger—or worse, an acquaintance's hands running over her body in search of weapons or contraband appalled her. "No."

"You're lucky then. I've been in places where they do strip searches on both sides."

Rebecca stared. Overnight, Jake had changed into a cold, hard man she barely recognized. The man she'd seen and feared the first day he'd come into the library. The lone wolf barely tolerating the trappings of civilization.

A caged wolf, now.

"I talked to Bob," she said quietly, not missing the strong flare of emotion in Jake's eyes, but she wasn't going to pretend she didn't know the man just to protect Jake's stubborn ego. If he wanted to object to her friendship with Bob Sutter, he'd better be prepared to explain why. "He was going to get a warrant to search Avery Dillenger's house for the tape of us last night and tapes of any other children he might have brought into the house."

"He did. Dillenger came in around midnight."

"You're kidding? He spent the night here?"

"His lawyer came by and sprang him an hour later."

Good Lord. She'd never even thought about paying Jake's bail. No matter. Jake wouldn't have let her, anyway. He was too proud for that. "Have you called a lawyer?"

Jake snorted. "Yeah, right."

Rebecca took offense. "What's wrong with that?"

"People like me, Rebecca, get public defenders. And mine is about as worthless as the one I had in Wyoming. I think he's usually a tax lawyer."

"Then let me find you a better one. We don't have to get one from Warner."

"I don't need a lawyer taking what's left of my money, Rebecca. Or yours. We all know where this is headed."

"You can't know that! Listen, Jake—"

"I violated my parole. That's an automatic one-way ticket back to the joint to serve the rest of my seven and a half-to-fifteen year bit. If Dillenger presses charges, which, after listening to him cry for an hour, I have no doubt he plans to do, I'll be there even longer."

Rebecca stared at him as his words sunk in. "You knew this would happen all along, didn't you?"

Jake simply stared back at her, his expression inscrutable.

"But you went to Avery's anyway. For Katie, and for me."

Jake shrugged as if it didn't matter. As if nothing mattered any more. "I did what I had to. Now Dillenger's going to do what he has to. That's life."

But all Rebecca could think of was Jake, her Jake, the Jake she'd loved since she was ten, claiming all he wanted was his freedom, then giving up that lifelong dream of freedom to rescue their daughter from a man whose personal mission was to see to it that Jacob Donovan spent as much of his life as possible behind bars.

Knowing even as he punched Avery Dillenger in the nose for insulting her that this would be his reward.

Rebecca forgot all about the guard standing by the door as she stepped forward, moving as close to Jake as she could, and said, "Marry me, Jake."

"What?"

"You heard me. I want to get married."

"Rebecca, are you out of your mind?"

"No. I'm completely sane."

184

Jake looked at her off-white suit again, and decided she'd worn it deliberately. He swore and closed his eyes. He knew what Rebecca thought she was doing. Coming to his rescue again. If they were married, she couldn't corroborate Dillenger's testimony that Jake had decked him. But the tape the cops had confiscated would take care of that. The tape Dillenger had edited before the cops had arrived.

Oh, yeah, he'd made sure Jake knew the score on that one.

"We could do it now," Rebecca was saying. "Get the magistrate down here and—"

"No way."

She stopped talking, looking stunned.

"Forget it, Rebecca. I'm not going to marry you."

She looked at him, hard, then swallowed and lifted her chin. Jake caught the determined glint in her eye and nearly groaned aloud, knowing a good talking to was coming. "Rebecca..." he began, but she held up a hand, shutting him down.

"I have loved you for over half of my life, Jake. I have borne you a child and made a home for you to the best of my ability. I have stood by you while you pushed me and the rest of the world away, again and again, and will continued to do so, without regret, for the rest of my natural life, if—"

"No, Rebecca. I'm telling you no."

She went silent, then searched his face slowly, her own face filling with resolve. "Then I'm walking out that door and never looking back. Do you understand? I won't be here for you when you come back the next time."

"What about Katie?"

"She loves you. And despite being teased and ostracized by her classmates over this…this *unholy* situation, she wants you to come home again, as soon as you can. She misses you as much, as deeply, as I do. But if you don't want us, you need to say so now, so that we can get on with our lives. We need to find a house and build a home. With or without you. We've been living in limbo far too long."

Involuntarily, Jake stepped forward and gripped the bars between them. "Are you saying the reason you never married or moved out of your aunt's garage apartment is me?"

Rebecca's gaze never wavered. "That's correct."

Jake closed his eyes and forced himself not to lean his forehead against the cold steel bars that separated them. He'd never guessed. Hoped, sure, but never thought he had a prayer of making a life with Rebecca. Now here she was, telling him if he refused to marry her, she was walking, and taking Katie with her.

She'd do it, too. He'd seen her walk away before. She'd made up her mind she didn't want that library job and hadn't looked back once.

But Jake knew he still had nothing to offer her or Katie. Less than nothing if Dillenger had his way. If the charges stuck, he'd be going up the road again. And if anything else happened, it would be three strikes and you're out. Jake couldn't live knowing that if he screwed up one more time, even just happened to be in the wrong place at the wrong time, Rebecca and Katie would pay the price. And with his luck, it was inevitable.

"I can't do it, Rebecca. I'm sorry."

Her determined façade wavered, exposing her deep vulnerability behind it. God, it killed him to know he was hurting her—again.

"Can't, or won't?"

If nothing else, eight years in prison had taught Jake how to lie like a pro. He looked the woman he loved dead in the eye, and lied for all he was worth. "Won't. I don't want you, Rebecca. If I did, we'd have been married years ago."

By the look in her eyes he knew he'd scored a direct hit. As she backed away from his cell, Jake nearly bent the bars between them to keep from reaching out to her. Ghostly pale, she lifted her chin and met his eyes, hers dark and wounded, but dry.

"Goodbye, Jake."

She stared at him a moment longer, then turned and snatched up her coat. As she strode toward the exit, head held high, the crack of her heels echoing like whiplashes in the cement room, Jake panicked, knowing this was it. If he let her go, he'd never see her again.

"Rebecca?"

She stopped, but didn't turn around. Jake refused to ask her to, terrified he'd see tears. Tears he'd caused, and tears he'd be helpless to do anything about. "I'll see that you get the house," he said. It was the least he could do for her and Katie.

"Keep it," she said, her voice colder than he'd ever heard it. So cold it even startled Savard, waiting by the door. "We don't need it."

****

"Visitor to see you, Donovan."

Jake looked up in surprise from where he'd spent the past

186

several hours, sitting on his cot, doing what he was destined to do for the rest of his life—mourning the loss of Rebecca and Katie with an ache that cut clear to his soul.

"Jake, my man, what's up?"

Watching FX approach his cell, a wide, warm smile on his face, Jake felt absurdly blessed. Jake shook his head and smiled back. "If I knew I'd tell you."

Both men remained silent as a big, burly guard pulled the orange chair from the corner and set it in front of Jake's cell. "Leave it right there, and we won't have any problems," the guard told FX, putting his hand on his nightstick. "Got that?"

"Got it, boss," FX said easily.

As the guard walked away, keys and cuffs jangling, FX's smile faded, warning Jake this wasn't a simple social call. FX cut one last look at the deputy, sat down, and leaned in close. "I'm not talkin' about what's got you sittin' here in this cozy suite at the Ritz," he said grimly. "I'm talkin' about that woman whose heart you done ripped out and stomped on."

Jake wrapped his hands around the bars in concern and frustrated hope. "Rebecca? She came to you?"

"Didn't have to. When she came in to serve lunch and asked me and some of the guys to help her move her stuff out of your house, it was written all over her face. You dumped her, not the other way around."

Jake swore ripely. "I told her she could have the house, FX. She doesn't want it."

"You stupid, as well as blind? That woman loves you. Why would she want to torture herself livin' in some house reminds her every damn day you don't want her? What the fuck you got for brains, Donovan, cuttin' loose a good woman like that?"

Jake swore and ran a hand through his hair before meeting FX's challenging glare. "I want her," he admitted in a low, rough voice, "and Katie, too."

"No news there," FX said dryly. "So what's holding you back?"

"Look at me, man. Look where I am. Look where I've been. I've got a record as long as my arm—"

"Juvie shit," FX interrupted, leaning forward again. "Seems to me you've grown up a little since then." He looked Jake in the eye. "It don't matter where you been, man. It's where you're going that counts."

"And I'm going back to hell."

187

"Maybe, maybe not. Word on the street is Dillenger's in a deep pile of shit." FX cast another quick look at the cop guarding the door. Jake didn't blame him, as he'd already figured out which ones were on Dillenger's dole. Mr. Prime Snitch was babysitting him this afternoon.

He let FX know with his eyes what the score was. FX lowered his voice even more. "This place is starting to give me the willies, man, so let me say my piece and go. You love the lady and I know she loves you. As for that little girl of yours—" When Jake opened his mouth to protest, FX cut him off with a look. "If that girl ain't yours, I'm George W."

Jake nodded. "She's mine."

"Right. That girl of yours is a real treasure, both of them are. They won't let anybody say a word against you, Jake. Little Katie's been tellin' everyone in the shelter how you rescued her from that slimeball Dillenger. She loves you, man, and so does her mama. Most men would kill for that kind of love, and you wanna throw it all away?"

"I'm locked up, FX. They deserve a life without me."

"Brother, they ain't gonna have no life without you in it, no matter how hard they try. You got real love here and you're lettin' it slip through your fingers. Why?"

Jake didn't have an answer for that. Not one he wanted to share with FX, anyway.

FX stood, knowing better than to offer his hand through the bars. He nodded. "Catch ya later."

Yeah, right, Jake thought, but nodded as well.

****

"Donovan."

What was this, Grand Central Station? Jake thought sourly, and rolled over from where he'd been dozing since FX's visit. He blinked the sleep from his eyes, and saw Robert Sutter himself standing outside his cell.

"Rebecca asked me to give this to you." He held up a small ivory envelope, already sliced open. Jake stared at it, recognizing it as the one he'd thrown into the wastebasket a week ago. The one from his grandmother.

"You Rebecca's errand boy now, Sutter?"

"I'm just doing the lady a favor. You want it or not?"

"You read it?"

"Nope. Just opened it for you."

They both knew he'd had to, to check for contraband. Jake

made no move to accept or decline the envelope. "You know, Donovan, you've got a real attitude problem. But I'm willing to overlook that, since it appears Rebecca was right. You're an innocent man."

"Say what?"

"I've been out of town for the past week, so my mail's been piling up, but I got a real interesting court order from Wyoming while I was gone." Sutter pulled a single sheet of folded paper from his breast pocket and offered it through the bars. While Jake read the two paragraph order for his release in stunned disbelief, Sutter continued conversationally, "Seems a Vincent Delgado confessed to killing Miss Christine Sanders two weeks ago when he was arrested for threatening to do the same to his current live-in. Apparently he saw your picture from the library rescue in the paper and started feeling the need to brag. Held a knife to his girlfriend's throat and told her he'd gotten away with murder before and didn't see any reason he couldn't do it again if she didn't see things his way. Once he let her go, she took her story straight to the police."

Jake stared, unable to believe what he was hearing.

Sutter shook his head wryly. "A real prince, Delgado. Still, he admitted to doing Sanders while you slept in the front room." Stunning Jake, Sutter then smiled. "We got your boot knife, too."

Jake blinked. Things were coming at him too hard and fast.

"The boys just brought it in," Sutter was saying. "We're going to need it a little longer, though, for evidence."

"Where's Dillenger?"

"Upstairs, being booked for attempted murder."

So where did that leave him? It hadn't escaped Jake that he was still standing in a cell.

"My guess is he's going to be too busy to worry about pressing charges against you," Sutter said, as if reading Jake's mind.

"So I'm a free man?"

"Not yet, but give me a couple of hours and I'll see what I can do. Paperwork. Here." He handed over the ivory embossed envelope.

Jake looked down at it, feeling more hopeful than he had in a long, long time. Looking up again, he met Sutter's eyes. "Thanks."

"I didn't have anything to do with it. I'm just glad to be the one giving you the news. Now, if you'll excuse me, I have a suspect to interrogate." Sutter turned to leave.

"Rebecca was right about you," Jake heard himself say.

Sutter looked pleasantly surprised. "Seems she was right about you, too. Turns out your grandmother's been trying to prove your innocence for years. Unfortunately, most of the PI's she hired were more interested in milking her for money. But this last one had been tailing Delgado for months. He was practically on the scene when Delgado was arrested, and from what I understand, she hired the lawyer that got your release pushed through so quickly."

****

"You're a lucky man, Donovan," Sutter announced less than two hours later, as he strode into the room with a fat set of keys. "Dillenger agreed to drop all charges against you in exchange for a lesser charge against himself, but from the looks of it, it won't do the slimy bastard any good," he said, and opened the door to Jake's cell. "Ever since word got out that we brought him in, my phone hasn't stopped ringing with calls from parents with a story to tell about him. No telling what's true and what's simply spite, but I'm sure there will be enough to send him away, especially if we can get him to crack on attempted murder. My brake cables," Sutter added almost cheerfully.

"Thanks," Jake said, and stepped out to freedom.

Sutter smiled. "You're welcome. Thought I'd let you go before we bring him down here. Unless you want to stick around for the show?"

Amazingly, Jake felt himself smiling back at the man he'd once considered his enemy—and rival for Rebecca. "Hell, no. I've got better things to do with my time."

Chapter Twenty-Two

His house was pitch dark, and silent as a tomb. Jake knew he had no one to blame but himself. He'd deliberately driven Rebecca away, and now he'd have to live with that choice.

Still, it hurt like hell when he stepped into his kitchen and saw she'd taken the oak table and chairs. The logical part of his brain understood she'd taken them because they were hers, but his heart ripped open at the sight of the room without them anyway.

The dining room was empty, too, but she'd left Mickey's old Zenith console, easy chair and couch in the living room. He forced himself to climb the stairs, and wondered why he bothered. He knew he'd be sleeping on the couch tonight.

As expected, both upstairs bedrooms had been cleaned out, and the bathroom. Not a pink bottle in sight. He stared at the empty sink and shelves, and felt like everything he and Rebecca and Katie had shared in the past month had been a figment of his imagination. But it hadn't, and the cold reality of their absence cut deep.

He braced himself and turned toward his room. The door was closed, which, in his dark mood, struck Jake as having a wealth of symbolism. He'd hurt her once too often, and now she'd closed the door on their relationship. Eighteen years of chances she'd given him, and he'd blown them all.

He reached out with a hand that shook, opened the door—and was shocked to see she'd left the antique rosewood bedroom set.

Maybe it hadn't fit in the truck, and she was coming back to get it. His heart skipped a beat when he spotted the note propped against the dresser mirror. If he was lucky, he'd get another chance to see her before he left town.

Because now that she'd left him, he had no choice but to leave. This was Rebecca's town. He refused to stick around as a reminder of what she was moving on from. He'd hurt her and Katie enough already.

He picked up the note, and prayed it would give him some kind of opening, any kind of opening, to see them again.

But all it was, was another note from his grandmother.

****

"Jacob. I wasn't expecting you so soon."

Jake looked past the maid who'd opened the front door, to the startled woman coming down the carpeted white marble staircase in her navy blue silk robe and slippers, and felt a twinge of guilt for surprising her this way. "I know your invitation was for tea, Mrs. Dillenger, but I didn't want to wait any longer. Sheriff Sutter told me about your efforts to prove my innocence, and I wanted to thank you for that, and for everything else you've done for me over the years."

Her eyes softened and she flushed, but recovered quickly, clearly used to hiding her emotions. They had something in common, then. "You're quite welcome, Jacob. Won't you come in?"

Jake took in the quiet elegance of his surroundings and felt like a bull in a china shop, but nodded politely. "I'd like that. I have some questions to ask, if you don't mind."

"Not at all. I expected as much. Have you had breakfast?" she asked, as if he hadn't barged in on her in her pajamas, as if he hadn't ignored every attempt she'd made to communicate with him over the past eight years.

"Yes, thank you," he lied. "Really, I didn't plan to stay long."

"Why not? We have quite a bit of catching up to do."

This, from the woman he'd spent his entire life believing she wanted nothing to do with him. Not for the first time in the past two days Jake wondered what might have happened had he bothered to open the letters she'd written to him so many years ago.

Regrets. It seemed he had nothing but.

"We'll take coffee in the dining room, Clarice," his grandmother said quietly, dismissing the maid who had opened the front door. Smiling at Jake, Margaret Mary Dillenger took his arm. "This way, Jacob."

Jake swallowed, desperately wishing Rebecca were with him, if only to keep him from making a fool of himself. He didn't know how to act in a place like this.

But Rebecca had left him, and he was where he'd always claimed he wanted to be—on his own.

As they settled into a pair of flowered chairs that flanked a dark, richly polished oval coffee table, Jake noticed the furniture matched the heavy floor to ceiling drapes. He looked at his grandmother, elegant even in her robe and slippers, and smiled. "I never expected to see the inside of this house."

"If your grandfather had had his way, you wouldn't have."

"So he was the one who didn't want me."

"Not after your father slandered him so horribly the night of your mother's funeral. He remained bitter about that to his grave. Forbade me to even mention the subject."

She doesn't know, Jake realized. She had no idea about what had happened to his cousin. Or was Dillenger lying again?

"So you wrote to me after he died."

"Immediately," she said, as if there had never been any doubt that she would.

"I'm sorry. I never read your letters. Never even opened them."

"I understand. I'm just grateful you're here now."

The coffee arrived. His grandmother dismissed the maid and poured them each a cup with graceful hands. As he settled back in his seat, she opened with, "You said you had some questions?"

"Yes. I'd like to know about my mother. What she was like as a girl—if it's not too painful."

She hesitated, then smiled wearily. "Painful it will always be, but you deserve to know the truth. Especially if you plan to have children of your own some day."

Jake stared into his coffee and thought of Katie. Another secret in a family with far too many.

His grandmother rang for Clarice and asked her to bring the family photo albums, then informed the maid she was not to be interrupted as long as her grandson was there. Jake looked up, startled by the reference, then was charmed by his grandmother's warm smile and whispered, "Get used to it, Jacob."

They moved to a loveseat to sit side by side, and went through the photo albums. Pictures of Conrad Dillenger were few and far between, which allowed Jake to focus on the shots of his mother. He saw Eileen winning tennis and horseback riding trophies, Eileen performing at piano recitals, Eileen sailing on the bay, skiing in Aspen, and spending her summers at Lake Banff.

But in none of the pictures did she look happy. The most disturbing of all were of Eileen's social debut.

"She looks miserable," Jake couldn't help but murmur, remembering the sad, introverted woman he'd known her to be.

"She was a sad girl, Jacob. Brilliant, athletic and talented, but never really happy. I was frantic when she eloped with your father who—no offense meant—seemed quite unstable."

"It's okay." Jake knew exactly how unstable Mickey had been.

"No one knows this except her doctors and I, but for most of her life, Eileen was on medication for depression. I was worried sick when I realized she'd left her pills behind when she eloped. I tried to give them to her when they returned from their honeymoon, but she refused to take them, insisting Mickey's love would save her."

"Save her?" Something niggled at the back of Jake's brain. "That's what she said? Save her?"

"Yes. Save her." His grandmother looked away, then sighed softly. "Maybe it was enough, in the beginning. She loved him desperately, and he was so different from anyone she'd ever known. Wild and carefree and full of adventure. But somewhere along the road things changed."

Unexpected tears welled in her eyes. She sniffed, then rummaged in her pocket for a lace-edged linen handkerchief. Not for the first or last time, Jake wished Rebecca was there. He had no idea how to handle a woman's tears. "I wish to God I'd known," she whispered fiercely, then blew her nose discretely.

"Known what?" Jake asked, feeling like he was heading into quicksand.

"She came to me, Jacob. The morning before she..." She lowered her head and buried her face in her handkerchief. "I should have known something was wrong."

"It wasn't your fault, Mrs. Dillenger," Jake felt compelled to say, feeling more off-balance than he'd ever felt in his life.

"But it was. It was *my* sleeping pills Eileen took. I had no idea they were missing until that night...until it was too late."

Feeling totally helpless, Jake gently gathered his grandmother into his arms. She was surprisingly fragile. As he held her while she cried, Jake finally understood his mother's suicide had not been his fault. She'd been sick from the start, and no matter how hard he'd tried, how good he'd tried to be, as long as she went without professional help, it wouldn't have made any difference. He *couldn't* have made her happy.

He hadn't broken her, therefore he couldn't fix her.

But who had broken her? Had it been Mickey? Her father? Or simply herself?

Finally Jake understood why his mother had stayed in bed for days on end. Why she'd rarely smiled. Why she hadn't been the kind of mother to him—or wife to Mickey—they'd wanted and needed.

Then Mickey, no saint to start with, had turned to the bottle in frustration and defeat.

Compassion, relief, sadness, grief and anger rolled around inside of Jake. He took a deep breath, wanting to nip the anger in the bud. Both of his parents had let him down. Both were gone now. It would serve no purpose to continue to blame them for not being there for him when it was clear to him now that they'd both been very broken people. They'd probably done the best they could for him, but their illnesses had won in the end.

He decided against delving any deeper into the ugly confrontation between Mickey and Conrad the night of Eileen's funeral. He would have to think of her as Eileen from now on, because if what he was beginning to suspect was true, he couldn't bear the thought of his own mother's pain. He'd loved his mother with all his heart, and just the thought of someone hurting her the way Avery Dillenger had planned to hurt Katie...

If Jake's guess was right, apparently Michael Donovan had known what a monster Conrad Dillenger was, because it had ruined his marriage. Clearly his 'unstable' father had done what he'd done to make Jake as much of an embarrassment as possible to old man Dillenger, in order to keep them apart.

The idea gave Jake a hell of a lot to think about.

But not right now.

Jake stayed for lunch and tea, but declined supper. He needed to go home and think, especially after his grandmother surprised him with his long lost leather jacket. Apparently her PI on the scene of Delgado's arrest had unearthed the jacket as well, wrapped in a property bag in the bowels of the Laramie County Courthouse.

She'd even had it professionally cleaned.

Four hours later, Jake rang the doorbell of the street-level door next to Barb's Antique Shop.

His heart nearly stopped when Rebecca pulled it open, smiling and wiping her hands on an apron. "Forget something?" she asked cheerfully, then stilled, her eyes wide with disbelief. Her smile vanished. "Jake. You're out of jail."

"Hello, Rebecca." He eyed the steep staircase behind her that led to the apartment above the shop, and wondered how he was going to make it to the top.

"I...I thought you were one of the guys. Someone forgot his cell phone."

Her moving crew, thanks to FX.

Rebecca blinked and stared. "Jake? Isn't that your old leather jacket? Where did you find it?"

He smiled, and wondered if she'd notice how much better it fit these days. It had been too big when she'd given it to him thirteen years ago, but he'd have died before refusing to wear it.

"It's a long story. Can I come in?"

"When did you get out?"

"Yesterday evening. Dillenger dropped his charges and Christine's killer confessed. Thanks to my grandmother, I'm a free man."

"Your grandmother?"

"That envelope you had Sutter give me was an invitation to tea. One of many. I finally took her up on it."

"Pardon? Did you say you're…free?"

Jake couldn't help but smile. "As a bird. Finally."

He wasn't sure what he'd expected, but it wasn't the tight mask of politeness that settled over her face. "Congratulations. I know it's what you've always wanted."

They stood there, in the drafty doorway at the bottom of the steps. Rebecca had to be freezing, with no coat on.

Jake finally realized she had no intention of letting him come in any farther. "Where's Katie?" he asked hopefully, looking past Rebecca's shoulder. Whatever got him through the door.

"Sleeping. The move wore her out."

"Oh." Jake studied her face again and found only resoluteness. She wasn't wearing his silver necklace anymore, either. He hoped she hadn't thrown it away. "I'm sorry I missed her."

"What do you want, Jake?"

Haven't you hurt us enough? her expression seemed to say. Had it really been only yesterday morning that he'd told her he'd never wanted her? It seemed like a lifetime, considering everything that had happened to him since. "I'm sorry, Rebecca. I never meant to hurt you."

"Been there, done that, Jake. It's getting old."

"I mean it, Rebecca."

"Right. And yesterday I offered you everything a woman can offer a man and you threw it back in my face, Jake. Deliberately. Tell me how you didn't expect that to hurt me."

"I was wrong. And I'm more sorry for that than you can imagine."

196

She studied him for a long moment, but still made no move to let him in. "Thank you for that much, anyway. Now, if you'll excuse me—"

Jake moved to block her way as she reached for the door. "Things have changed, Rebecca."

She looked up at him, her eyes flashing fury. "Not for me, Jake. I've had it with being jerked around by you."

"Marry me."

She blinked, clearly shocked. "What did you say?"

Jake swallowed, hard, and felt a strong appreciation for the courage Rebecca had shown yesterday outside his cell. If she'd felt even a fraction of the fear he was feeling now...

"I asked you to marry me. Please."

She stared at him for an endless, frozen moment, then drew a deep, shaky breath. "No."

Jake's cheeks went hot with embarrassment as he stared at her, shaken to the core. Was she saying she didn't love him anymore?

Rebecca closed her eyes and took another deep breath, apparently struggling with something. Jake's hopes lifted. If there was any chance at all that she still cared...

She opened her eyes again, her expression sadder than any he'd ever seen on her, but completely resolute.

"You don't love me," she said with quiet dignity. "I deserve to be loved by the man I marry."

Jake nearly dropped to his knees in relief. But he refused to tell her what she'd waited to hear for eighteen years at the bottom of some cold, dimly lit stairwell while she damn near froze to death from stubbornness.

A stubbornness he actually liked. He smiled and touched her arm, "C'mon Becca, let's—"

"Let's nothing," she snapped, jerking away from his touch. "It's over, Jake. You have your life and I have mine. So please, just...just leave us alone." Her voice cracked at the end and she swore, then turned and ran up the stairs.

Jake went right up after her. "Rebecca—"

She slammed the door in his face.

Jake stood there for a stunned moment, then took a deep breath to gather himself. "Rebecca. Wait. I need to tell you something. Please. Open the door."

Nothing.

Damn it, he'd have been better off telling her in the stairwell.

Now he'd have to do it through a door.

"Rebecca. I love you. I always have. Since we were kids."

Nothing.

"Rebecca?"

The door opened slowly, her eyes all wet and wounded looking. She seemed a little shaky, too. "What did you say?"

"I said I love you. Can I come in now?"

She stepped back, still looking pale and shaky, and more than a little wary. It killed him to know that he'd finally told her and she didn't believe him.

"It's true," he said, then stepped inside and off to the side of the doorway. The place was a mess, mostly boxes and packing paper. "I've been thinking a lot these past two days, and I finally realized that when my mom killed herself, I thought it was my fault, because, hard as I tried, I couldn't make her happy.

"So I tried doubly hard to please Mickey, but the only thing he ever seemed to notice or approve of was my getting in trouble. Since my grandparents didn't seem to want anything to do with me, either, I guess I convinced myself I was defective as a person. Unlovable. By the time I was ten, all I could think of was leaving town, getting as far away from Warner and all the people in my life who didn't want me. I'd show them, I thought." He smiled wanly. "The classic runaway fantasy.

"But then you moved in next door, and suddenly being stuck in Warner didn't seem so bad anymore. But you were full of hopes and dreams, dreams I knew I couldn't possibly make happen for you, even though you had no idea what it meant to me that you shared them with me. Then you started to fill out. Whoa. I thought I could handle it, but...That's when I knew I had to leave Warner for good, to give you the chance to fulfill all those dreams with someone else."

"Jake..."

He held up a hand. "Hear me out, Becca, please. You deserve to know all of it. You want to know why no other guys in town ever came around you? Why I got to be the first to kiss you, that night before I left for the army? It wasn't because of Chloe, like you thought. It was because of me. You were mine, Becca, and every guy in town knew it—even though I never made a move on you. It was one of those things that was just understood. I might not have been sleeping with you, or even dating you, but I sure as hell wasn't going to let anyone else get next to you, either. I'm sorry, Becca, I was being just plain selfish."

She blinked up at him as if she were in shock. Jake supposed she was. He took a deep breath and ran a shaky hand through his hair. He'd never talked so much at once in his life, and the worst of it was he was nowhere near finished yet.

But Rebecca was still listening, so...

"For some stupid reason, I thought the army would cure me of wanting you, but it only made me miss you more. So the minute I got out, I came looking for you. I told myself I just wanted to make sure you were okay before I hit the road, but it was more than that. The whole time I was gone, the whole time we were writing to each other, there was a part of me that felt like you were my girl back home. Every time I got a letter, I couldn't wait to get back to my bunk and read it. Over and over and over again."

At this, Rebecca seemed to finally regain some of her spunk. "Come on, Jake. You expect me to believe you never dated after you left Warner?"

"Sure I went out with other women, but not nearly as much as you might think. Not like I did here. And I hardly ever slept with one. Because when I did, it always felt like I was cheating—on you. But when I came back and found out you were practically engaged, I knew I'd missed my chance. You'd moved on with your life and it was time for me to do the same."

He looked into her eyes, willing her to believe what he had to say next. He wished he could touch her, some how, some way, but that decision had to be hers. "But then we made love. It was the most incredible night of my life, Rebecca. I swear it. But in the morning I knew I had to leave. Everything you'd ever said you wanted was within your reach. I couldn't ruin that for you. I wouldn't."

Rebecca was shaking her head, one hand covering her mouth. "Oh, God, Jake." Tears trickled down her cheeks.

He took a chance and stepped closer, reached out to touch one hot tear. It broke his heart to see her crying, but maybe when he was done, she'd be able to find it in her heart to forgive him. "I left you not because I didn't want you Becca, but because I wanted you too much. It was Christine who told me I was in love with you. She also told me if I ever wanted to be happy, to get my ass back home to you and fight Kane for you if I had to. Then she told me to spend the rest of my life letting you know how much I love you."

His own eyes misted as hers overflowed with tears. "That's what I was coming back to do when I was arrested for killing her," he ended quietly. "I was coming home to you."

"Oh, Jake!" She was in his arms before he knew it, kissing him like there was no tomorrow. He kissed her back for all he was worth, and inside it was just like the first time, and every other time he'd ever kissed her. It felt like home. Like where he was meant to be.

Finally he broke the kiss, and, still holding her, buried his face in her sweet, strawberry-scented hair before saying, "I could have died of shame when I got your first letter in prison. I'd hoped so hard you'd never find out what happened to me. But your letters kept coming, and I read them so many times I can still recite them from memory. Thinking of you, remembering your goodness, was the only thing that kept me sane."

He stroked her hair, determined to get it all out. "Since you never mentioned Kane in your letters while I was in the service, I wasn't surprised you didn't mention him later. I knew there was something going on and you weren't telling me, but I didn't think I had the right to ask. Your letters were too upbeat, too cheery, you know? All I could think of was you weren't sure if I was guilty, or you'd gotten back together with Kane and didn't know how to tell me. When the letters stopped coming, I decided it was Kane, and you'd married him."

"Never," Rebecca whispered fiercely, making Jake smile. She still hadn't lifted her head from his chest, but that was fine by him. She felt so good in his arms that if she leaned back and looked up at him, Jake knew he would kiss her and not stop for a long, long time.

"Those were the darkest years of my life, but part of me was glad you were finally living the life you'd always wanted. I spent years torturing myself, thinking about what your life with him was like. When I came back here to sell the house, you were the last person I expected to see. But when I realized you were still speaking to me, after the way I'd treated you, I started wanting you all over again."

At that, she squeezed him even tighter, but Jake could tell it was a happy hug. Still, he wasn't finished yet.

"But when I saw the life you'd created for yourself here, I knew it wouldn't work. There was no way I could make you happy when all I had to offer you was trouble. Finding out Katie was mine shocked the hell out of me, but it also thrilled me more than I could say.

"Then I started hating myself for abandoning you the way I did. I thought that to claim her would mean putting you through the hell of letting everyone know I was the sorry bastard who got you pregnant and left you to raise Katie alone. I'd rather have left Warner forever than put you or Katie through the shame of calling you mine."

This time, she did lean back, her cornflower blue eyes still wet but more militant than wounded-looking. "There would have been no shame in it Jake, or blame, for any of us."

He smiled and shook his head. His avenging angel was back and telling him what time it was. "I know I didn't act like it, when you asked me to marry you yesterday, but it was the most humbling moment of my life. After all I'd done to you, after all I'd put you through, you still loved me."

He reached up to brush her hair away from her face. "I'll never forget that, Becca, or how you looked when I turned you down. It killed me to see you hurting so bad, but I couldn't get past my own insecurities. I couldn't let you throw your life away on me. You deserve so much better."

He met her eyes, his own solemn. "You still deserve better, Becca, but the truth is I can't stay away from you. I never could. My feelings for you are the reason I keep leaving—keep running away—and the reason I keep coming back. For eighteen years I've been trying to outrun my feelings for you, and I've finally realized...I can't. I don't want to."

"All these years," Rebecca whispered, "You never said a word."

"I never dreamt of having a home and family, Rebecca, because I didn't know how to. Living with Eileen and Mickey, I never learned how to." Jake couldn't resist any longer. He smiled and kissed Rebecca on the forehead. "But then you and Katie showed me how special being part of a family could be. How happy I could be simply working at something I love, then coming home to share dinner and watch a movie or chase lightning bugs across the yard. When I walked into my empty house two nights ago, I knew *you* were what I had been searching for all this time, and *you* were why I kept coming back. Not to Warner, but to you. Because you, and only you, can give me the home and family I want. The home and family I need."

She was crying again, hard. But somehow Jake knew that this time it was different. He smiled and offered to get her a tissue. As he handed it to her, he said, "I want to spend the rest of my life with you, Rebecca Reed. I want to be a real father to our daughter. I want to make up to you both for all the years I've been too bullheaded to see what was right in front of my face. All these years I've been too scared to reach for happiness, because I couldn't believe it was simply there for the taking."

"Oh, Jake." Tears still coming, she reached out and stroked his hair. "I love you so much."

"For real? Enough to marry me?"

She bit her lower lip, a smile in her eyes he hadn't seen since the night they'd made love. "For real. Enough to marry you."

"Thank God." He pulled her into his arms and kissed her long and hard. She wrapped her arms around his neck and held on as if she never wanted to let him go. Ending the kiss, he pulled back and smiled. "Two more things. Let me get them out now, because I may never talk this much again."

"Oh, you'll talk to me, Donovan. I'll see to that."

He grinned, glad to see her feistiness return. "Before I came here, I went to see Feeney. He's still willing to sell me the station. I'm ready to buy it now, if it's okay with you. I also want to tell Katie and the rest of the world she's mine as soon as you give the go ahead."

Rebecca nodded, tears welling again. "We'll tell her tomorrow. Will you stay the night?"

Startled, Jake looked around the living room, saw there was no couch, and felt his hopes soar. "Are you sure? What about Katie?"

Rebecca gave him a watery smile. "I doubt she'll mind when she hears the news. I should warn you, though. It's a single bed. There wasn't room for anything else."

Jake laughed. "Do you have any idea how long I've wanted to get you alone on a single bed?"

"I don't know. Fourteen or fifteen years?"

"At least. But tomorrow we'll move back to my place. Even if I have to haul every last piece of furniture down those steps myself. Sound good to you?"

She laughed, sending his heart soaring, then smiled. "Sounds perfect. Now let's see about that bed."

Jake smiled when he saw his silver heart on the nightstand. He picked it up and let it dangle from his fingers. "I was sure you'd thrown it away."

Rebecca sat down on the bed, smiling and shaking her head. "I thought about it. Thought about chucking it right into the bay. But I decided to save it for Katie."

Jake looked at her, patiently waiting for him to join her, and swallowed hard. "You're a good woman, Rebecca Reed."

She reached out her hand. "And you're a good man."

A word about the author...

Liana Laverentz got hooked on reading in the second grade, when the exchange gift she received was a Nancy Drew mystery. Her love of writing followed shortly thereafter, but she didn't start writing for publication until 1988.

Her first novel, Ashton's Secret, a murder mystery romance published by Meteor/Kismet, was released in 1993. She is a member of Romance Writers of America, the Washington Romance Writers, and a charter member of Pennwriters, Inc., where she has served as their critique coordinator, contest coordinator, conference coordinator, treasurer and president. In 1998, she won the Pennwriters Meritorious Service Award.

She then took some time off to rearrange her priorities and "just be a Mom." She started writing for publication again in 2002. Her widely acclaimed contemporary romance Thin Ice was published by The Wild Rose Press in 2007. Her first novel, Ashton's Secret, will be re-released by The Wild Rose Press in 2008. After that, she has another romantic suspense planned.

Liana's hobbies include reading, writing, mixed martial arts, soup making, and road trips. She lives in Pennsylvania with her son and three cats.

You can reach her at www.lianalaverentz.com or
www.polkadotbanner.com.